A HOLE IN
NO•WHERE

A NOVEL

DeNisf

Dedicated to my Mother and Father

ACKNOWLEDGEMENT

With very special thanks to DeLon H. Smith for the hours and hours and days and days and years and years. There are not enough words to express my thanks and love to you.

In loving memory of Kathryn J. Watson.

Thanks to DeNette H. Wheelwright, Alice M. Henson and Lucille Bullard for their encouragement and love.

Much love and gratitude to Pat Seay, for all that you are.

Thank you to the best parts of me for always believing in me. Nicholas Pawlikowski, Matthew Pawlikowski, Jodie Pawlikowski & Nevaeh Cason, live happy, be strong and always know I love you.

To Tim Wood, thanks for EVERYTHING my love.

PROLOGUE
Winter 1990

She held her breath, her eyes tightly closed. Her knuckles were white as she held a death grip clutch on the steering wheel. She felt beads of sweat forming on her forehead as she pressed firmly on the brake, both feet planted, pushing down as far as the floorboard would allow. She prayed she would stop. She wanted to scream, but finally, after what seemed like an eternity, her body flew sideways slamming her shoulder into the door as the car bounced off a tree. She and the car came to a rest on the edge of the road. Slowly she wiped her brow, expelled her breath and opened her eyes, thankful to be alive.

Eliza Johnson sat wondering what to do. She was shaken and sore. She needed help. She looked around. Her headlights reflected only glistening white. As far-off as she could see, which was not very far, her view was filled with snow, snow piled upon snow. She decided to get out of the car hoping to improve her line of sight; eager to see a light off in the distance, hoping to see anything at all.

Eliza stepped out of her car, pulling her coat on. She was freezing. She turned a full three-hundred-sixty degrees scanning the sky, the trees and even the ground for some source of light beyond her own headlights. There were only dark shadows staring back. Her body began to shake with chills. She did not know if it was the darkness, the night air, or the distress of her death ride making her shiver, but she buttoned her coat, pulling the collar up tightly around her neck and walked around the car looking for damage. She found a small dent in her bumper, but stopped at her tire and cussed.

When the tire blew it scared her. She was going too fast for the road conditions and she panicked, slamming her brakes on, throwing her car into an uncontrollable spin. As she looked down at the source of her trouble she shook her head. "I can't change that." A chilly breeze blew sending her shoulder length auburn hair dancing into her face. Her checks were turning pink and she shoved her hands deep into her dress length ivory coat. Her boots were the same shade of ivory as her coat, but not snow boots. As she kicked at the flat tire she wondered if she had indeed, packed her snow boots.

Eliza was on her way to Houston for a new job. She planned on stopping at her parents' house before she made her way down south. She wanted to look her best. Now she wished she had flown. If she had not bought the eight year old car, she would have had enough money for the airplane ticket, but Houston is a different city; you need a car to get around in Houston.

She wanted her parents to see her now, to see what she had done with her life. She was not the same little girl full of attitude, who stormed out of her parents' house, with a boy, when she was seventeen. She had a college degree now and a good job waiting for her. Her parents had told her she would amount to nothing if she ran off with "him." She had almost failed in life. She had been on a fast road, no, make that the express lane to nothing, but she had turned her life around. Now she had a great job and a great apartment waiting for her. She wanted to show them they were wrong. She was not a hooker, she was not on drugs, and she was not homeless on the streets.

So much for pride Eliza thought as she climbed back into her car. "I should have flown." She started the engine. She was freezing and turned the heater on for a few moments. She wondered how long until a car would pass. She turned the radio on. She looked outside. The sky was getting darker as the moonlight and stars were being shrouded by clouds. *I hope someone comes by soon* she thought as she turned the heater to high. She checked the gas gauge, almost a full tank. She needed a few minutes longer with the heater on; it was so cold out there.

No one passed and nothing moved except the snow blowing in a circular motion right before it fell to the windshield of her car. Eliza was getting tired. She had been driving all day and the warmth from the heat was making her drowsy. She decided to turn the car off. She had heard stories of people dying while trying to stay warm. She did not want to die. She was looking forward to a bright future. Dying in a car, sitting on the side of a road someplace in Kentucky, was not in her plans.

I'm not staying here all night! Eliza thought. *What should I do? Get up and walk away from the warmth of the car, into the unknown of the outside world?* "No!" Eliza yelled to no one. She would stay by the safety of her car even if it took all night.

Maybe I should try to change the tire she mused as she got back out of the car and looked again at the tire. "I don't even know how to get you off." She was completely clueless. "Damn you!" She shouted into the evening air. She felt a tear slip from her eye. She quickly wiped it away. "There are plenty of women that don't know how to change a stupid flat." Her thoughts then mocked back, *and there are plenty that do.* She covered her ears as if to keep the voice that was nagging her out and yelled, "Shut up, shut up, shut up!"

She got back into the car and stared at her reflection in the rearview mirror. "Don't look at me like that; you're just as stupid as I am." She began to laugh even though her tears were flowing and her nose was running. "I've gone mad. I'm sitting in this car talking to myself and I've gone mad." She was not sure why she was crying, but she thought she was scared. She checked the doors to make sure they were locked and tried to relax. *Hurry up morning; I'm not walking in the dark.* Her mind was made up and not another thought was given again to stepping outside of the car; at least during the darkness of the night.

Eliza began singing to herself. A silly little song she was making up as she sat there. "Here I am, sitting here. I wish I were sitting someplace else. But here I sit all by myself. I'm so lost in the world today. I was not lost until I came this way. But here I sit all by myself, wishing I were sitting somewhere else."

She pulled a blanket out of the backseat and wrapped herself in it. She slumped down in the seat. She was no longer looking out of the window or in the mirror. She tapped her foot on the brake as she sang, keeping a beat to the silly little song. She turned the car back on just to take the chill off and sang, the words getting slower and slower as sleep drew her in. She turned the car off and laid the seat back stretching her legs out with her foot now resting solidly on the brake. She quickly fell into a deep sleep.

A loud tap on the window startled Eliza awake.

"Hey, you need some help? I saw your brake lights." A man's voice boomed through the night.

Eliza sat up and screamed. Not a little scream, but a scream which echoed throughout the car and into the night. Then it was not just one scream, it was a series of small screams that came and went as she inhaled and exhaled. Her hand reached for the horn and she pushed as hard as she could sending the person standing next to the car back, as her screams along with the horn, startled him.

"Hey I'm sorry; I didn't mean to scare you. I saw your lights. I thought you might need some help. My name is Chris, Chris Peters," he said.

Her voice began to leave her as her mind finally comprehended the words the man spoke. She bowed her head trying to catch her breath. She touched the window with her hand, as a giant smile of relief crossed her face. "I'm sorry. Thank God you stopped." She reached for the door handle, trying to open the door. "What's wrong with this stupid thing?" She said as she pulled back and forth on the door handle. She then tried the window. She reached for the handle realizing there was not one there. She started to panic. "Let me out, I can't get out!" She yelled, now thinking she was in a nightmare. She then remembered she had electric windows, but they did not work either. She could feel the man staring at her as she fought with the door handle and the window buttons. She dare not look up at him as her task required all of her attention.

Chris tapped again on the window. "Turn the car on," he requested.

"What?" Eliza said.

"Turn the car on and put the window down or unlock the door, whatever you think you'll be able to accomplish." His words were light as if he was amused by her actions.

She found herself almost laughing at her own stupidity. She felt foolish, but now was not the time to reflect on that. She turned to the voice and looked at the body of the man standing outside her car. In his left hand he held up a flashlight. As he lowered the flashlight the beam of light crossed his face. Eliza saw his face. She stopped moving her hand on the car's ignition and stared at the man. Her goofy smile turned into a look of shock as her brain took in what she was looking at.

A large scar ran the length of his face, starting at his chin and running up to his hairline. His forehead was caved in where part of his skull was missing. On his head, the skin grafts were tight, dry, patchy and hairless. There were smaller scars by the outside of his empty left eye socket and zigzag sunken scars across his left cheek. He did not have front teeth. His mouth when closed exposed a gaping hole where full lips should have been. The disfigurement continued to his nose which had the appearance of being two holes tightly sewn together; there was no cartilage or bridge, just two holes sticking out on his face. It appeared he was trying to grow a beard, but with so many missing hair follicles the patches only added to his gruesome looks.

"Look, it is really cold out here. Do you want some help or not?" Chris was shaking his flashlight as he spoke to her, shining it back and forth between his face and hers; the grin no longer on his face either.

Eliza was frightened again, but this time she knew why as she looked in his other hand and down his body. He carried a tire iron and his jacket was stained with a reddish brown substance.

"No!" She shook her head and yelled, "I don't need your help; just go away, you can go now." She looked him in the face and shuddered at what she saw. "Just leave me alone, I don't need your help, just go away!" She screamed, "Leave me alone!"

"Are you sure lady? No one is going to be down this road tonight. In fact, you are really lucky I happened down here. This old road leads to the plant and it's been closed for three months now. Why are you on it?" He rubbed his cheek with the back of his gloved hand, making his already distorted face look even worse.

"I said, Leave Me Alone! I don't need your help. You can go." She now went from angry to pleading as if she were begging for her life. "Please just leave." She looked at the door lock and put her arm across it making sure the button was down as she spoke.

"Alright, but I don't know how anyone is going to find you out here." He shouted through the closed window.

"I don't need any help I said. I'm not some helpless woman. I know how to change a stupid flat tire and I have protection, right here. I have a gun. Right here in my purse, I have a gun." Eliza patted the purse next to her hoping he would just go away. She knew the only thing in her purse that could do any harm was a fingernail file. She would have to be really close to the person to use it, and the little damage it would do would probably just tick off the person trying to attack her.

"Well okay then, there's a bad blizzard coming in tonight. I hope you know what you are doing." Chris bent down beside her car.

What the hell is he doing now? She wondered compelling herself not to look as she prepared herself for an attack.

Chris knocked on the window again.

"I told you to go away!" She yelled. "You just go!" Her own face was now distorted.

"Hey, you dropped this out of your car, Eliza." He held the card up to the window.

Eliza's mind began to race and she dare not look at him again. He knows my name. Oh my God, he knows my name. "That's not mine! Please just leave! Just leave me ALONE!" She yelled through the window.

"Well alright, but I'll be back just to make sure you got help. You could freeze to death out here. You don't have to be afraid of me, afraid of the way I look. Anyway, tonight is not the night I eat people." He laughed as he spoke the words.

Eliza heard his words. She remembered a movie she had seen, it was based on a true story, about a family that ate people. She was now scared to death!

Eliza watched him walk to his truck. His head was shaking back and forth. He looked back at her and smiled. His smile did nothing for his face. He put his hands out as if to ask her one last time if she needed help. She turned away from the window. She wondered, just for a moment what had happened to him, but the moment passed as she heard the truck start. *Thank God* she thought.

He pulled his truck next to the car. "I'll call my sister Mary at the sheriff's department and ask her to send Doug out to help you. You'll like Doug, you'll like the way he looks." He yelled out of the open window.

She did not turn toward him as he spoke. She could hear the disdain in his voice. She could not tell if he was telling the truth about his sister or not. She did not care. She wanted him to leave and take his grossly deformed face with him.

The truck idled beside her another moment and then quickly pulled away. As Eliza watched the taillights disappear, she breathed a sigh of relief. *Those are the people mothers warn their little girls about.* As the thought ran through her mind, a shiver ran through her body. She turned the engine on; she knew she could not stay there. She was scared. If in fact, this was the road to a plant that had been closed for a while; she knew she was not going to find help, any safe help. She wondered how bad it would be to drive on the rim, but she did not care. "Damn, I should have flown," she said again. She put the car in gear and turned the car around. The red from the car's taillights lit up the snow as Eliza and her car disappeared into the night.

1
Summer 2005

"EJ, wake up," Eliza shook her son lightly. "EJ COME ON, we have got to go. Please EJ, you NEED to get up." She shook him firmly. It mattered not if she spoke softly or yelled in an earsplitting tone. It was not the sound of words EJ responded to. EJ was deaf and no matter how loud she spoke; he would not, could not, hear her. Now as Eliza thought about it a tear clouded her eye, but she swept it away before it could spill onto her cheek. It had not always been that way; when EJ was a small baby he would coo at her voice, follow her sound, and find comfort in her soothing tone. That was ages ago and now EJ was deaf. She taught him to sign both visually and in her hand, for this was the way they communicated during the darkness of the nights and there were thousands of dark nights.

Eliza often wondered if he remembered the sound of sounds. As much as she wished he could hear, there were times she was thankful he did not. The pain some sounds cause is better left unheard, and there were plenty of sounds Eliza knew EJ should have never been a witness to. Being unable to hear made it possible for EJ to at least block out the horrible sounds surrounding them. Eliza hoped he had closed his eyes tight as he hid under the small bed, regulating his breath in and out so he was not seen or heard. "What a child's life he has had. What a pitiful life for a little boy." Eliza whispered.

Stop it! Eliza thought. *I had no control then; everything was out of control, everything is still out of control. God help me to find the control I need. God, just please help me.* She touched EJ again. "Come on EJ," her voice sounding stern, "Wake up!" She reached down and kissed him on his forehead.

Eliza looked down upon her son. He was only a shadow in the darkness. She then looked at the small window which held her and her family captive. A new day was beginning to dawn. Although the sun had begun making its way across the sky, it had yet to reach the small window that would brighten up the insufficient quarters she shared with her son and his baby sister.

"Damn it EJ, come on, we've got to go! The sun is coming and we've got to go if we want food. We've got to go if we want freedom. We have got to go now, if we want to live!" Eliza pulled his almost lifeless body up from the pallet he slept on and placed him on her lap. His body was that of a small child, but to Eliza he seemed to be a hundred years old. The son she held now was skin and bones, but his mother knew he would live at least today. She knew so very little, but this she did know. She unbuttoned her worn out shirt and placed her breast beside his mouth. "Here EJ, take the milk." She could not let him starve. She would let him feed for only a few minutes, she needed milk for her other child. She had yet to reach the point of choosing which child would live or which would die.

EJ sat up and tried to look at his mother. He tried to open his eyes, but his lids were heavy with sleep. He tried to lift his arms, but they too were heavy. His mother held his head to her breast, and he suckled her nipple, like an infant child. His belly thanked him for the food and a surge of energy ran through him. He opened his eyes. He could feel the vibration of his mother as she spoke to him. He could read her lips when he could see them, but there was still not enough light. He did not move from his mother's lap. EJ was tired. Not that he had done anything to take his energy away; he had no energy, because he had no food. His body was eating him alive. It seemed his surge of energy ended with his eyes opening. He leaned into his mother and begged sleep to return to him.

Eliza spoke aloud to him because she always had. She wanted to be sure he could read lips in case he found a way out if she died. A way out; that thought had consumed her for more years than she herself had even known.

After a moment EJ grabbed his mother's hand and placed his fingers in her palm. His question was a simple one, but caused his mother pain. She pulled her hand back with surprise, startling EJ, and making the meager boy jump.

The words echoed through his mother's head as if he had spoken aloud, "ARE we going to live?"

Eliza wanted nothing more but to tell him, *yes*. She could not. She did not have the answer. She had no answers other than the bars on the window, which held them in their prison, were loose. Her son, her daughter and she herself could now fit through the tiny hole. She grabbed his hand and signed back, "With all my heart, I pray yes."

"We must go son," she signed into his small fragile hand. She lifted him off her lap and placed him on the floor, in the far corner, by his sister. Gradually, ever so slowly, the light began to seep into the room.

Eliza peered around the place she called home for so long, so very long. It was one room with old clothes, a pallet of blankets and a twin bed. There were books; some still full of their pages, others just a shell; empty, used for toilet paper and napkins. A bucket with a thin pipe they used for a sink and a larger pipe they used as a toilet, stood in the right corner of the room, near the window. The walls, made of cinder block, were cold and the floor made of concrete, was littered with an assortment of clothes, to keep their feet warm. The room had smells they cared not to notice. It was a dark, dingy place, a cage where all hopes and dreams die. She was ready to go, ready to leave. She was ready to be free.

She pulled the bars from the window and broke the glass which was already cracked. She tossed a blanket on the glass, so her son would not cut himself, knowing deep inside, any loss of blood for him, could mean death. She lifted her lightweight son through the window, and then went back for her baby daughter. She handed the baby to her son, who was bent down looking back into the hole. She then pulled herself up through the opening to freedom.

Eliza had an urge to turn, to look again; back into the room which had held her for so long, but decided against it. She knew every nook and cranny. She knew every bug that ever managed to find a way in, hoping to follow it out. She resisted the security the room held, at least there, she had shelter. Her children had shelter. She was afraid. *What if we do not make it? What if he finds us? What if we die?* She had visited death many times over the years. *It would just be better if we died. No, no, no* her mind would not stay in that place. *What if we make it?* It was the thought of success that refused to let her turn around and look back. After many years of pain, hunger, and hopelessness, it was time to leave this place, her hole in no·where.

She grabbed her son's hand and spoke into his anxious palm. "We will make it." EJ turned his face up. Eliza saw he matched the smile she had placed on her face. As the sun drifted into the sky, he smiled. She took the baby from him and held the little infant close to her heart. She grabbed EJ's hand and walked him toward the trees. She knew they needed cover to survive, an open field would not do.

EJ was overwhelmed; his mouth fell open and he wanted to stop. He jerked his hand from his mother's and looked at the grass, the trees, the shrubs and the ferns which surrounded them. The wonders of the world came alive to him. All colors, not flat ones like he had seen in books, but bright brilliant colors enhanced by the magnificence of their ever changing shades. The light of the sun filtering through the white clouds came alive. He had never seen such beauty! He was entranced. His mother tried to pull him along, but he pulled back. The sights of the morning absorbed him as birds took their morning flight and wind wrestled with the leaves on the trees. He stood with his eyes wide open and his mouth ajar as his arms reached out to touch the marvel of the world before him. He could feel his mother jerking on him, but he did not want to move.

EJ fell to the ground, crossed his legs and refused to budge. A giant smile was still plastered on his face. The grass, with its morning dew, felt wet to his fingers. He lifted his hands to look at his fingers, amazed at the moisture covering the ground. The grass beneath his fingertips rebounded, causing EJ to push it down again and again. His arms took flight, as his eyes caught movement in the sky. He moved his arms as though he were flying through the sky, mocking the birds which were soaring into the white clouds. EJ wanted to close his eyes and pretend to follow the birds, but he was so taken in by the greatness of everything, he refused to close them, even straining before he blinked.

Eliza caught his hand as it was taking its imaginary flight. Although she had been locked up for many years, and just the smell of fresh clean air made her want to gulp it all in, her mind was on getting away, not looking at the morning. "We have to go," she signed into his hand. She pulled him again.

EJ jerked his hand back not even looking at his mother.

Eliza caught his hand again. "Do you want him to find us? He will if we stay out here. Is that what you want, for him to find us? Do you want to go back in there? Do you want to live there forever? We need to go. Get up EJ. We need to go now!"

The smile disappeared from the little boy's face, as if his mother had slapped him. He got up off the ground, grabbed his mother's hand and looked her straight in the face as his hands began to talk. "Will he come back? Will he put me there again? I will be good. I will be a good boy, mommy, please." He vocalized, "Ood oy," struggling with the words as they came from his mouth.

Tears appeared in his eyes. His mother felt guilty for the harsh words, but she needed him to get up. She was too weak to carry him and his baby sister. She wished she were stronger. She wished so many things.

She pulled him close to her and hugged him. "We need to go to be safe." She dragged him to the cover of trees which lined the field they were in. They headed away from the area, not a fast walk, but not a slow one either. They needed to get away. She wanted to remember landmarks of the area they were in, but it was all just too much to take in. There was too much field, too many trees and too many hills they had to climb.

If they managed to get away, there would be more mornings; a lifetime full of mornings to enjoy the sights, sounds and smells of each new day. If they escaped they could explore new places, learning new things and hopefully forget where they came from. For now though, their journey had just begun. It would be a long journey, one for which she had no maps, but she was ready to find a way. She stopped once to check her pocket, just to make sure she had her old license, and the hundred dollar bill inside. It was money she had hidden inside an old book. It had to be enough to get them someplace, someplace far from here. She wanted to think of happy thoughts, of a life in another place; but she needed to remember the way they had lived. The pain and the misery fueled their passage into freedom.

2

It was a beautiful warm morning. The sun dried the dew and the slight morning fog had disappeared. The birds were singing as Mary Owen drove into work. She was having pleasant thoughts of the night before with her husband. She could not keep the smile from her face, replaying the night, over and over in her mind. *What a beautiful day*, Mary thought. *Nothing is going to spoil this day.* She finished her drive, parked and went into work.

Last night was the first night she let Bryan make love to her. It had been weeks since they were intimate because of the accident. Doug Moore, the sheriff, brought her the terrible news; her brother was dead. Mary insisted on seeing his body. She had to be sure it was Chris, but she was not prepared for what she saw. Chris' head was smashed completely in. The scar which held his face together was ripped open and pieces of skull and brain matter oozed from its former containment. She collapsed. The last few weeks were a blur, except her last image of Chris which was burned into her brain. The tears came often, and she thought working would take her mind off the pain and loss she felt. Bryan held her when she cried, and laughed with her when she laughed. Bryan was more than her husband; he was her best friend and the rock of their marriage.

She put her thoughts of Chris away, and forced a smile to her lips as she walked into the sheriff's station. She was a deputy for her hometown and took pride in her position. She enjoyed her job, and although she had had a few problems with the people she worked with during the years, she still respected most of them. The citizens of her community were pretty good considering the day and age she lived in. Crime, even major ones, had never been a problem in the area.

In the early years, Cider Bend had been known for hard drinking, but the religious right moved in and soon the only drinking done in the town was iced tea on a warm summer day. A dry county kept alcohol at bay or at least miles away in a different county.

Cider Bend was located on the northern most edge of Blue Grass country, in the mists of the hills and valleys of Kentucky. The roads twist and turn, dropping and climbing. Those not familiar with the area usually ended up losing their stomach or worse, their lunch. Farms litter the outskirts of town; while in the town, old wood framed houses stood the test of time. The town itself was small; where everyone knows your name and gossip keeps the tongues of both the ladies and gentlemen busy throughout the day, and at times, into the night.

Farming was the industry which sustained the community for more than half of its existence, but soon, unable to create enough income, many of the residents in the area went to work at the plant or worked in other communities. The farms on the outskirts of town, continued to grow fresh vegetables, sharing their crops with their friends and neighbors. The future of the small town was uncertain for a while due to the plant closing. Many moved on leaving behind the true spirit of the community, the families of the original settlers. They were still farmers at heart; they learned to put away for the lean times. It had been fifteen years of lean time, but the town was still surviving.

Mary smiled and greeted the other two people in the station, then sat down at her small desk. There were five desks in the main station area and one behind a wall of glass. That office belonged to the sheriff. There were three other rooms. On one end was lock-up, containing two cells that stayed empty most of the time. On the other end of the station a small hall led to the back door and the bathrooms; the women's room to the right, men's room to the left. In between the hall and the cells was another room. It contained small kitchen equipment, a table and some chairs. It was referred to as the donut room, because every morning the local donut shop dropped off fresh hot donuts for the station.

Robert Messer walked in a few minutes after Mary. He was a short, round man, friendly and kind. His hair had begun falling out about three years earlier to become a noticeable bald spot, but he kept brushing it over, as if it were still there, hoping no one would notice. No one ever said a word for fear of hurting his feelings; and no one in town or on the outskirts of town would dare do that. A loveable man in his mid-forties, he had grown up on the farm where he now resided with his wife and two children.

Robert bought a motorcycle a few months earlier, against the wishes of his wife and everyone who knew him. His body was not that of a biker. His stomach measurement was almost wider than his height. He spent half the day sucking in his belly to pull his pants up only to have them fall down below his tummy as soon as he finished.

"Robert, I saw you pull up on that darn bike. You are going to kill yourself on that thing one day. Aren't you ready to give it up?" Mary jabbed.

"I'm still a new rider, give me a break. I get a little wobbly when I have to turn then stop," he replied as he removed his helmet.

"Yea, just make sure it's not me picking up the pieces off the road, ok?" Mary said and winked at him.

"Deal, if I ever lay the bike down, I'll request you not be sent to the scene, even if you're the only one working. I'll just wait till the next shift comes in." Robert smiled back at Mary and laughed a hearty laugh that shook his whole body. "It's good to see you back Mary."

"So, what's on the agenda for today?" Mary looked at John and Jeff.

John Armstrong and Jeff Wilkes were finishing their night shift. Both were part-time employees. John was older, in his late fifties. He had worked for the sheriff's department for as long as Mary could remember, but never ran for sheriff. He was happy doing what he was doing without having total responsibility. Jeff was young, only twenty-three. He had been with the sheriff's department for about a year.

There was no news and nothing happening. It seemed to be a typical day at the station. Occasionally, there was some trouble to report. There was Mrs. Wisdom who called every week and a few of the high school kids getting into trouble every now and again. Mostly the department just rode around the streets and let the community know they were there, just in case they were needed.

Mary and Robert flipped a coin to see who was going out on patrol first. They had always done this. Mary said it kept the job fresh since you never knew what you were doing first; answering the phones or meeting with the people you protected and served. Robert thought she was nuts, but almost every day for the last seventeen years he flipped a coin for Mary. He never called heads or tails, he just flipped for Mary and always without fail he would yell, "It's heads, no it's tails, I think I see an arm, no that's a leg." Mary thought he enjoyed it regardless of what he told everyone else.

So began their day; Mary in the station answering the phones for six hours and Robert on the streets for six hours. After the six-hour period they would switch.

Mary had been married for twelve years and had a beautiful baby boy. For years, she and her husband Bryan had tried to have children, but with no luck. Then out of the blue, four years ago, she found out she was going to have a child. They were ecstatic. Mary kept working and all seemed well until her sixth month. Her water broke when she went to the bathroom. She had gone into labor. Robert, whom was on the shift with her at the time, rushed her to the hospital. By the time Bryan arrived, she had given birth to a baby girl. She lived for twenty-eight minutes; just long enough for her parents to kiss her goodbye. They named her Joy, even though her life was so short. Neither had ever felt such "joy" in their hearts as they did when they held her or such sadness when they lost her. The doctors were unsure why Mary lost her baby. A year later, almost to the day, Mary gave birth again. Bryan insisted on her taking a leave from her position during her pregnancy. She hated being told what to do by a man, but she agreed. Putting your heart out like that, twice, takes courage. Protecting your heart only takes common sense. Charley screamed into the world bringing with him pleasure and delight, easing their heartache.

The day was somewhat boring for a Saturday. The office phones were silent and no one stopped by. Mary worked a crossword puzzle she kept in her desk, drank coffee and called home. She glanced at the clock on the wall and begged for the hours to creep by faster. She settled back into her book, hoping for the answer to a question. At eleven thirty nature called and she left her post to visit the ladies room.

Mary checked her reflection in the mirror as she was washing her hands. She was five feet-six inches tall and even after having a child so late in life, she was quick to lose the weight. She was nearing forty, but thought she still looked pretty good. Her hair had changed shades through the years, but she thought the, "coffee with cream" color fit her perfectly. Her eyes, still a dark brown, had kept their sparkle over the years and enticed those that had just met her. Most people wondered how they could lose themselves in a person's eyes; Mary always said her soul was so pure it just pulled people in. She finished washing her hands and while grabbing some paper towels to dry them, the bell on the outside door jingled.

"I'll be right out," she yelled, quickly dropping the spent paper in the waste basket. She checked her hair once more in the mirror, then left the room with a smile and her eyes sparkling. She closed the door behind her and turned toward the front of the station. Her smile, her sparkle and her voice left her when she entered the room.

"Can you help us?" A minuscule voice asked, coming from a small woman. She was tiny, less than eighty pounds. Her hair hung down her back in a braid, but swung out to the side as the woman spoke and looked down at her children. Her skin was translucent, showing the blue of her veins. Her face was dirty and also carried scars from wounds of long ago. Mary wondered how old the woman was, but dare not guess. She had a very small baby and another young child with her. To Mary, she looked old, tired and beaten. She looked a feather's throw close to death.

The woman wore old, torn, thin pants that might have been a pair of blue jeans at one time, with an old sweater that had puffy shoulders despite the eighty-five degree weather outside. Her shoes were high top tennis shoes, each lace tied in multiple places. Mary remembered her days from the eighties, as she looked at the woman, and wondered why she had chosen these clothes to wear.

Her eyes were sunken in with deep dark circles. The whites of her eyes were slightly yellow and bloodshot. Her eye coloring was a magnificent shade of blue green that reminded Mary of a lagoon. As Mary looked at her eyes she was sure she had seen them before somewhere, but she could not place where. The lady's cheekbones stood out and her jaw was very pronounced. The skin around her mouth was tight, but with her mouth hanging a tad open it gave the woman a slightly dumb look. Mary wondered if she was a mentally retarded woman who needed help getting to her home.

The child next to her held on to her leg. The adolescent appeared to be four or five and Mary could not make out if it was a boy or a girl. The child was also skinny and had his own share of scars. His skin color, like the woman's, was also an ashy, translucent color. The child's outfit was a large shirt, appearing to belong at one time, to the mother. His sunken eyes carried the same strange blue green shade, only his eyes held a little fear beneath his color. His cheekbones and jaw like his mother's, were very prominent. His face was not round like that of a healthy child, but more like that of a dying child. It was like the faces and bodies of the children of Africa Mary had seen on TV asking for money.

The woman carried a blanket in her arms. The blanket was not a typical baby blanket, full of pale blues, yellows and pinks, but appeared to be an old, dirty and extremely stained bedspread frayed and ripped. Mary saw a skinny little arm appear then disappear, back into the makeshift cover.

Mary took a step toward the family and was hit with the most nauseating smell she had ever experienced in her life. Her hand automatically went to her nose. The stench was so bad Mary's eyes began to water.

The woman took a step back, and then turned to leave the station.

"Never mind, we don't need any help," the woman said, shoving her son back toward the door.

"Wait, please don't go." Mary put her other hand out and stopped advancing.

The mother and both children appeared to have legs and arms that looked like stick limbs a child would draw on paper. The child in her arms whimpered a moment, and then stopped as the mother shook it gently. The woman slowly turned back around.

"I really can't let you leave. Please wait, I don't think you will get very far. You all just look so tired and maybe a little hungry. Please just stay." Mary's voice was cajoling but firm. She knew she would have to fill out a report about this woman, but more importantly she knew she would have to help this woman. She was bewildered; she had never in her life seen people that looked like this. There was no way she was letting them walk out of the door; at least no way she was letting the children go with the woman.

"I asked if you could help us please," the woman spoke again. Her voice was queer, shaky and thin.

Mary took another small step forward and said, "I can try to help you. Please come in and sit down and we can see what I can do for you. I don't want you to leave, at least not yet." She sounded cheerful, as if she were inviting a guest into her home. She pointed to the chairs in the donut room behind her and said, "There is food in there. Please help yourselves. I have to make a call."

"Who are you calling?" The woman sounded fearful as she asked.

"Oh, I want to get you some more food. We only have a little in there and there is no milk for the baby. I bet the baby is hungry. Can I see her or is it a little boy?" Mary was being really nice and she knew she might come across as fake if she were not careful.

The woman responded, "She is a girl. I've named her Hope. Can we leave if we want?" She asked Mary.

"Yes you can, but you need some things for the children first. Please let me get you some food and nothing will happen to you." Mary crossed her fingers behind her back. She did not want to lie to the woman however; she knew if she said anything the woman did not like, she would have to fight her to get the children away. She did not want to hurt a wounded animal and that is what the woman looked like to Mary.

After Mary got the family settled in the room, she went back to her desk. She picked up the phone, hit the speed dial button and was quickly connected to Doctor Denton's office. While finishing her conversation with the doctor's office, she retrieved the radio and called Robert to return to the station.

"Mary it's early yet, are you that bored?" Robert asked.

"Robert hold on, I have to call you right back." Mary put the microphone down and went back to the room.

"What kind of milk does the baby take?" Mary inquired.

"Breast milk, but I'm dry. She has never had anything else. I didn't have anything else to give her. I just don't know what else to give her."

"Well, I guess a little powered baby milk won't do her too much harm until the doctor gets here," Mary said.

"Doctor, what doctor? I don't want to see a doctor. We just need a little help to get away from here!" The woman exclaimed.

Mary thought for a moment searching for the right words. She then carefully told the woman, "The doctor needs to make sure the baby gets the right formula."

The lady did not move or say anything. After a few minutes, Mary looked down at the small child and said, "What's your name sweetie?"

The child was looking at the donuts not paying attention to Mary.

"His name is EJ and I'm Eliza Johnson. Have you heard of me? Have I been reported missing?" Eliza looked up at Mary.

"No, I'm sorry dear, I have not heard of you and there haven't been any missing person's reports from this area. Who reported you missing?"

"I don't know. Nobody I guess. I, oh, never mind." Eliza put her head down.

"Do you need anything else for the children? What about yourself? I will get Robert to pick it up on the way in." Mary, still using her happy tone, asked. Right now she did not want to push her too hard.

"You called someone else? We can't stay here. We only came in here because you are a woman. I don't want to be around men. We can't stay if you're bringing in a man." The woman started gathering the children up to leave.

"I just want to get you some food. Please just wait. I can't help you if won't let me and you really look as if you need help. And you don't have to worry about Robert. He's such a good guy. He is nice and funny and he wouldn't hurt a fly," Mary said.

"We don't want to be any trouble. We just need some help to get away from here. We really can't stay that long," the woman responded. The boy was still staring at the donuts on the table.

"Please help yourselves to those donuts. They won't be eaten and will just get thrown out." Mary walked around the table to the donuts and pushed the box forward. She noticed the strong odor accompanying the family, seemed to be dissipating. "There are some cups over there on the counter and there is coffee and water." She pointed toward the coffee pot and the sink. Mary noticed the change cup sitting there and added, "There is no charge. The cup is just for the people who work here."

Mary did not know if the woman was married or not. She looked down at her finger in hopes of finding a ring, and then she realized, if there had in fact been a ring on her finger, it would have long been gone. Her fingers held no ring. Only a thin, pale sheet of skin covered her deformed bones. Mary wondered if she was born with a deformity or if they had grown mangled after being broken. Either way, it still did not answer her question about marriage, so she plunged ahead and said, "Mrs. Johnson, where is your husband?"

"Husband?" She asked, as if Mary was speaking in tongues. "I'm not married." Eliza, for the first time in her children's life, realized she was indeed, an unmarried woman with children.

"What should I call you?" Mary tried to manage a smile, but the more she heard from the woman the more she thought *white trash*. She shook her head trying to get the phrase from her mind.

"Eliza. Just call me Eliza. It's been a really long time since anyone has called me by my name."

"You've got it Eliza and you can call me Mary." As the words left her lips, she knew she was pushing the happiness thing too far. She was not happy about a woman bringing two small children, starved, into her office; and the woman was not even married! Mary knew she should not think it, but her church background crept in and she thought, *what a whore*, before she could stop herself. Thank God she did not say it out loud. She hated the fact her tax dollars went to support people like that; people popping out children, people who refused to work to support them, and people having babies out of wedlock. Girls used to take pride in their bodies, now they just opened their legs to every Tom, Dick or Harry. Mary felt disgusted.

Mary felt her anger growing. She needed to get out of the room before she said something she might regret. "I need to call Robert and let him know what to pick up." Mary walked out of the room, closing the door behind her. She gulped in the fresh air and realized she was not getting used to the pungent smell.

She called Robert back. "Bring baby milk from the store and some kind of food with you please."

"Hey, I'm not your husband picking up your grocery list," Robert said laughing. Then quickly added, "What do you need Hon?"

"Robert now is not the time to joke. Please, just get here and get here quick. You won't believe what I'm looking at. I can't explain over the radio. Please, just hurry; I need you here." She turned the volume down on the receiver in hopes the lady did not hear Robert.

"I'll be there in a minute; I'm right down the road. Are you okay?" Robert picked up the tension in her voice.

"Yes I'm fine, but you really have to see this," she said back.

"Why don't I just come there first?" He questioned.

"No, bring the food and the milk. Whatever you do Robert, please, don't forget the milk."

"I just pulled up to the store. Did you find a cat or something Mary?"

"Robert, you have known me for a long time, would I call you for a stupid cat?" She found herself almost yelling into the microphone.

"Sorry Mary." His voice was soft and Mary regretted not using the fake, nice voice she used on the lady.

"Is this personal or business? I need to know how to pay." Robert's voice was now professional.

"Business, I'm sorry Robert, I've got to go." She ended their conversation. She felt bad, but Robert would get over his hurt feelings soon.

Mary turned and stared back through the glass of the donut room. The woman was tearing small bits of donuts for the boy, giving him a piece at a time. She ate one for every three she gave him. Mary thought he was very well behaved for a child of his age, who was starving, and with food sitting before him. From time to time, Eliza would rub her fingers over the lips of the baby, as if this were the only food the little one would get for the day. She decided to wait for Robert, before she talked to the woman again. Mary sat at her desk, watching and waiting not believing her own eyes.

3

It seemed an eternity before Robert made his way to the station. Mary watched the clock on the wall when she was not watching the family. She watched seconds pass as though they were minutes. Five hundred twenty-three seconds later, Robert walked in with milk and a plastic bag full of various snack foods.

"Now, what's so important it has you nuts?" Robert asked, his nose picking up a slight odor. "And what's that smell?" He wrinkled his nose as he looked at Mary, waiting for an answer. As he placed the milk and snacks on her desk, Mary pointed in the direction of the donut room. Robert's eyes followed her finger. He stood staring at the woman, the child, and baby in the room.

Eliza looked up. She could feel new eyes staring at her and it made her uncomfortable. She did not like being on display. She looked to Mary. She wanted to get up and leave. She wondered where the back door was. Maybe she could sneak out. She looked at EJ. He needed food. She looked back up at the man. He waved at her with a fake smile plastered on his face. Eliza turned away.

"Robert, I said baby milk." Mary picked up the whole milk rolling her eyes.

Robert turned back toward Mary and spoke, "What the hell? Who is she and what is going on? And as for the milk, I got what they had."

Mary got out of her chair, shook her head, looked to the woman and said, "I don't know what is going on. I gave them some donuts and waited for you. I have never seen anything like this before. They need help. I'm not sure what kind of help they need, but they need help. So be a good man, walk in there and help them. The woman is Eliza. Good luck and I'll wait right here for you." She planted herself next to her desk and gestured toward the room. She then added, "By the way, she hates men!"

"Oh no dear lady, she came to you so you can help. Anyway, I am no good with children. And what do you mean she hates men? What did I ever do to her?"

"Please Robert, I have seen you with your children, you are really great. And I don't know why she hates men. We didn't get that far. I suspect it has something to do with the way she looks. I think she's been beaten for a long time, possibly years," Mary said.

"Well, I'm not that good with kids. My kids walk all over me. Their mom is the mean one and I am the play guy. Really pisses her off," Robert laughed. He then got a serious look on his face. "She really does look bad, doesn't she?"

"Okay, we do this together. Come on in, let me introduce you." Mary headed to the room.

"Come on Robert, don't lag behind and grab the milk and food. You did get food didn't you?" Mary went to the door, took a deep breath, and opened it.

Mary and Robert went into the small room. Robert put the milk on the table, grabbed his nose and dumped the bag of snacks out. EJ's eyes got huge.

Mary grabbed two cups, filled them with milk, and then asked, "Is there a bottle for the baby?"

"No, none of my children ever had a bottle." The woman looked to her chest. "I have no milk now. It dried up. I tried to make it last, but I had no control. My body just will not produce milk anymore. I gave them all I had."

Mary's mind raced, "Robert, go to my vehicle; I'm sure there's a bottle from Charley there." She reached into her pocket and pulled out the keys. "Here, here are the keys." Robert took them and quickly left the room. Mary then went to the window and opened it. Although the station had air conditioning, fresh air seemed more important to Mary than the bill for cooling the outside.

Mary knew Robert was thankful for being able to get away from the smell for a moment. He was after all gasping for breath by her desk. She knew he would have a hard time dealing with not only the smell, but also how the family looked. Mary knew Robert would need to talk to her. She wondered if he could sit in a room talking to this woman, and not throw up. She wondered if she herself could.

The small child looked at the food, then to his mother. Finally his mother said he could have something. "Only one EJ, we really don't want to be a bother. Go on my little boy and you can have the milk. It's good for you." The little boy looked from his mother to the food; she finally pushed a packet of crackers to him. He tore open the packet and quickly ate the whole thing.

"I'm sorry. It's been a few days since he's had food. I mean we ate some raw vegetables I took from a garden, but that's all we've had to eat." She looked down at the baby. "My milk ran out this morning. I expected it to be there, but then it just stopped flowing. I guess you have to eat to have milk flow. I let EJ feed too, when I had milk. How could I deny him? His life has been so hard." The baby began to fuss as Robert returned.

"I found this one. It's dirty. I took the top off and smelled it." He pointed the bottle to Mary while giving her a funny look. "It's got a really bad smell and Mary; it's not the only thing ..."

"I'll be right back," Mary said, cutting Robert off mid-sentence.

"No. Please don't leave him here with me," the woman begged.

"I think we should call the Doctor and see what's keeping him. I'm not leaving Robert in here with you; he's coming out with me." Mary said yanking Robert by the arm.

Robert, still holding the bottle in his hand, still looking at the woman and the two children that were with her, let himself be drug out of the room by Mary.

"Call Doc and see what's keeping him. Tell him to get over here quickly. I know they stink, but right now that's not the important thing. Now, I'm going to clean this bottle and get the baby some milk to drink." Mary looked Robert straight in the face and added, "Robert, do not let them leave. I mean it. If she tries to leave, she cannot take the children. Do you see how skinny they all are?"

"Oh, for God sake Mary, I'm not stupid or blind. What has she done to those children? What kind of a person would do that to their own kids? Even if a man did beat her, she is a mother and mothers are supposed to protect their children. Fathers are supposed to protect their children." Robert wiped a tear from his eye.

"I'm sorry Robert; I don't know what has happened to her. Just call the doctor please." Mary touched him on his arm as she spoke.

"What's the number? I know it but, I just, I just don't know it now." Robert said as he reached for the phone.

Mary pointed to the phone numbers programmed on her desk phone. "I'll get the bottle cleaned for the baby now." Mary did not know what else to say.

She went to the restroom and cleaned the bottle. She used paper towels and hand soap, and then ran the hottest water she could in the bottle. She went back into the donut room, filled the bottle with more hot water, and then set the timer on the microwave oven so the water would heat, cleaning anything she missed.

"Is there anyone you would like to call?" Mary asked Eliza.

Eliza sat for a moment then decided, "Yes, my mom."

Robert made his call sitting at Mary's desk. Mary knew he did not want to enter the room again since he lingered long after hanging up the phone.

"Robert." Mary poked her head out of the open door. "Bring the phone over here please."

Mary asked for the number and dialed on speakerphone. When the phone was answered, Eliza made no attempt to pick up the handset so Mary listened.

"Hello?" The voice on the other end was old and frail, belonging to a woman.

"Momma, is that you?" Eliza's eyes filled with tears.

"Who is this? Is anyone there?"

"Momma, it's me Eliza. Are you there Mom? Are you there?" Even though it had been years since Eliza heard her mother's voice she knew her, she knew her sweet mother's voice.

"Eliza, is that you? It's been so long, we thought you were dead."

"No momma. I'm not dead."

"Where are you Eliza?"

"Oh mom you would not believe what I've been through. Mom, I need help." Eliza's voice begged.

"Eliza, it's been so long. Why haven't you called or come to see us?"

"I was going to see you, I wanted to call you. I, I need your help. You are the only family I have. I have no place else to turn."

"Eliza where are you? What's going on?"

"I am in a police station."

"Oh, we will not get you out of jail. Is it drugs or something? Are you one of those whores? Did you kill someone? You have not talked to us for so long. I hope you didn't do anything too bad. We just can't help you; even if we had the money to get you out of there. We just don't have any money; after your father's heart attack and the doctor bills, the cost of medicine. No, we just can't get you out of jail."

"No Mom, I didn't do anything. It's just that my kids and I," Eliza began but was interrupted by her mother.

"Call your husband to help you. You haven't needed us or spoken to us in years. You said you were coming by. You said you had a new job in Texas. You forgot all about us. We just can't help you. You've broken our hearts. Just call your husband."

"Mom, I don't have a husband."

A male voice could now be heard through the receiver. "Who is on the phone Martha?"

"It's Eliza. She's in jail. She doesn't have a husband and she has kids."

"Did your husband die Eliza?" The woman asked in a soft voice.

Eliza was shaking her head as she answered, "No mom, I never got married. Mom, will you listen to me?"

"She never got married. She has kids and she never got married."

A male's voice was now yelling, not into the phone, but to Eliza's mother. "Just hang up the phone. She's a tramp. I told you our daughter is a tramp. Let her be dead. Go on Martha, hang up the damn phone." The voice belonged to Eliza's father.

"Daddy, is that you?" Eliza whispered as the phone line went dead. She cried out. "I guess I have no one now."

Mary could hear Eliza, but did not want to look at her. She was not sure what to say and thought it best to say nothing.

Mary cleaned the bottle's nipple and let it sit in the hot water for a full minute, hoping it would take away any germs that might lurk on the bottle and nipple. She ran the cold water to cool the bottle, and then filled it with milk. She heated the bottle for a few seconds then finally, before she handed it to Eliza, she said, "I'm sorry about your parents."

Eliza stopped crying and reached for the bottle. Mary knew Eliza must still be upset at the rejection of her parents. Eliza started to give the bottle to the baby.

"Wait!" Mary yelled, taking the woman by surprise and making her jump. "You need to check the temperature on your arm first."

"Oh, sorry, I've never used one of these before." Eliza was holding the bottle as though she had never seen one, much less used one before.

Finally Mary asked, "Is there anyone else to call, anyone at all?"

Eliza simply said, "No."

"Can we talk about what happened to you now?" Mary thought it was time for answers. Enough time had passed and it was time to get to the bottom of what was going on.

"I've been kidnapped. Please help me. We don't need a doctor, just a way out of here." Eliza begged. "Please help us before he finds out we're missing. We need to be safe. I don't know what he'll do to us if he finds out we're gone."

"Kidnapped? When? My God! How long did he keep you and the children?" Mary's voice was anxious. "Do you know who did this to you? Where were you kept?" Mary leaned on the back of the chair she was standing next to. "Where did he go? How did you escape?"

"Please, there is no time to go into all of this. We got out yesterday and we walked forever. No, I'm not sure who did this and I don't care. I do care, but he will kill me. Do you understand if he finds me and my children, he will kill me and he might kill them too?" Eliza stood up, "If you can't help me, we have to go. We have to go now. Any day now he'll be back and any day now he'll start looking."

"Please wait. No one is going to come into this office and take you and kill you. You are safe. As long as you are with us, you are safe. Please, please sit back down in the chair and let us help you. That's what our job is, to help you." Mary motioned in the direction of the chair. She saw the reaction of the woman and wanted to help her. Mary knew if Eliza did go out on the street, this man, may see her and her kids. Although they took up little space on the earth, they stood out and would call attention to themselves.

Mary went to the door after the woman sat back down and called for Robert. "We need to call Doug. He needs to be aware of this situation."

Mary turned facing Eliza and touched her hand softly, "I'm sorry. Doug is our sheriff; he's been out of town. We'll call him and I'm sure he'll be back soon. Nothing like this has ever happened here before. We live in a quiet, small town and things like this just don't happen here." Mary paused for a moment and looked away, and then more to herself than to anyone else in the room she added, "At least I didn't think so."

Mary turned back to the lady letting her hand go and said in an incredibly professional voice, "We'll take down a statement, don't you worry; whoever did this to you and your children will pay."

4

Robert walked into the room and said, "Mary, can I speak to you for a moment; outside?" He motioned with his head.

Mary walked out leaving the door slightly ajar.

"Doc is on his way and I called the sheriff. I told him we had a kidnapping."

"What did he say?" Mary asked.

"He said to get all the information we could. He'll be here in the morning, said he would drive all night. Doug also said to keep a lid on this. No one else is to know. He really stressed no one else; like I would call the media or something." Robert whispered.

"What did he say about Saul?"

"I didn't ask about Saul, but you had better call him if you want to keep your job Mary."

Mary called Saul Schultz; the deputy left in charge, and told him what was going on. She asked him to find some diapers for the baby.

Saul reluctantly agreed to stop and make the purchase. Unlike most law enforcement personnel that worked together, Mary and Saul did not. Saul had made sexual advances toward her years earlier. He had never gotten over the fact that, not only had she turned him down, but she told her husband and the sheriff about his unwanted advances. Since then, they were never scheduled the same shift together. Mary was uncomfortable in his presence. Right now, however, she had no choice but to call him in; the sheriff was out of town and he was left in charge.

Mary and Robert walked back into the room. Mary said, "There will be another officer coming in soon. His name is Saul. We are all here to help you any way we can, so if you need anything, I mean anything at all, please let us know." Mary reached out to touch the woman, but Eliza jerked her arm back quickly.

"Please just let me feed the children and go. I do not want a question and answer session. Just give me a bus schedule, a ride out of town or anything that will take me and my children as far away from here as possible." Eliza pleaded.

Mary chose to ignore her and asked, "How old is your baby and the other child? Would you like me to take the child while you eat?"

"I will keep my children with me. He said you would take my children if I ever went to the police. At times I wanted you to. I wanted nothing to remind me of this time. I wanted my children safe, but I had no way of getting out. I held on to life so I could somehow protect them. I left because we needed food. There had not been any food for a long time. It had been longer, longer than ever before. When the earthquake came, the window broke and the bars that covered the window came loose. I was so afraid he would come and notice the cracked window. I was afraid he would know the bars were loose. He did not come. I didn't know if he would ever come back. We had to get out. The opening was so small. You know, if I weighed what I did before, I would never have fit through that window. I tried; I broke the window and tried." Eliza spoke taking Mary by surprise.

"We walked in the woods covered by the trees. I didn't know where I was going; I just walked and walked at times dragging EJ. We slept and then walked some more. I don't know where I am. Can you help me please? I need to get away from here, far, far away." Eliza was now crying.

"But where is the father of these children? Would you like us to call him? I'm sure he would like to know where his children are." Mary was confused. The lady was making no sense to her, but she waited for a name or number.

"You just don't understand, do you? Do you not understand what I am trying to tell you?" Eliza asked as a man walked through the doorway.

"Here are the diapers," Saul walked into the room. Mary could tell he was fuming about having to stop and get them in the first place. He threw the small bag of diapers at Mary, almost hitting her in the face. Saul's forward stride faulted as he moved further into the room. He looked at the family, and then looked back at Mary and Robert. "Mary, I need to talk to you and Robert for a minute, outside." Saul's fingers blocked his nasal passages as he backed out of the room.

Mary opened the bag and gave a diaper to Eliza and wet some paper towels for her. "The baby needs to be changed."

Saul poked his head in the room again and said, "Mary."

Mary glared back at him turning her hand up gesturing for him to wait. She looked at Robert, rolled her eyes, and turned, walking out of the room. Robert followed not saying a word.

"I told you we had a kidnapping." Mary said before Saul could speak.

"Yes, you did and now that I'm here, I'll take care of it," Saul said. He was a tall thin man in his mid-forties. His dark hair had begun to turn gray, but only in the temple area.

"What?" Mary responded a little louder than she wanted to.

"Mary, you stay out here and answer the phones. Has anyone bothered to call the Doctor? What about Doug? Don't look at me like that Mary. I'm in charge and this case is just too big for you. We need an open mind in there and face it Mary, everyone knows that women are emotional thinkers." Although his voice was powerful, Mary stared at him as though he had lost his mind. She knew he was an ass, but to drop back to the middle ages with a comment like that seemed a little too much for Mary.

"No, I'm not answering the phones. I need to be in there. This lady needs to have a woman with her, emotional thinker or not." She folded her arms not budging; she was going in that room come hell or high water.

"Mary, I don't think so."

Mary grabbed her notebook out of her top pocket and said, "We've already started." She walked into the room and pulled a chair next to Eliza.

Saul followed her into the room. "Mary!" He said, almost shouting.

Mary looked to Saul and said very calmly, "She'll be more comfortable with a woman in here."

"Mary, I'm not asking you."

"Saul, please, I told you she feels more comfortable with a woman here; that's why she came in, because I'm a woman. I'm not going to leave her, at least not now."

Saul's face turned red. Mary knew her defiance was angering him. He pointed and shouted, "I need to speak to you right now, out there!"

The woman spoke. Her voice at first afraid and quiet; it was just above a whisper. "I want her here or I'll leave. You men think you run the world. You make me sick. I will not speak to you; not now, not ever. I don't like men and I don't like you. You think you can do this to me, to her?" Her voice grew stronger as she spoke. It was drawn from deep inside of her soul and everyone in the small room was shocked. The meek woman that had walked into the office was now full of rage and anger. Her voice did not raise much above a whisper, but her attitude changed as did the look on her face. The way she accented certain words, took her from a small meek woman to a giant. Her son was clinging to her and weeping. The baby had also finally found her own voice, and was screaming.

"Please Miss, don't get upset," Mary patted her fragile hand. "Let me just go out there and speak to him and see what we need to do. I tell you what; there's a bathroom in that room over there, why don't you let Robert take you over there, he'll wait outside. You can clean up and change the baby, use the restroom, and maybe wash a little." Mary's voice was soft. She noticed Eliza had not put the clean diaper on the baby. She also failed to mention the fact the family stunk. How would you work that into a conversation?

Eliza said, "No, we'll wait here for you."

Mary left the room with Saul and simply said, "She has had a really bad time. I know you are in charge right now, but that woman needs tender care. When it's time to take down the bad guy, you can go all out and be a big man. Right now, we need to yield to her needs, so we can find out what the hell has happened." Mary felt like she was eating crow, but she really had no other choice at this moment.

"Where do you get off talking to me like that?" Saul asked.

Mary was about to answer, when the door to the sheriff's office opened.

Doctor Denton walked in carrying a small black bag with him. He was sixty-three years old, but had only been living in the area for five years. He wanted to move to a small community, but still practice medicine. He picked Cider Bend. He walked with a slight limp and hunched to one side. The talk in town was he had gotten mugged in the city and wanted a safe place. Boy was he in for a shock, Mary thought.

"Well, what do we have here?" Doc asked, and then peered into the windowed room. "Wow, is it drugs? Has that woman said anything about drugs? You know, I saw this in the city, women starving themselves and their children just to get that high. I better get in there." He walked into the room not waiting for answers to any of his questions.

For a man with a limp, the Doctor moved fast. By the time Mary and Saul entered the room, he had his black bag opened and was starting to work with the lady first. He asked her questions as he examined her.

Before he reached for the boy, Doc asked the woman, "Can the boy hear?"

"No," she replied.

"I didn't think so. You know you can tell these things. He never looks up when the door opens until he sees something. How old is this child?"

"I don't know. I don't know when his birthday is. I tried to keep track of time, but it slipped away," Eliza answered her eyes lowering as she spoke.

"I bet this child is eight or nine years old. Look at his size. You know the mouth gives these things away. They are all in poor health. The baby should recover. I see things I don't like. The boy, hard to tell; does he speak at all?" Doc waited for an answer.

"Yes, I taught him the best I could," Eliza answered.

"I'm going to take some blood from all of you and see. I think all of you should go to the hospital," Doc said.

"No, the children will not leave me and we are leaving this town today." Eliza jumped up from her seat and then added, "Please, if you just take us to the bus stop. I have a little money; we'll catch the bus and be gone." She pulled the folded up hundred dollar bill from her pocket. "It's the only money I have. I managed to hide it for all these years. It has to be enough to get us away from here."

"Look lady, your children are sick and you are sick. You need help, you all need help. Now, I'm not saying I can put you back to a hundred percent, but we can get you food, some clothes, and I'm sure, we can find you a place to stay for a few weeks. My advice is to get the doctoring you need. How far will your kids get if you drop dead? Malnutrition puts a strain on the heart and you could fall over dead at any moment. How will that help these kids? How will that help you? Now if you won't go to the hospital, I want to see you and the children first thing in the morning and plan on spending the day. I will arrange a room at the motel by my office, and if you won't take care of you and these children, I'll do it. And if it has to be by force, well I can do that also. This is just bad, this is just real bad." The doctor was shaking his head as he spoke.

He looked at Mary. "She's not on drugs that I can tell and not throwing up her food. She needs to eat and get some weight on. She has bones that were broken and were not set to heal properly and the ear thing and the scars, well I'm sure there is a long sad story. That is your department. I'm sure if I hook her up and run test, we will find she has heart problems. There is just so much that could be wrong with her. I'm afraid the boy has some serious problems too, but let's not get into that right now. Tomorrow, we will run the proper test. And by the way, you might want to get some pictures for both of our files." He began drawing blood. The lady sat still. The baby cried. The boy had to be held down. No one there thought the boy would have such strength. Before Doctor Denton left, he said to everyone in the room, "And for God sake, get this family cleaned up, they stink!"

Robert took the necessary pictures of the children and handed the camera to Saul. Saul handed the camera to Mary and said, "Mary, help this woman clean up the kids and take the rest of the pictures. We will need pictures if this goes to court and this has to be done right."

Mary grabbed two tee shirts from the Sheriff department's bike ride last fall. She then went to her SUV to grab a pair of extra uniform pants she kept there.

Mary led Eliza, her boy and the baby to the bathroom. She then helped the mother clean the children. The baby was skinny, but seemed to have no other problems. The boy had scars everywhere on his little body. His bones could be seen through his transparent skin and Mary could count the ribs on the little boy's stomach and back. As she snapped the pictures, tears filled her eyes more than once. Eliza changed in the bathroom stall. Mary could only imagine what horrors her frail body held.

5

Mary grabbed some paper and pens for the boy to draw with. She called her husband to check in on Charley, keeping in tears as she spoke to him. She ordered food from the diner up the street for Eliza and her son. Her shift was about to end, but she was not leaving. She wondered; was it because this was the biggest thing that had ever happened in their small town or did she really feel a strange connection to this woman and her children, wanting them to be safe. She hoped it was the latter, but maybe it was a mixture of the two.

Saul and Robert also stayed. When Jeff and John arrived, John was sent out on the street. Jeff stayed in the station to answer the phones.

Mary, Saul and Robert sat in the room with the lady. A tape recorder on the table was turned on ready to record her story. Mary thought that after the family had hot food, Eliza would feel better and could tell them everything she and her children had gone through. Mary made a makeshift bed for the little baby. Eliza at first resisted, and then laid the child down. The baby, now full with milk and clean, fell asleep despite the florescent lights beaming from above. The boy lay on the ground next to his mother, clinging to her leg with all his might.

"I'm not stupid; do you know I have a college degree? I know who I am and I know my children's names, all but one. I gave him a pet name, the child I lost. I wanted to give him a strong name, but the monster would not let me. I only had my first son a few weeks. I was scared and confused. I had lost so much blood. I was still weak." Tears ran down her cheeks and Mary reached for the box of tissues, which was kept in the room.

"My name is Eliza, EJ is my son and Hope is the baby." She looked over at the sleeping child. "I really don't know where to start. There's just so much, many years worth. If EJ is as old as the doctor said, then how old is the other boy I had before EJ?" Eliza looked to Mary and asked, "What year is this?"

"2005," Mary said as she looked at the calendar on the wall. "July 10th 2005."

"1990. Fifteen years gone in the blink of a lifetime. I thought I would die there. I spent fifteen and a half years in hell." She sounded shocked.

"Can we get on with this story already?" Saul seemed restless shifting back and forth in his chair.

"Look, I just want to get out of here, not tell you my life story." Eliza responded.

"I think you came to us, we did not go out looking for you." Saul retorted.

Eliza stood up, "I'll just leave. You can't help me anyway."

Mary looked at Eliza saying, "Go on, it's okay, he won't say another word. Please just sit down. We will help you." She eyed Saul again making sure he would not open his big mouth. "Why don't you just start at the beginning? That's always a good place to start. You can start at the beginning."

"I don't know who did this to me. I don't know if I ever saw him," she reluctantly began. "He never showed his face. When I had the flat tire, I saw this awful looking man, it could have been him. My captor's voice was mean and cold, his hands cruel on my body.

He would come at night, under the cover of darkness, but never on a full moon. We lived in darkness, except for a small window that let a tiny bit of light in during the morning. I was always awake then. I would lift EJ up to get some sun. I thought he needed that. Kids need sunlight." Eliza looked at Mary waiting for her to agree. Mary's head nodded in agreement with Eliza's.

"Do you know I could have had a great life? That's what I wanted, a really great life. I've had a hard life. How could I leave these children? They kept me sane. I didn't want them. I've lost time. I don't know how old the children are." Eliza again looked at Mary.

"Wait a minute, you're losing me. I thought we said you were going to start at the beginning, and now you have run through a ton of material, but have not said anything. Why don't we start again and this time I need, we need to know, how a woman spends fifteen years in another world. How did you get there, what happened once you were there and finally, how did you get out? You must not leave anything out. In order for us to help you, you must tell us everything, no matter what it is. Now collect your thoughts and let's begin at the beginning. Can you go back in your mind and remember what happened?" Mary touched the small hand of the woman. "It's okay. You're in good hands."

"Yes, I can start from the beginning. I've thought about that day, about that night; every moment since my capture. I have it burned in my brain. I wondered what I could have done differently, what I should have done differently," Eliza said.

6

"My name is Eliza Johnson. I was born on September 13, 1965. I ran away from home when I was seventeen. I was madly in love, he was not. My parents tried to get me to stop seeing him, but all that did was make me want him even more. I ended up running away with him and got pregnant." Eliza's voice was steady as she spoke, but as she stopped to take a breath Saul spoke.

"What are you talking about? Does this have anything to do with why you're here?"

"Perhaps he should wait in the other room. I'm talking about a lot of years that happened and if I have to stop and answer questions, I might as well not tell you what happened." Eliza spoke to Mary as though she was the only person in the room.

"No, no one will ask you anything until you have told us what's going on. We may have some questions for you to answer after, but right now we are going to sit here and listen to you speak." Mary looked at Saul as if to say, '*Shut the hell up.*'

"My boyfriend left me in New York. I had no money and couldn't call my parents, not after what happened. I lived on the streets for a few weeks, and then moved into a shelter. Everyone there was so nice to me. They helped me learn skills to get a job and to be a good mother.

"After a month, there was a terrible fight at the shelter. A man had come to get his wife and was not taking no for an answer. He grabbed her by the hair, pulling her through the house, to the outside stoop. She was fighting him and screaming. I ran up to try to help her. He pushed me with such force that I fell down the front steps. I could feel the pain radiating through my midsection. I knew something was wrong. When I looked down all I could see was blood. There was so much blood!

"I was five months along when I lost the baby. She was a little girl. Angel was born in the ambulance on the way to the hospital. They let me see her tiny little body before they took her away. I cried for what seemed like days, and then Linda, the director, came to see me. She spoke about my future; I spoke about my past. There was nothing that could be done for the little girl I lost, but I could hold her little memory in my heart forever. I needed to make something of myself, so her brothers or sisters would never have to know the horrors, I thought I had seen and gone through. That was such a lie. Some people are damned, a dark cloud that follows them wherever they go. Oh never mind." Eliza stared off into space.

"Does any of this have anything at all to do with why you are here?" Saul asked.

Mary shot Saul a look rolling her eyes and shaking her head slightly side to side.

Eliza ignored him. "I took it as a sign from God, that I was not ready for a family. I had to take care of me first, and then I could have a family. I found a job and went to school. I worked so hard. I didn't go out or play around. I put my goals first; going to college and studying really hard. I worked extra shifts during the holidays and took the mini semester at school so I could finish.

"I finally finished school in December of 1989. I was at the top of my class. I was so proud of myself. I put in applications everywhere I thought I would like to work. I was not settling for just any job. I wanted a job with a future, as far away from

New York City as I could get. A firm with an office in Houston responded; they wanted an interview. I went to the interview and I swear some other person took over for me. The time I spent in school and with the interviewing class I had taken at the shelter, it just all came together. I was not the mousy person that I had been. I was confident and answered all the questions like a pro. They offered me the job. The money was so good and they would put me up in an apartment for six months, until I could get my own place. I was made for the position. I got the job. And not just any job; I got the job I had been training for and studying for and oh, how I celebrated! I was on my way. I felt like that woman in that TV show. You know the one where she throws her hat in the air. I did throw my hat, only it was in my apartment." She looked off past the glass, as though it was a window into her apartment. She laughed and smiled.

"I had a little money and three weeks to make the trip to Houston. One of the girls I worked with at the store had a brother that was selling a car. It was not a new car by any means, but I could fit my few belongings in and drive down there. I heard Houston was different than New York and most people needed a car just to go to the store for food. I jumped at the chance and bought the car. I was on my way.

"I bought a map and planned my trip to Houston. I decided to stop, no, needed to stop and see my family on the drive down. I wanted them to see me and I craved them and their blessing for my life. I needed them to know just what I had accomplished. I wanted them to see, I was not the failure that they thought I was. I was so proud of what I had done. I wanted my parents to see the degree that I worked for and to know that I had turned out okay. I had gone so long without things that people take for granted. Sometimes there was little food to last until I got paid. I didn't have a TV or phone. The heater would almost freeze before I would turn it on and I had so few clothes. It was easy to fit everything I owned in a car." Eliza spoke as if trying to convince the onlookers that she had earned a better life.

"I left early in the morning of January twenty-ninth. I packed the car the night before and didn't sleep much. I was nervous about the trip. I knew once I got on the road I would be fine. I'm not sure if it was because I was going to see my parents, which I had not seen for many years, or if it was the new job awaiting me."

Saul looked up then, marked on his pad, and then, as if he really couldn't help himself, he said, as if in total shock, "Are you thirty-nine?" He looked at her again, and then added, "No way, you have to be at least sixty! Look at how you look!"

Eliza's hands went up to her face and Mary could hear her sobbing quietly.

"That's it Saul! You're out of here," Mary could no longer control herself. "There is something wrong with you." She knew there was plenty about Saul she didn't like, but she never knew he could be so rude to a complete stranger; to a stranger that had obviously been through hell.

"I don't know who you think you are Mary, but I am not going anywhere." Saul folded his arms, and then sat back in his chair.

"Robert, will you do something," Mary begged. Eliza was still sobbing.

"Would you mind, Saul? Can I please talk to you, outside?" Robert asked.

"You know Robert, I like you; you are good for a laugh every now and again. Please don't get in the middle of this," Saul said, and then added, "Both of you know when the sheriff is out, I am in charge and last I heard, he would be out until tomorrow, is that right Robert?"

"Robert, please take Eliza out to the front, and I will be there in a moment," Mary said.

Eliza did not want to go at first. She shook her head and stayed planted in her seat. Mary touched her hand, and then whispered in her ear, "Please, I need a few minutes to talk to Saul. I know you are scared, but you must go with Robert. Just for a few minutes, I promise."

7

Robert helped gather the children. He carried the baby while Eliza carried EJ. They went to the front of the station and sat at Mary's desk. "Is this her husband and child?" Eliza asked, looking at a picture of Charley with Bryan.

"Oh yes, they are her pride and joy. Can I get you anything?" Robert asked.

"I wish all men were like you. Is her husband like you?" Eliza asked, still looking at the picture.

"Oh Bryan, he's a nice guy, I'm better looking, but he's a nice guy." Robert laughed and Eliza cracked a smile. Robert was glad Eliza was finally relaxing and Robert himself relaxed a little.

The station; still quite, went on as usual. Mary and Saul stayed in the donut room. Eliza sat in the chair and waited. A part of her was scared. A part of her was screaming happiness from the inside. After all this time, her kids were safe and she was safe. She asked Robert if she could walk outside for a while. The air from the air conditioner was cold on her face, arms, and legs. She did not have any body fat and the chill went straight to her bones. They left the station through the back door and Eliza soaked in the warmth of the sunlight.

The sky was still bright, although the clock read six-thirty as she went outside. It was summer, darkness was still hours away. She looked at the cars driving down the street and the clothes that the people wore, and then said aloud, "I am not dreaming. We made it out and we made it out alive."

Eliza smiled at EJ and pointed to the cars on the street. She made a few hand signs, and then turned back to Robert. "My son is very smart for a boy that can't hear. He was not born this way you know? He was perfect. He had ten fingers and ten toes. He was a happy, perfect baby. I wish I had a picture of him then, before all of this, but he was born into this life. What kind of life is it that you have to wish for the simple things? Why can't it all just be easy? You know officer, I just wanted an easy life, now look at me. Look at my children. Look at what kind of life we've had. We deserve better. We all deserve better."

Robert looked at them, and then found a word that he prayed would comfort the woman. Finally he said, "Faith, Miss, you have faith and no one can ever take that away from you. You will be fine now."

8

The room that contained Mary and Saul was quiet. Neither said a word. They were both in separate corners waiting for the match to start. They failed to shake hands and neither requested a fair fight.

Saul sat still in his chair with his arms folded and his lips tightly closed. His body language shouted annoyed and his eyes pierced through Mary, unsettling her. She waited for him to say something, say anything. He said nothing.

Mary wore the carpet out in her corner. Back and forth she went, never far, only two steps in each direction. She did not want to say anything stupid. Her mind was full of things to say, awful things to say to him. She could feel herself getting angrier and angrier and she was trying to bite her lip. She could no longer stand it and like a pot that finally boiled over, she started yelling. "How dare you talk to a person like that? Just who in the hell do you think you are? We do not treat people like that in here. Never do we treat people like that. I have had enough of you and if you don't leave right now, I'm calling the state police. They can take this case and then YOU can explain to Doug why our office can't handle a problem that comes in here! Now you have a choice and I hope to God you make the right one." Mary was red in the face. She was irate and she felt her blood pressure rise higher with every word she spoke.

"That's it! I have had enough of you. I know you think you should be in charge, but you are just ... look at the way you are yelling at me. Doug was so right about you. And to THINK; I felt just a tad sorry for you when I took your place, when you left to have that child of yours, but do you know what? You don't deserve to be in charge. You think you control everything in this station. You think I have to listen to you? You are such a bitch Mary, and after this, you will not have a job in this station or anyplace in this state. If you think I am joking, you better think again. Now, I want you to leave this station. I mean right now, just go home." Saul found his feet and was now standing directly in front of Mary.

"Mary, I never should have let you in there to talk to that woman. You really don't know what you are doing. Do you think that we are not going to check out her story? You think that we just believe everyone that walks in through that door? How stupid do you think we are? No, I take that back, how stupid do you think I am? I'm taking this case and if you are not careful, I'll charge you with interfering with a criminal investigation." Saul was now pointing his finger at Mary.

"Do you WANT to have a pissing contest with me Saul? Do you honestly think that I'm walking out of here and leaving that lady and her children with you? You better get another thought because that one is coming straight from your ass! I'm now walking out of this office and I'm taking the lady and those children. I'm calling the state police and if you think you are going to follow me, you'd best think again. And get that damn finger out of my face!" Mary grabbed the door handle, opened the door and walked out.

Saul followed her out of the interrogation room, but went straight into Doug's office. He picked up the phone and turned his back to the glass. Mary was sure he was calling Doug and her heart was beating. What the hell would Doug say? She had never behaved like this in her life. She was a God fearing lady for goodness sake!

She had been so unprofessional and for all of this to happen in front of a victim, she was ashamed and embarrassed by her behavior.

Mary stood watching Saul. She wished he would turn around so she could see his face. She was pretty good at reading people's faces, but all she could see was the back of his head and his arms moving up and down and back and forth. He turned once, but Mary darted her eyes back to the donut room. As she looked through the glass, she noticed that the recorder was still there and still recording. She went back into the room, picked up the tape recorder, and headed back to her desk.

She looked at Jeff, who was now staring at her, and then said, "WHAT?" Her tone was quite rude and the expression on her face was, well, it made her look, mean.

"Nothing," he said and shrank back a few steps.

"No, you look like you just have to say something, so go ahead, and say what's on your mind." She stood waiting for him to say something smart to her about her fight with Saul. She was ready to jump down his throat. She was on a roll and even if she thought it was unprofessional, she had nothing to lose, but more temper, so she was ready.

"I thought you were going to ask me where they are," his voice was gentle and soft. Mary felt guilty, she was ready to pounce and he was just doing his job.

Embarrassment took over and Mary felt the blood rushing into her face.

"Are you okay Mary? Your face is red." He went over to her and led her to a chair.

"You better sit down while I go get them. They walked outside for a few minutes." He headed for the door, then turned and smiled at Mary.

"Remind me never to piss you off," Jeff laughed and Mary felt a smile cross her lips.

"Shut up," she drawled, as she shook her head, smiling.

Robert came in a few minutes later, the family and Jeff in tow. "Mary, are you okay?" Robert asked.

"Some people just can't keep their mouths shut around here I see," she looked toward Jeff and smiled.

"He asked, and what was I supposed to do, lie?" Jeff shrugged.

Mary turned serious and asked Jeff to take the family back to the interrogation room, and then addressed Robert.

"Saul went into Doug's office, so I think he's calling him. I'll wait here and see what he says. If it's to leave them here, I will not do that. Wait till he hears what Saul said." Mary was looking into Doug's office at Saul's back. She could feel her temperature rise as she spoke. Her conversation with Saul was still fresh in her mind.

Mary got up and began pacing the floor, and then unexpectedly said, "I'm leaving. I'm taking her and the kids with me. I need to know they are safe, and with Saul, I just don't think they will be. Tomorrow, I'm taking them to the state police in Lexington. They need one good night's sleep and they should at least have that, before they see the doctor. I will bring them to him in the morning. They need help and to be honest, I just don't think they will get it here, not with Saul." She went into the room and gathered the family to leave.

A moment later, Saul reappeared in the room and simply said, "Doug is going to call me at home when he gets in tonight. This is not over Mary, but if I were you, I would wait until tomorrow before you take them to the state police. If that woman came from this area and you screw this up by taking her someplace else, Doug will fire you; if he doesn't fire you for your mouth. That my dear, you can bank on!" Saul walked to the door.

"I'm not now, nor will I ever be, 'your dear'!" Mary turned her back as Saul turned around.

Saul shook his head and said to Robert and Jeff who were watching him, waiting for his reaction, "Remember this you guys. Remember how she's acting." He was looking straight at Robert.

"Goodnight and good-bye Saul," Robert said.

"Goodnight gentlemen and lady." Saul turned toward the woman as if waiting for a response.

Eliza turned away showing she wanted nothing to do with him.

After Saul left, Robert looked at Mary, "Don't worry Mary, I'll tell Doug what happened."

"You know, it's getting kind of late. I'm going to take Eliza and the children to the hotel for the night. Maybe I can get the story."

"I'm sorry you had to see this. Please forgive us." Mary touched Eliza on the shoulder.

As Robert helped Mary get the family into her SUV, she asked him to call Bryan and tell him to bring some clothes for Eliza and the baby. She then asked Robert if his son had any clothes EJ could borrow.

The baby sat in Charley's car seat and EJ sat next to his mother in the backseat. She drove the few blocks to the hotel and got the room for the family.

While Eliza settled the children in the hotel room, Mary sat outside. She played the recorder over and over. She had really lost her temper. *A pissing contest, what was I thinking? I watch too much TV.* Mary thought to herself.

Bryan came down to the hotel with Charley. Mary was so happy to see them. Charley brought his mother a picture he had drawn and Bryan brought the bag of clothes Mary requested through Robert.

Robert appeared moments later. He also carried a bag of clothes and a few toys. Mary smiled and thanked him. "Here are some of Peter's old clothes. Martha thought I was throwing them out, but when I explained, she threw the toys in."

"You tell that wife of yours, thank you please." Mary hugged Robert and whispered, "Go home; tomorrow will be a long day. Will you be here with me at eight?"

"All you have to do is ask," Robert said.

Robert drove off and Mary knocked on the door of Eliza's room. Eliza asked, "Who is it?" She sounded afraid.

"It's me, Mary. I have some clothes for you and the children." Mary could see Eliza open the curtain and peek out. *She must be afraid* Mary thought. Eliza slowly opened the door.

Mary handed the bags of clothes to Eliza, turned, and then pointed toward her husband. "This is Bryan and my son Charley. They wanted to meet you." Bryan stepped forward with his hand out, but Eliza pulled the door closed with just her face sticking out.

Mary noticed Eliza's reaction and simply told Bryan, "Now is really not a good time to meet Eliza. Perhaps another day would be better, after Eliza is healthier and has had some rest."

"It's nice to meet you," Eliza said with her head down, and then she mumbled, "I better get the children down. Thank you for the clothes, I'll get them back to you soon." She began closing the door.

"No!" Mary yelled scaring Eliza. Eliza froze, looking up at Mary.

"I'm sorry Eliza; I just wanted to tell you those clothes are for you and the children to keep. Go get the kids in bed and we'll talk soon. It is okay Eliza, you and the children are going to be okay now. I'm going to be here for a while. You and the children are safe." Mary then pulled the door closed.

"Not such a perfect world, is it?" Mary asked Bryan.

"Wow," was all Bryan could manage to say.

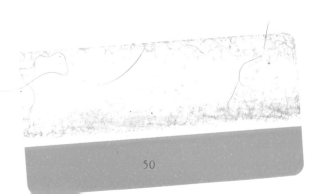

9

Mary watched the window for the light in the room to finally dim. She wanted to give Eliza time with her children and Mary herself wanted to spend a little time with her own family.

Moments later she quietly knocked on the door, not wanting to wake the children.

"Eliza, I'm sending Bryan to the store to pick up a few items. Is there anything that you need?" Mary asked as Eliza cautiously answered the door.

"I don't have a lot of money, but I really, only, want a soda. I haven't had a soda for many years and I saw the machine earlier as we passed it. Would you mind? I don't have any change though. I'll pay you back." Eliza sounded almost desperate.

"You could have asked me for the world and you chose a soda?" Mary laughed. "A soda it is. I'll be back in a few minutes. What about the children, do they need anything or are they sleeping? I know today has been a big day for them."

"Well, EJ fell asleep watching the television. I tried to turn it off, but he threw a fit. It is so new to him. Everything is just so new to him. A soft clean bed; such a simple thing, he has never had that before." Eliza's face grew sad.

"He'll enjoy it Eliza. Think of the fun you can have with him traveling through life showing and teaching him all the things everyone else takes for granted." Mary touched Eliza's arm.

Eliza pulled her arm away. "Would you mind if I take a bath? I feel so dirty. I don't think I'll ever feel clean again."

"I don't mind at all if you take a bath. Eliza my dear, you are a free woman, you can do what you want. That means taking a bath or shouting from the rooftop. You don't have to answer to anyone any longer." Mary smiled.

"Bryan, go ahead and go to the store. I'll wait here. Charley come and stay with Mommy." Mary put her arms out and Charley came running up.

"Charley, I would like you to meet a nice lady. Her name is Miss Eliza and she has some children also." Mary picked up Charley.

Charley smiled at Eliza, "Me play with the kids?"

"Not tonight Charley, Miss Eliza's children are sleeping. Why don't we play with them another night. Will you go with me to get Miss Eliza a soda from the machine? I'll let you push the button!" Mary said to Charley.

"I push the buttons, yea!" Charley wiggled out of his mother's arms and started for the machine.

Eliza's eyes filled with tears. "It could have been this way with EJ and me."

"No Eliza, it WILL be this way with you and EJ. You'll see. He's still young and you are a bright woman. You three have the whole world in front of you."

"Mommy, come on. I want soda too," Charley said.

Mary grabbed the change out of her pocket and said, "I'm coming Charley." She winked at Eliza as she turned to go. "Kids."

Mary heard the door close softly behind her and headed to the machine. Charley squealed as Mary picked him up. "I love you so much." She planted a giant kiss on his cheek. "Can you put the money in that slot right there?"

Bryan pulled in a short time later. "What time do you think you might be coming home?" He asked as he handed a bag to Mary.

"I don't know. When I'm done I guess. Oh Bryan, I feel so bad for her and the children. What kind of life have they had? Look at us. We've had almost the perfect life with the perfect child." Mary said, leaning against Bryan.

"Everybody has their crosses to bear. Our cross was Joy. We carried it and we came through. She will do the same thing." Bryan kissed Mary gently on the forehead and pulled away from her. "Go make her cross easier to bear."

Bryan turned to Charley, "Come on Charley, Mommy has to work and you have to go to bed. Kiss mommy goodbye and hop in the truck."

With kisses finished for the night and all the "I love you" that their hearts could carry, Bryan and Charley left. As they drove away, Mary smiled and waved, but her mind was on the door that stood between her and the story that was on the other side. She knew Eliza was ready to talk, and she was ready to listen.

10

Eliza had watched Mary play with her child and race with her child and laugh with her child. She shut the door to her room and climbed on the bed with EJ. "Soon it will be that way for us also, just you wait and see." She closed her eyes and fell fast asleep rubbing EJ's head.

When Mary knocked on the door it scared her. She had not meant to fall asleep and was confused when she awoke. She finally heard Mary's voice softly calling her, and went to the door.

"Here is a soda for now and one for later," Mary said, as the door opened.

"Thank you," Eliza said, as she opened the door a little wider. "Your family, have they gone?"

"Charley has to get to bed, we need to talk and you still need that bath." Mary gave Eliza the bags. "Please Eliza, go take your bath. I'll stay with the children. I won't let anything happen to them, I promise."

Eliza opened the bags and smiled. Mary had thought of everything. There were bubbles for the children and for her, powder and lotion. All of which smelled wonderful. The shampoo and conditioner smelled of lilac. There were toothbrushes and toothpaste, and hair brushes and a comb. Eliza looked into the other bags that were given to her. The clothes in the bag were in perfect shape. There were dresses, shorts, blue jeans and beautiful tops. There were three pair of shoes; one a sandal, one a tennis shoe and one a slip-on. There were clothes for her children also; sleepers for the baby and shorts, pants and cute shirts for EJ. And there were toys; not many, but one was more than EJ had ever had in his life. He would be happy in the morning, Eliza was sure.

Eliza looked at Mary, tears falling down her cheeks and said, "Thank you." Mary smiled at her, nodded and Eliza felt okay. Mary then turned her focus to the television glancing between the children and the TV. "We are good out here Eliza, go on and take your bath."

The bubbles were pure white and the water hot. Steam filled the room and crept around the cracked door to where the children slept. Eliza was worried about the kids, but felt she could trust Mary. Some things you just know about people, she believed, but just in case she left the bathroom door cracked just a bit.

Eliza washed her hair, scrubbed her body, and then soaked her fears away. Well, some of them anyway. She could not wait until EJ awoke in the morning. What a nice bath he would have. What a nice breakfast, lunch, dinner, hell, what a nice rest of his life he would have. *Oh yes, what a wonderful rest of your life you will have*, Eliza thought to herself; *I will not fail my children again*. She thought she was a bad mother because she let everything happen. *Yes*, she thought, *I was a bad mother, but not now. From this day forward I'll be the best mother ever. I will protect my children and give them love. Maybe one day EJ will forget about this time in his life, grow to become a wonderful man and know the right way to treat women.*

When Eliza emerged from the bathroom she had a towel wrapped around her body. She sensed Mary's eyes on her. She felt embarrassed. She wished Mary would look away, but she would not ask her to.

Eliza stood looking at herself and Mary in the mirror, "Funny thing about life is no matter what, it keeps on going. If I don't make it through this, my kids will keep on going. They are the proof that I existed. My blood flows in their veins. I am them, they are me."

Eliza could see Mary's reflection staring back and wondered what she was thinking. She hoped Mary would not stay all night. *If Mary left soon there is a chance we might be able to get a ride out of town and far away. Probably not, but it was at least worth a thought.* Eliza laughed softly to herself, *it's doubtful.*

11

Mary held the camera out. "Eliza, I need to take some pictures of you. We may need them for evidence." She did not want to take the pictures. She knew Eliza was embarrassed by her body, but she pushed on. "Eliza, I'm sorry I have to take the pictures."

"What do you want to see?" Eliza grabbed the towel tightly around her body.

"Eliza, I need to see everything."

"Oh." Eliza turned away from Mary. She lowered her head as the towel slipped to the floor.

Mary gasped. She could not believe how Eliza actually looked without clothes. Her clavicles stuck out and her shoulder blades appeared to almost pierce through her skin. Eliza's rib cage and pelvic reminded Mary of pictures of the holocaust, her arms and her legs did not appear to contain muscle or fat and her feet actually looked like that of a skeleton. As much as Mary wanted to turn her eyes from the woman standing before her, she felt drawn to look.

The room grew silent except the sound of the instant camera as it spit out picture after picture. Eliza's body tensed with every flash.

"Can you put your arms up?" Mary asked gently.

Eliza turned and Mary saw tears slipping down her sunken cheeks. *I'm sorry* Mary thought. *I'm so very sorry.*

"Eliza, I'm done." Mary spoke gently, turning away before wiping tears from her own eyes. She could not say another word. There were no words, just images of Eliza's body; bones covered with scarred encrusted skin.

Eliza bent down and picked up the towel, her eyes slowly opening.

"Would you help me cut my hair?" Eliza asked finally breaking the silence.

Mary sat Eliza in the chair and cut her hair. When she finished she walked Eliza to the mirror and waited for her reaction.

"Do you like the hair cut?" Mary was having a hard time reading Eliza's face.

"Well, I just don't look like me. This is not the face I remember, the hair I remember or the body I remember. I think I was pretty once. I don't mean a model or anything like that, I mean I looked okay. I had plenty guys ask me out; I never went, school was much more important, but I still looked nice. My hair was a little longer and it was a beautiful auburn color. My face was clear, no scars or lines. My teeth were almost perfect and I never wore braces a day in my life. Now look at them." Some were knocked out, but more were rotten. "I'm sorry if my breath stinks. I saw you put a toothbrush for EJ and me in the bag. Oh Mary, I feel like you are my friend, the only friend I've had in so many years. Thank you for being so kind to the children and me. Thank you for the food and getting us these clothes. Thank you." Eliza had tears running down her cheeks. Mary leaned into Eliza and hugged her.

"Come on Eliza, you should get dressed now." Feeling Eliza's bones made Mary uncomfortable.

"I guess I should." Eliza looked through the bag of clothes to find something to wear. All of the pants in the bag were too big, just like the ones Mary had given her earlier. Eliza settled on a dress.

Mary looked at the dress and realized it was the same dress she was wearing when Saul made a pass at her. She had forgotten it was in the bag, but couldn't tell Eliza to take it off. All Mary said to Eliza was she would bring her a few more dresses tomorrow. Bryan had picked up underwear from the store and although they were a little big for her, Eliza pulled them on under the dress.

"Maybe I'll gain a little weight while I'm sleeping. What are the chances of them fitting in the morning?" She held them up, as she made her way to sit on the chair by the small desk, next to the TV in the room.

"Eliza, it's going to be okay. I don't think the panties will fit in the morning, but they make smaller undies. You are safe now. Tomorrow is the start of a new life. So now I need to ask, do you want to go on with your story or wait until the sheriff comes in the morning? I can record it, and then the sheriff can just ask you any questions he might have. The decision is yours. You need to tell me what to do. I know you are tired."

"I want to talk to you. I don't want to talk to him. Most men are like that man, that guy Saul. No, tonight we talk, tomorrow I may answer questions." Eliza spoke now like a woman that had made a decision.

Mary walked out to her SUV and grabbed the tape recorder they had been using earlier. The sun had almost disappeared over the hill and Mary hoped the woman would get her story out without any interruption. She wanted to help this woman very much, but the day was also coming to an end. She knew the next day would also be a long one and the fight with Saul had really worked tension into her shoulders. She wanted to go home, climb into a hot bath and soak her own problems away.

Mary walked back into the room. She held the recorder, looking for the best place to put the machine. "Give me just a moment and I'll be ready." Mary settled on the table then hit the play button. She wanted the recorder to pick up where Eliza left off; however she also wanted everything Saul said on the tape. She stopped the tape and decided to put a new one in. She was still getting everything set up when Eliza began to speak.

"I should have never left home. That was a mistake." Eliza's voice was steady and without emotion. Her words were precise and to the point and Mary, who had waited all this time for her to start, told her to stop.

"Eliza, I need just a moment."

Eliza appeared not to hear Mary and she continued to speak. Mary finally walked over to the chair and touched her shoulder. Eliza jumped.

"Eliza I need you to start again dear. I'm sorry, I was not quite ready."

Eliza smiled and said, "I'm sorry, I thought you were ready. Sometimes my mind just wanders. I hate to say that, but for years I got myself prepared to tell my story. I would go over it time and again in my head and now I have a chance to tell."

"You can start anytime you want now. I'm ready." Mary sat next to the recorder she had placed on the table.

Eliza began again. This time she spoke without interruption and at times failed to breathe, or take a breath. Mary's emotions changed from anger to disbelief to shock and horror. Mary found herself inside the place that held Eliza, as if she were floating above the room seeing all the things that Eliza saw, experiencing all the pain and terror that Eliza went through. She did not break in nor did she let Eliza hear her gasp or see her mouth fall open or see the tears that fell down her cheeks. She simply sat and listened as Eliza told her story.

12

Eliza slipped back into time quickly; off into the place she called both home and hell for the last fifteen years. Although this life took place years ago, it was all she thought about. Her remembering was what kept her sane during the time she spent in her hole. She began to speak and started by showing no emotion. Her voice was monotone. "I should have never left home. That was a mistake. I should have listened to my parents. I guess at times they really know best. I worked my way through school after everything that happened in New York, but I could not stay there. I got the job in Houston to start a new, better life. It was all the way across the world, but I was going. The pay was great and they say everyone is friendly there. I was happy and anxious all at once.

"The roads were bad that day. There had been lots of snow, but I thought I could make the fourteen hour drive and be at my parents' house before midnight. I decided to stay on the highways as much as possible. The road crews usually keep those roads pretty clear. As I drove I sang along with the radio and heard the occasional weather report. The day was warming and the sun was melting the snow. I hoped for good weather and at the time, the weather seemed to be working with me. Around six that evening my luck had changed. An eighteen wheeler had jackknifed on the road ahead, and the delay would be hours due to a chemical spill. I was still a few hundred miles from my family home and didn't have directions for side roads.

"I stayed in the ever-growing line of cars and trucks on the interstate and waited. Around eight that evening, I heard on the radio, the state police were shutting down a five mile section of freeway for the rest of the night. The spill, it seemed, had leaked out of the truck and soaked into the ground.

"I then joined the ever-growing crowd of cars, which were now turning around, heading back in the opposite direction. As I approached the first small city, I got gas, and purchased a road map of the United States. I wanted to pick a new route for my trip. I found a coffee shop and sat down reading the map, plotting a new course.

"The sky was completely dark and as I left the diner, snow began to fall again. The night air gave me a chill and I rushed to my car, turning the heater on full blast. I looked at my small clock on the car radio and was surprised I had spent so much time in the small coffee shop. I hated driving at night, but hated worse, driving in the snow. I was still hours from my parents' house and it was getting late. I debated with myself about staying the night and finally gave into the idea. Although I hadn't counted on the extra expense, it might be well worth the effort to go back inside and find the closest place to stay. In the morning I could resume my driving and be at my parents' by noon.

"The young girl, working at the counter, had been friendly enough when I was ordering my food, but now she seemed impatient with me as I asked for directions. She gave me some directions really fast. I wanted to get some paper to write them down, but a man's voice impatiently called for her. I remember her saying, 'You'll see it on the left side. I've got to go; the weather is getting bad and we're closing. I'm sorry, my boyfriend is calling me. You have to leave now.'

"I stood outside of the door the girl had practically pushed me out of and stared at the closed sign and the back part of a window shade. I looked around the streets of the town, hoping to find a business open, but there were none. The street stood silent, except for a wind whipping up the snow.

"The chill finally got to me and I made my way back to my car. I sat in my car, not knowing what to do. I then started the engine. I decided I should go back to the interstate and wait for the road to open. I drove down the street with the radio off. I have no sense of direction and as I drove, I realized that nothing I passed looked as if I had ever seen it before.

"After driving a little ways; I saw a sign that looked like the sign I had seen before I came into town. I turned. I should have paid more attention while driving into town. I could not remember how long I was on the road after I left the freeway. There was a little traffic earlier and I blindly followed, not really paying attention. Stupid, stupid, God I was so stupid. The sky had been clear and there were lights from all the businesses drawing me in.

"I kept driving; and as the road turned, so did I, and when that road ended, I turned around. I didn't know where I was. I was lost and I was getting scared. I was trying to drive my car slowly, but I was getting really anxious. The next thing I knew, I hit something and the car started swerving and spinning. Whatever I hit, it gave me a flat.

"The car landed on the side of the road. There were no houses that I could see and I cried for what seemed like forever. I finally managed to get out of the car and looked at the tire, to see if I could change it. I had never changed a tire before in my life. Now here I was, out in the cold and snow, I didn't think now would be the best time to start. I climbed back into the car, turned the heater on and off, and sang.

"A man knocked on the window and scared me. I was stupid. I should have taken his help, but I didn't. His face had a scar that ran from his forehead to his chin. He just scared me. The things he said and the look on his face, I sent him away. I waited for a short time, and then I decided to drive on the tire rim. I needed to get back on a main road; maybe someone would see me and help me. It might have been that man that did this to me. I saw him again right before I was captured. I just don't know. After I was taken, I really never saw the man. Do you know that man Mary? Do you know who that man is?"

Mary shook her head. Silence filled the room. Neither Mary nor Eliza spoke for a few minutes.

"I drove slowly and I think I got on the main road. My foot hovered over the brakes and I applied pressure trying to keep the car under control, but it was no use. I could see nothing and the car was slipping. The snowfall had turned into some sort of blizzard now. I was uncertain of what to do; but I drove on, hoping against hope, I would soon find a town, the freeway, or even just a house I could stop at for the night. It was so very hard to see, even inches in front of me.

"My wipers did not work as fast as the snow fell from the sky. As soon as the blades cleared a spot on the windshield, it was full of snow again. The road, now completely covered with ice and snow, disappeared from my view. I was foolish. I drove and drove, then turned around and drove back. I took turn after turn, but I wasn't getting anywhere. I was driving in circles I think, although I didn't see the same thing twice. The snow changes things I think. There was no light in the sky, even the moon was hidden. It was just snow, snow and more snow.

"I started to panic. I remember my heart beating and my eyes watering. I started crying and it made it even harder to see. I was not just a little lost, I was totally lost. There was no place to stop and ask for help like in the city. I was out driving in the country, in a state I had never, ever been in. I didn't even know what town I was in. I tried to look at the map when I would see a sign, but I just couldn't find the road I was on. My head hurt and my eyes were tired.

"The car was so hard to control. I would slip and slide all over the road. I'm not even sure how much damage I was doing to the car, but I didn't care. I had to find help, I needed to find help. I was not stopping until I found it; no matter what happened to the car, the tire or the rim.

"I had a horrible thought; what if I was no longer on the road? The snow kept falling and as I inched my way, I kept looking for anything that would tell me I was still on the road. I just knew I was now driving in a field someplace. That thought quickly left my mind however, because what happened was worse. My car started sliding and the brakes refused to work this time. The car was slipping and sliding and then it was going down at an angle. The car was picking up speed and no matter what I did I could not stop. I started screaming when my car flipped over. The car went upside down, sideways and finally right side up, coming to a rest at the bottom of a hill.

"At first I thought I was dead. I had bumped my head on the steering wheel or the roof. I tried to get out of the car, but it hurt so much to move. I struggled to get the car turned off.

"I'm not sure how long I was there. When I opened my eyes I found the sun was bright in the sky. The pain in my head was overwhelming and I reached up and felt a big knot on my head. The snow that seemed to shoot across the sky last night now lay still on the ground. I tried the doors, but could not get them to open. I struggled getting the car turned on and was ready to give up, but the engine finally caught. I put the window down and crawled through the open space. The wind which ran through my clothes yesterday now seemed a distant thought. The air was cold and the sunlight hurt my eyes. I looked at where the car was and knew it would take a tow truck to pull it out. I know I yelled and fell to the ground and cried."

Eliza looked up at Mary then said, "If I could do it all over again, knowing now what I didn't know then, I would have died in that car crash. I would have just stayed there and died."

Mary said nothing, but looked over at the two children that were sleeping.

"Oh, I know, I wouldn't have my children if I had died, but what a life EJ has had. I wonder if he himself would not have wished to be dead at times. I never talked about death to him. He knows death, but chose life. I don't know why he chose life because the life he knows is worse than any death."

Eliza sat staring into space. Moments later, a visible tremor ran through her body, shaking her from her daze. "Where was I?" Eliza asked. She had been staring toward the children, but not quite looking at them. "Oh yea, I remember, the stupid car and me, after I crashed. I was hungry, thirsty and in pain. I remember it so clearly; it was the first time I awoke feeling that way. Not the last time, mind you, but the very first time I ever remember waking up feeling that way. Only then, I still believed I would be okay. Stupid me; I really thought I would be okay.

"I got out and stared at the car, and then kicked it. My trip was not going as planned and I was taking my anger out on the poor car. I wanted to know how badly I had damaged the car. I needed to know if maybe, just maybe I could get it to move. I climbed back into the driver's seat. I put the car into gear and pushed the gas. The car didn't move. I pushed harder; I could hear the tires spinning. Well, it could be worse, at least it ran. I was a little disappointed. I left the car in neutral, got out and tried to push it. What a bad idea that was. I fell flat on my face. The car was stuck on something. Pulling it back up the hill was the only way I could think of to get out of this mess. I turned the car off in disgust.

"I had bought a few snack items for the trip; some crackers, nuts, chips and sodas. I reached into the backseat and pulled out a package of peanut butter crackers and a soda. I had my breakfast. It was still early, the sun not full in the sky. The stupid clock, in the car, stopped running when I crashed, so I'm not sure what time it was. I decided I had to walk. I didn't even know if I could be seen from the road. I had not heard a car or anything pass since I crashed.

I needed a phone to call a tow truck or find someone willing to pull my stranded car up the hill.

"I looked at my surroundings. The trees all around me looked dead. Their leaves had long left their branches replaced with icicles dangling from their branches. The ground was covered with snow. My car, slightly tilted, was sitting at the bottom of the hill. I was ready to go and headed in the direction of the steep incline. The snow, covering the ground, gave way as I walked. I tried to climb the hill, but only fell back down, ripping my jeans and tearing my coat. One of my boot heels broke, but that really didn't matter, they sucked at keeping my feet warm anyway. I went back to my car, I needed to change clothes.

"I put on two pair of socks and changed shoes. I found a long sleeve tee-shirt which I put on under two sweaters. Underneath my warm-up pants, I added leggings. I looked at my torn dress coat, and decided I needed my old familiar jacket; the gaping hole would not keep me warm. I took a blanket, throwing it over my shoulder. I filled a bag with some snack foods and grabbed a soda.

"I went back to the front of the car, deciding I should maybe leave a note. I found my purse sitting on the front seat and the keys still in the ignition. I remember thinking I was stupid for forgetting them in the first place. The note went on the windshield and as I walked away, I stopped to look back at the car, hoping I was not forgetting anything that I might need.

"I decided to walk at the bottom of the hill until I could get up without killing myself. Soon I was able to climb up easily, using a tree branch for leverage. When I reached the top I found what I thought was a road. It was hard to tell though. I went to the side and moved snow until I saw the asphalt under my feet. I was happy. I walked, following the road, not wanting to get lost any more then I was. I tied strips of an old shirt I had to some of the trees as I passed. I wanted to be able to find my way back to my car and all my worldly belongings.

"After what seemed like hours, the road finally came to an end. A large iron gate sat before a winding drive. I was so glad. I could feel my face light up. I climbed the metal gate and started running. I saw a house and a barn and I made my way yelling, 'Help, is somebody home? I need help. Please, let somebody be home.' I begged God.

"I looked over the house as I ran to the door. It seemed quite new for the area. The cabin style home had a large porch that seemed to wrap around the whole house. The trim was colored in a bright green. The door was set back just a bit, and the windows across the front had green shutters that were open. There were lace curtains with butterflies that covered them. The stone chimney was quite grand and appeared to the left of the house. I stared at the top; hoping, wishing, I could see smoke creeping out. Why would I think my luck had changed any? There was nothing coming from the stack.

"I finally reached the door and knocked loudly. No answer. I banged on the door this time and waited. Still there was no answer. Sitting on the porch there were two chairs and a beautiful wood table. I looked around at the view. It was beautiful. The hills in front of the house were large and covered with snow. There were pine trees all around the property, giving the grounds a little color. I looked in the windows. I could see the house was almost empty. Somebody had to live there or at least stop by and check on the house. It was just in too good of shape.

"I was tired from my morning hunt to find help. To be honest, I just didn't think I could go any further. I had to sit down. I needed to rest. My head still hurt and my eyes began to get blurry from the headache. If no one was home now, maybe in a little while they would return; if not, I would break a window and enter the house. I was hoping that the house belonged to someone that lived there, and was not like a hunting lodge that was used only a few times a year.

"Even though it was cold outside, I guess I had been sweating. I could feel my body begin to chill as I cooled off. I found one of the chairs and pulled the covers tight around me and fell fast asleep.

"When I awoke, I could tell by the sun that it was mid-afternoon. I was almost frozen and decided to break into the house. I was just so cold. I was shaking, but I don't know if it was due to the cold, or the fact that I was about to break the law. Surely the police would understand. I didn't know the punishment I would face at that time. How could I have known?

"I went to the back of the house looking for a way in. I picked up a piece of firewood that sat on the side of the porch, and broke a window on the back door. I managed to get the door open, and then went inside. The house was smaller than I thought.

"There was a sink, a stove, some counters, a few cabinets and a refrigerator in the kitchen, all bare. The living room was separated from the kitchen with a long counter. Opposite the counter was the stone fireplace I had seen outside. In front of the fireplace was a small green sofa with a dark maroon pattern running through it. There was no phone in either room.

"Off the living room there was a door leading to a bedroom. The room was empty except for a mattress and a bed frame. Still there was no phone. I tried the next door and saw it led to a basement. I reached for the light switch, waiting as the florescent bulb caught, and then I slowly descended the steps, one at a time, sticking close to the wall as I crept down. I found the room empty. It was not even a finished room. I ran back up the stairs closing the door behind me.

"The last door led to a bathroom. I was surprised at the bathroom. It was very clean. In fact, the whole house was spotless and I knew no one lived there. I looked at the tub. It was a thing of beauty. It was cast iron and had the cutest feet holding it up. I went in because looking at it made me have to go. I really had to use the restroom.

"I looked in the mirror and noticed how dirty I was. I looked a mess. I was no great beauty by any means, but right now I looked like a homeless woman that had been beaten up. Well, if that doesn't beat all; I was a homeless woman, beaten, but by my car. I laughed at my silly thoughts and winced at the figure staring back at me. My eyes had dark circles and appeared blood shot. The large bump on my head stretched the skin as far as it would go. It stuck out about an inch and was purple, yellow and green. No wonder it hurt so badly. My face was dirty and my clothes followed suit. I had made up my mind; if there was running water, I was taking a bath. I hoped no one would come in on me, so I locked the little door, as though it would keep someone out.

"I ran the bath water; it was icy cold at first, but soon warmed to steaming hot. I found shampoo under the sink and a fresh bar of soap along with two towels. I stripped my clothes off and double checked the door making sure it was locked. I felt funny taking a bath, but as I stepped into the hot tub, my body began to melt and the room filled with steam. It took only moments for the mirror to fog over and although the water felt great, I quickly washed, cleaned my hair and drained the water. I would have spent more time in that tub if I'd known it would be the last bath I would have for all these years.

"I really had no idea how dirty I was, until the water began draining and a large ring stayed behind. I looked for cleaning supplies as I dried. I didn't find any, but remembered shampoo cleans, so I used the washcloth and shampoo to scrub the tub. There was no way I was leaving a mess behind.

"I decided on my leggings and the long sweater that could have been a dress. I put on the cleanest socks I had and decided to go without panties. I had no clean panties. I placed my dirty clothes in the lined waste paper basket, unsure of what to do with them.

"I brushed my hair and put on a little makeup which I found in my purse. 'Well, look at you now, still no beauty queen, but at least you don't look like something the cat drug in.'

"When I left the bathroom it was turning dusk. I decided I should just stay there for the night and tomorrow I would go and find help. My head was hurting again and my stomach was grumbling.

"I sat on the sofa, eating some crackers, trying to decide if I should turn on a light; giving myself away if someone arrived home. Then I heard a vehicle drive up. I went to the window like I owned the house and an unexpected guest had arrived. A man stepped from the truck and walked toward the porch. I was nervous. How was I going to explain being in this man's house? Should I meet him at the door? Should I wait until he walks in, and then spring myself on him? I would pay for the broken window of course. I would mention that first. I would explain what happened to me and he would understand.

"He was a good looking man. He had dark hair and a great face. He was slender in the waist, making his broad shoulders and great ass much more pleasant to stare at. As he put his jacket on, I knew I needed to check myself in the mirror before I confronted the man. I knew then, I would wait until he came in to meet with him. I needed the time to go over what I was going to say. As I stepped back from the window, another vehicle drove up.

"The man, who had almost reached the door, stopped, then went to meet the new arrival. As I looked at the truck pulling up, I noticed it closely resembled the truck from the night before. When the man exited the truck, I recognized him. It was the man from the night before; the one that stopped to change my tire. I watched the two men as they talked. Neither saw me, as they seemed to be caught up in their conversation. As they began walking in the direction of the house, I had a complete feeling of dread. I fled to the bedroom and hid in the empty closet.

"They walked into the house and I could hear the deep tones of their voices, but could not make out what they were saying. I needed to get out of there, but I was trapped. I had no way of getting out; so I stayed and waited.

"After a while, I realized I had left my purse and my dirty clothes in the bathroom. There was no way of getting them. I prayed neither would have to go; or else I would be exposed. I had visions of both men tearing through the house and finding me hiding in the closet.

"My ear was stuck to the door, listening for any movement toward me. After what seemed like an eternity, I heard the front door close, both trucks start, and then drive away. I was stupid. I should've made myself known to them. I mean, there I was. I had lost my opportunity to let anyone know I was there; to use a phone, or to get help of any kind. The one man scared me; he was so ugly with all the scars. The other man, the one that looked so great, his looks scared me too. I mean there they were; two men the complete opposite of each other; why were they together?

"I considered leaving the house. I was unsure which of the two men owned the house or if they would be back that night. I didn't know what to do. I thought I should leave. I gathered my things and I went outside. The night air chilled me instantaneously. I quickly went back inside. I was just too cold. It was just too cold to survive through the night. It was dark and I had to find my way back down the road, this house was a dead end. My head was woozy and I needed to lie down. I lay on the small bed in the bedroom and although I was still hungry, hurt, and scared, I fell asleep.

"I don't know how long I slept, but I awoke with a start. I listened. The only sound I could hear was my own breath, in and out. It was still dark outside. I needed to get out of there. I needed some "real" food and I needed to find help. Staying where I was, was not going to get me the help I needed, or get me food and I was famished. I wanted to wait until the sun rose, but as I sat there waiting, I knew I needed to go. The place was starting to creep me out. I bundled up and followed the light from the moon and stars.

"I headed down the path, away from the house. I got to the gate, it was locked. I climbed the gate again and made my way down the road. As I got further from the house I could hear a strange noise. The sound echoed through the leafless trees, as it made its way around the bends of the road toward me. I walked on.

"Headlights blinded me as they came around the bend. I put my hand up, over my face, as the truck came to a halt before me. I was saved! The truck turned on another set of lights, almost like a spotlight that shone directly in my eyes. The light beam blinded my sight. The darkness of the night ensured that the color of the monster's truck would elude me, even to this day.

"'Hello!' I yelled out. 'Hello!' I was starting to get scared as I noticed the person driving the truck was not getting out. I stopped moving forward as a chill ran through my body. I turned and started to run, back down the road toward the house. No, that was not a good idea. I needed to run past the truck, away from the dead end road. It was dark and I just was not sure what to do. There had to be help in the other direction. Someone had to help me. I started screaming and yelling, as my legs carried my body, as fast as I could go. The cold took my breath quickly, but I made my way past the truck. The lights from the truck disappeared, but I could hear the rumble of the engine pulsing through the night air. The road was slick with ice. I ran and ran. I fell and I got up and I ran some more. There was always the rumble of the engine close by. I dare not look behind me, but I was drawn to. I didn't want to know how close he was to me, but I needed to know. Why couldn't he just help me? Why was he doing this to me? Who was this person scaring me? Were they going to hurt me? Kill me? Why was this happening to me? What had I ever done in my life to be put through this? I looked over the edge of the road and there was my car; right where I had left it. I needed to get to it. I could hide in it. I was tired of running. The pain in my legs, side and chest were unbearable. I slid down the hill keeping my eye on my car. I stumbled, falling forward, and then found myself air bound; the rumble of the truck's engine, haunting me. I remember nothing after that. I don't even remember landing.

"That's it. I know nothing else. I don't know who did this. I don't have a face, I don't have a name. I can't even tell you what the person looks like. I have my suspicions though. I think it was one of the men who were at that house. Who else would drive down that road at that time of the night, morning? Why did he do this to me? Why?"

13

Mary said nothing. She knew the man Eliza was talking about, but she would not tell her who he was, at least not right now. The man she knew would not, no make that could not, do anything to hurt another human. The man she knew was loving and caring and would give anyone the shirt off his back. The man she knew was dead. *He's not in hell. No, not my brother, he had his own hell on earth, he didn't do this* Mary thought. She knew the house that Eliza was speaking of. She had been in it many times over the last 15 years. She helped hang the lace curtains with pretty little butterflies, which all seemed to float.

"I don't know what happened after that. I just don't remember." Eliza looked up at Mary and said, "How could a person forget the most important thing?"

Mary sat looking at her, and then said, "Maybe it was so traumatic that you just blocked it from your mind." She was busy thinking about the house Eliza described; she knew the place inside and out. It was her brother's house. He bought it about 15 years ago.

Mary said nothing about her brother, the accident, or the fact that she knew the house intimately. Her brother was dead now. There was no use bringing him up to this woman, at least not right now.

There was a chance it was someone else. Eliza was afraid of Saul and the way he acted around her. Come to think about it, Saul had moved to town about the same time this would have happened. He lived in a cabin over by the river. Mary had never been to his house. Saul was unmarried; it would be easy to keep a woman locked up if no one ever came around. Saul hated company. There were other men in the community that could have done this, but most were married or old. Mary made a mental list of the men that lived in the area all those years ago. She tried to remember what kind of cars and trucks were owned back then, but it was no use. She only knew her brother's truck, a pick-up with lights across the top. It sat in the barn beside his house, the house in which Eliza described.

Mary decided it was best to keep an open mind and a closed mouth. Someone in the community hid a deep dark secret. Mary was not certain which of the men knew more then they were telling; but she knew she would find out, one way or another.

"Yea, I guess that's it. The hell that happened all of these years was not traumatic at all, but how I ended up in a place like that, yea, that was the traumatic event of my life." Eliza voice was full of sarcasm.

"I'm getting tired. I think I want to lie down." Eliza made her way to the bed. She walked like a duck holding her underwear up.

Mary regretted opening her mouth, but did not want to upset Eliza any further. She thought it best to say nothing. She watched Eliza waddle across the room knowing that if it was any other circumstance she might laugh. Mary turned away. When she turned back to Eliza she saw her head on the pillow and her eyes closed. *Damn*, Mary thought, *I lost her*.

14

There was an uneasy silence in the room. Eliza waited. She could feel the rage building inside of her. *How dare this woman question my memory of what took place!* She knew Mary did not mean to upset her, but she had to rest her mind a bit. Telling the next part of her story would be almost as hard as living it. She had survived it once. She knew at this moment she was safe, but telling her full story would take her mind back into the bowels of hell. She wanted Mary to record the story of her life and let her leave. She never wanted to tell her story again. She was ready to move on, to leave this place. *For God sake, I got out of my hellhole. I want to start living again. Today, right now.* She wanted to wake the children and run as fast as she could to get away. She did not want to tell the rest. She opened her eyes and saw Mary looking at her.

"Your turn," Eliza said out of the blue.

"I'm sorry, what?" Mary sounded baffled.

"Tell me something about yourself, Officer Mary." Eliza, now propped up on her elbow was looking at her.

"There is really nothing to tell. I'm married and have a 3 year old son. He was a joyful surprise after the miscarriage of my daughter. I grew up around here and have lived here my whole life. I attend church right up the road and when I'm not working, I teach Sunday school. We are not rich people, but we make enough and for the most part I'm happy." Mary moved to the table and chairs and waited for Eliza to start again.

"What? No unhappy times? I wish I were happy for the most part. You know, even now, after getting out and getting free, my life will never be, happy for the most part. Tell me Mary, you seem like a smart lady; why would God make you happy for the most part and make me take sign language in college? Was that the big plan for me; to fill up French class and force me to take sign language? His big plan for me, was to keep me locked up for all those years and torture me, so my son could learn to talk? What kind of a messed up God are we dealing with here?" Eliza collapsed back on the pillow and was now staring at the ceiling of the small room.

"Well, that's not true. I've had hard times. My father died when I was young and my mother doesn't know who I am when I visit her. My brother died a few weeks ago, when his tractor overturned, while mowing for the county. His crushed body was found by the sheriff. I didn't even get to say good-bye. So hard times, yes I've had my share." Mary wiped a tear from her eye. "I'm sorry my life story does not compare to yours, but I did not put you in that hole. I'm here to help you. I'm here to make sure you are safe from this day until, well, until you can make your own self safe."

"Please, I'm begging you. Please let us leave before he finds us." Eliza was pleading, her breath short and her face now red.

Mary went to the bedside. She held Eliza and rocked her in her arms. "You are safe now Eliza. You are going to be just fine."

Eliza closed her eyes and regulated her breath. She felt Mary cradled her like a mother holding a child. "I wish you would have gone on with your story," Mary quietly said as she got off the bed.

Eliza felt the bed shift gently. She sat up, took a drink of the soda next to the bed and began her story.

Mary, still standing, pushed record and listened.

15

"I awoke in a hallucinogenic like state. My mind tried to focus. Everything around me was fuzzy. I didn't move. I was cold. I felt shivers run up and down my body. I tried to reach for covers knowing my body was naked. My arms didn't move. I'm dreaming. 'Wake up,' I said. 'Wake up.' I was scared, my head doing flip flops. I didn't know where I was or what I was doing. I thought I was dead. Wait, I thought; I'm thinking. I must not be dead, but if I am not dead, then what's going on? If I'm alive, why can't I move? Where am I? How did I get here? What's going on? I tried to remember. I tried to remember everything that happened, yesterday, today? How long had I been there, wherever there was? I wanted to get up. I wanted to leave this place. I wanted to go home. I could feel a wet, warm tear run from my eye, to my temple and disappear into my hair. 'Oh my God what was going on?'

"My mind played back the very last thing I could remember. I was running away from something; no, it was somebody. I found my car and I jumped. Oh my God! I've broken all of my bones; no, maybe just my neck. I tried to look around. It was dark. I tried to move my head, tried to lift it, tried to turn it. The reality of me being alive and hurt and broken came over me. I tried yelling and screaming, but at that moment, I couldn't find my voice. I gathered all my strength and managed to lift my head. My arms and legs still wouldn't move. I started to feel a tingling sensation throughout my body; and with the sensation I had both movement and pain in my extremities. I jerked my arms and legs up and down. I was strapped to something. My legs and my arms were being held to something. I jerked with all of my might to loosen my body from the straps which held me. I felt my flesh tear as they cut into my wrist. I tried to get up. I tried to leave. I was scared. I was full of panic.

"I wasn't sleeping in a dream, I was in a nightmare. I could feel pain fill every pore of my body. 'Wake up,' I said to myself, 'Wake up, please, wake me up, will someone just wake me up?'

"I laid quietly listening for any movement; I couldn't see. I strained to hear things like talking, walking or anything, anything at all. I heard sounds in the room with me. Whatever was with me was scampering across the floor. It was small, but the noise it made was loud as it echoed throughout the room. I was in a room. But where was I? What room was I in? I tried to see the thing making the noise on the floor. I hoped it was not coming my way. I was frozen with fear. What was it? Where was the noise coming from? Was it coming toward me? Was it going to eat me? The noise stopped. I waited for it to start again. I waited for the sound that I dreaded hearing. The covers I lay upon moved, not much, but just enough to let me know I was not alone on the bed. I was on a bed. My mind was working in two directions at the same time; one trying to figure out what was going on, the next trying to be as still as I could with this thing on the bed with me. I held my breath. I didn't move. My skin started to crawl and a shiver ran through my body. I could feel it touch me. I panicked. I freaked out.

"I yelled and screamed until my voice left me. My arms and legs jerked only an inch or so up and down, but the whole of my body jerked and shook. I heard a hiss through my screaming, and then I heard it run away. I tried again to get up. I wanted to leave.

"At that moment, I didn't care what HAD happened to me. If I didn't know, there would be nothing for me to forget, nothing to tell. 'I didn't see you!' I yelled into the room. 'Just let me go!' I shouted over and over. I tried to control myself, but I couldn't. Panic had taken hold and there was nothing I could do to make it go away. I was scared to death. Finally exhausted, I laid quietly, my heart pounding. I tried to go back to sleep; to wake up again someplace else. I couldn't. I listened for any movement. I couldn't see as tears stung my eyes and the darkness folded in on me. I used my ears again; waiting, listening for any sound; any sound of the rodent, any sound of a person, any sound at all.

"I heard nothing in the room with me, but I could hear the wind outside. No voice; I had no voice left. I struggled against the straps again, though the pain in my arms and legs was unbearable. I prayed. I lay in the darkness forever. I was dead. I had gone to hell. I cried. My eyes ached, my head pounded, my heart broke for me. I must have done something really bad in my life, and this was how I would pay for it. I thought I had jumped to my car and landed, not on the ground beneath, but passed through, landing in hell, where all my sins had come to me. The punishment for my life was to lay in the darkness of hell forever and ever, amen. So be it! And it was. I stayed in HELL forever!

"I guess I fell asleep, exhausted after a while. I felt my mind slip away. I did not know how many days I was there and I did not want to think about it. I just wanted the whole thing over.

"I woke again. This time there was light coming in from a window. It was a little window about the size you would see in a small bathroom. My throat was dry and hurt when I swallowed. The straps had been removed from me. A white sheet covered me. Under the sheet, I wore nothing but black and blue marks. I grabbed the sheet around me. I tried to cry out as pain seized my every movement. No sound escaped my voice. I reached for my throat and the pain seemed to overwhelm me. I slowly lifted my pounding head from the bed.

"I looked around the room, it was small. I was on a bed that sat against the wall. The walls were made of cinder block. I appeared to be in a basement. There was a sink of sorts and a large pipe with a paper that said "toilet" above it on one side of the room. On the other side of the room it looked as if my car had been spilled out. Everything I had packed into the car was there in the room with me. My clothes, my books from school, and my purse; everything I owned was there.

"I looked at my arms and legs and pulled the sheet close to my body. There were cuts on my wrist and my ankles. My body bruised with welts. My mind was trying to take it all in. I could not believe this was happening; I could not believe this was happening to me!

"I jumped off the bed. My legs felt like limp noodles and would not hold me up. I fell to the floor, hurting my already beaten body. I looked up at the bed and saw the straps that held my arms and legs. They were connected to the bed, hanging to the floor.

"I was awake. I pinched my arm to make sure. Where was I and why was I there? I was cold. My body began to shiver and goose bumps consumed me. My teeth began to chatter. My wrists hurt. The blood had dried from the cuts of the straps, but movement of my arms and legs hurt. Hell, movement of my whole body hurt. I moaned as I drug myself along the floor. I went to my clothes and quickly got dressed. I wrapped my arms and legs with strips from an old shirt. I pulled myself back on the bed and waited. I don't know what I was waiting for, but I would be ready.

"I looked around the room again. There was no door. I was in a room without a door. How could that be? I noticed the small window had bars on it. I remember thinking there has to be a door. All rooms have doors. I looked up to the ceiling. There, in the ceiling, above the room, was the door. It was made of wood and tin. It came from the sky. There was no way to reach it. I tried. I looked around for anything I could find to stand on, to try and get out. I pulled the bed over and jumped up to the door. I jumped and held things to push up on the door; it was no use, it refused to move. Finally, I was able to reach the knob. I grabbed it and hung on to it, my feet dangling above the bed below. I guess my weight was too much because it broke off in my hands. The knob and I fell to the bed below. I remember thinking, now I'll never get out. I had broken the door. No one could get in, but I could never get out. I cried and screamed; and my throat, I had damaged it. I know I did. It was so long before my voice came back to me. I cursed the door as though it had put me in that place. I collapsed on the bed exhausted. I think I went into shock. I lay there unable to move, unable to think.

"I awoke some time later. I got off the bed and looked again for anything to help me get out. I went to the window this time. It was so small. The bars were on the inside, but I could reach the window. I broke it, but it did no good. The cold air rushed in, freezing my face as though I had walked into a freezer. I tried to yell out the window, but I could not. I had no voice. I banged things against the bars, but I saw nothing or heard no one.

"I was out in the middle of nowhere. I could see the snow that covered the ground and some trees and a hill. The air was so cold and my body hurt. My arms and legs ached. I was so full of dread too. What was I going to do?

"I didn't know if I should eat or drink. I thought about it for a long time before I did. I went to the sink area and moved the lever. The water flowed into the bucket that sat below it. The water flowed clear. I drank as though I had never drank before. The water was cold and felt good on my throat. The bucket overflowed and the water spilled to the floor. I turned it off quickly, not wanting to have to sit in a wet area, until I could get out.

"I felt hungry and found some food in my bag. There were crackers, I was so hungry. The crackers scratched my throat, but I ate them anyway. I was not dead. I was alive. I ate slowly as I planned my escape.

"I had no plan. I had to wait until someone came. I thought I could make them see. I said the words over and over in my head. I said them differently each time I spoke. 'Please, just let me go. You can have anything you want, just please let me go!' I begged.

"I waited for days. The sun came and went. No one showed up. I stayed awake as long as I could. I slept, but I heard every sound around me. I waited for the sound of the door to open.

"I tried to clean the place I was kept in. I folded my clothes. I had to have some kind of order in my life; although I controlled nothing. I cleaned myself with water that would never get hot. I thanked God that I bought soap and things before I left. I needed to stay clean. My life was so dirty.

"I looked down at the food I had left. There was almost none. I had eaten very little every day, but now I was near the end. One package of 4 cheese crackers was all that was left. I thought, now I would die. I would starve to death. I sang as I ate the last bite. I prayed to God to bless the food I ate.

"He came to me that night after dark. I had a book in my hand. I decided I might need something to defend myself with, so I began taking a book to bed with me. I heard the door squeak and I sat up. There was total darkness in the room. I could hear him. He was mumbling something to himself, and then I heard him curse. He lowered something into the room. It was a ladder. I heard it creak as he climbed down.

"I jumped off the bed and went to the sound. 'Please, help me, please help me. Don't leave me here to die,' I begged. Then I got scared. I wondered if I should hide from him. I saw the light. It ran across the top of the ceiling and down the side wall and then the light found me. The bright light went straight into my eyes. I could not move. I froze and I felt a chill run through my body, I felt woozy and thought I was going to pass out.

"I could not see anything, but the bright light coming closer to me. I finally moved my arm up to shade my eyes and saw the book I held in my hand. 'Who is it? What do you want?' I yelled. I was really scared. He made his way toward me. I could hear his footsteps, I could hear him breathing. As the light moved closer to my eyes, I swung the book I had in my hands at the dark figure approaching me. The light that blinded my sight disappeared. I heard a bang as the flashlight hit the floor.

'"You bitch!' he bellowed. His breathing intensified. I could hear him getting closer to me.

'"Stay away from me!' I screamed. What a stupid thing to do, to yell like that. I should have run away. I should have hid. I felt him grab me and I yelled and fought. The room was total darkness, but he found me and he grabbed me.

'"Stop fighting me,' he growled in my ear.

'"Leave me alone!' I screamed back. I fought like I had never fought anyone in my life. He slapped me. How could he see my face when I could not see his? I refused to scream in pain. I wanted the pain to drive my fighting. I kicked and I hit back at him. My hand hurt as it made contact with his face. It was not his face; it was a mask, a leather mask that zipped in the back. I ran my hands over it and over it not believing what I was feeling. When I got to the eyes, he jerked my hands away and pushed me back. I fell on the bed, but I quickly got to my feet again.

"Blind people have what is known as a second sight. It keeps them from running into things. I developed one over the years, but at that time I was new to the game. Being a baby to this game, I didn't know a punch was coming toward my face. I didn't watch, or I should say, listen for the break in the air. I fell flat on the bed and the pain overwhelmed me. I tasted the blood that ran down my face and into my mouth. My eye caught part of the blow and every nerve in my body stood on end, waiting for the next hit.

"I had to fight. My mind said, don't let him take you, fight; come on, get up and fight. My body and my mind worked differently. I think my brain finally got it when he held a blade to my neck.

I always thought I would rather die than have someone rape me. I didn't want to die, I wanted to live. He pulled me up to the top of the bed. He ripped the clothes from my body and I didn't move. I couldn't move as he put the straps back on my arms and legs. I wanted to, but I couldn't move, I clung to wanting to live. Damn me, I wanted to live.

"I felt him enter me. I screamed as my flesh ripped open. 'Get off me! Stop, please get off me!' I felt the tears run from my eyes. 'Please,' I moaned; my body jerked and twisted, 'don't do this to me. You don't have to do this to me.'

"He moaned as he deposited his hate inside me. I cried as I understood what had happened.

"'Now that's more like it,' he whispered in my ear.

"'What are you saying? You raped me!' I yelled at him crying, my body jerking with sobs.

"His breath smelled of booze; that sweet, sick, smell. Not beer, but whiskey, hard drinking whiskey.

"I told him I wanted to leave. I didn't want to stay. He had gotten what he wanted. I didn't see his face. 'No one has to know,' I told him, 'No one has to know.'

"He told me, the only way out was death. He climbed on top of me again for the second time that night. I fought him as best I could. He hurt me. He ripped at my flesh and tore at my breast. I tried to fight him. I struggled. His hands were on my throat, I had no air. He was deep inside me. My insides screamed in pain. He let go of my throat and I yelled.

"'Oh, I know you like it, don't you whore? You know you like to feel me inside of you. Do you want more of me? I know you do. Oh, this is so much better than when you were out of it. I like it when you struggle.'

"Oh my God, he raped me when I was out of it? Did I hear him right? He violated me and I was not even aware? What kind of sick monster was he? I would soon find out.

"I bit his arm and he smashed my face again. This time it was my left side that took a beating. I felt him finish. I wanted him out of me. I wanted his body out of mine! I pushed with my insides and I wormed around, but he stayed in me while he spoke. His breath was short as he spoke in my ear, 'If you bite me again, I'll rip your teeth out, one by one. Is that what you want you whore?' He slid out of me and I could feel his deposit slide out with him. He climbed off of me and I could see the figure of a man. He was tall and big; not fat, but his shoulders, legs and arms were big. He grabbed his shirt then said, 'I like it when you fight; I know who's in charge when you fight and I win.' He laughed. He bent down; and I swear to you, he laughed in my face and then left. He went up the ladder, to the opening.

"He stopped, and then came back. 'Now you be a good little whore and stay put.' I felt him at the straps and I felt the blood rush back to my hands and feet.

"'Please tell me where I am,' I whispered.

"'You are in a hole, a hole in no·where.' He laughed and hit me again.

"'I see you broke the window. I'll only replace it once. There is no one to hear you screaming. If you want to freeze, that's fine with me, but your death will be on your own hands, not mine.'

"He had taken the straps off me, but I dare not move. The room was so dark and my body hurt. I rolled up in a ball. I could smell his sweat on me. My nostrils burned with his scent. I was so dirty; I remember feeling I would always be dirty. I stayed in the bed and cried. I cried until I had no tears in my eyes. I slept for days and days. I would watch the sun come and go through the little window.

"Finally my body demanded food and I had to get up. Sometime during my sleep, he brought food with a note that read, '*Use sparingly.*' He had brought a couple of boxes of crackers and twenty cans of potted meat, a jar of peanut butter, and some dry cereal.

A large pack of toilet paper and eight bars of soap completed his shopping spree. The window remained broken and I spent my days yelling out for help. No one ever came. My yells fell in the hills.

"He's keeping me. This psycho thinks I'm his toy or something and he's keeping me. I yelled into the room, 'I'm not a doll! You can't take me out when you want to play and put me up when I bore you! Let me out of here, I swear, I'll never tell a soul!'

"I refused to eat anything he brought into the room. Soon I began to starve. I was weak, but I refused to give in. My arms were heavy and it took all the energy I had, to crawl to the bathroom area to throw up. I had eaten nothing and my body was throwing up bile.

"My mind wanted to die, but my body did not. I crawled to the food and I ate like a mad person. I ate until there was almost no food left. I ate until all I had eaten, I threw up. I went days again with very little food.

"The water was always there. I couldn't clean myself like my body wanted. I felt so dirty. The water was cold too. My skin would crawl when I tried to wash. I covered myself, not sure if he was watching me or not. I wanted him to have no pleasure from watching me. I took to holding up a blanket when I used the restroom and when I cleaned myself. I wanted him to have nothing of me given to him freely.

"He brought food when he came. He made me say thank you. The man was crazy. He refused to let me leave. He would rape and beat me and then make me say thank you?

"He finally replaced the window. I wanted to break it again, but I knew only I would suffer. He was right; there was no one to hear me screaming. Don't you see there was no one to hear me scream?" Eliza was now crying as though she were reliving it all over again.

Mary looked sympathetically at Eliza.

"He would come in the night and I would fight. I never bit him again. I knew his threat was real and I just couldn't do it. He would win, he always won and my body paid what my mind would not. I blocked him out of my head after each fight. I tried to distance my mind from my body during his rapes. Sometime it worked, most times it didn't.

"I slept and planned my escape. It consumed my mind. I would think of getting out day and night. I thought one day I would take him by surprise and I would win the fight; but the fighting just turned him on, making him crazy with rough sex.

"He would thrust deep into me...and the pain; I felt him rip through my body and into my soul. I found it hard to get up after he finished with me. I soon learned to just lay still. Let him do what he wanted; hating him with every inch of my body. He hated it when I didn't fight. Soon he began leaving the straps off of my arms, and then off my legs. I knew I could never take this man in a fight and win, but the beatings that came with the fights, were less than the ones, where I refused to fight. Eventually, I bought into his way of thinking and gave him what he wanted. I gave him a fight.

"He had broken me like a cowboy breaks a horse. The horse follows the command, but wants to kill the rider. That was me; I became the horse. Once, when he was on top, I finally did it. I took him by surprise and bucked him to the ground. I took off to the ladder. He recovered too soon. He grabbed me before I was even halfway up. He pulled me down by my legs.

"I struggled; I held the rings of the ladder until the wood ripped my flesh from the bone of my arm. I screamed or blacked out or something. I'm not sure what happened, but before I knew it I was in his arms. My blood was running down my arm, dripping to the floor below. He took me back to the bed and wrapped up my injured flesh. At that moment, I thought he was human. I forgot everything else. I forgot about the abuse, the isolation, the torment. I cried tears of relief that this man had compassion.

"I paid for that mistake, the mistake of thinking of that monster as a man. He came back the next night, and as he entered every hole my body had to offer, a part of me shriveled up and died. The taste of him in my mouth, with the taste of me; I had to keep from gagging. The knife at my throat, kept me from biting his manhood off.

"Time slipped away from me. I lost track of days and nights. I could sleep for days at a time; not moving even to use the bathroom. I was a lifeless human. He had sucked the life right out of me." Eliza looked at the scars that were buried deep into her shallow skin and rubbed her hand on her neck. Mary noticed her neck looked as though it had been cut in two.

"He would complain about the smell in my hole. Tell me how I didn't take care of myself. As he descended the steps, he sprayed cans of freshener in the room. He would tie me up and clean me. The cold water froze my body. The brush he used would leave me raw.

"The sun came and went. The moon passed and I guess time just slipped away. I ate when given food and drank the water, but I wanted to die. I just wanted to die and end the madness of where I was and whom I was with.

"I awoke one morning just to watch the sun rise above my bed. I could not take the pain any longer. I knew at that moment, I would never get out. I would live forever in this hell that I was in. I tried to kill myself by hanging. I took the sheet from the bed and tied it to the bars that were on the window. He found me though and took the sheets from the bed. I could not understand why this man wanted me alive. Why did he want me to live? So he could have some poor girl as a sex slave, to have as his own personal slut? There are so many girls out there giving it away for free, why was he keeping me here like this?

"My period appeared one day. When I stopped flowing, I prayed every night I was not carrying this man's child. I never had any signs that I was pregnant and soon, I guess I lost track. I knew the body would react to stress and strain; so after months and months of not having one, I thought I never would. When the bleeding started, I was unprepared. It was like I was a small girl getting her first period and not being told what it was. I saw the blood and felt the cramping. I was unsure what was going on. I thought maybe he had ruptured something inside of me. I feared I was going to die there; bleed out. A part of me had wished this for so long. A part of me prayed I would one day be set free. If it was to die; in this bed, at this time, in this way, I was ready. I was prepared to die. I lay in the bed for hours; waiting for my time on earth to end. Waiting for the hell I was living in to be over. I prayed to God to let me in Heaven, I prayed for my sins to be forgiven. I was ready to go; I was ready to be lifted up to heaven, because I had done my time in hell.

"When I finally realized it was my period, I was happy and depressed all at once. I laughed at my own stupidity. I had been having periods for years before I was kidnapped. I was a grown woman without a thought of a simple monthly cycle. I finally realized my body had adjusted to the state I was kept in. Then I had another fear. It consumed my every thought. It ate at my mind. If I was now bleeding again, did that mean I could have a child by this monster? I tried to remember everything I was taught about my cycle and when pregnancy could occur. He was away from me for long periods of time then. I lucked out for months, but my life was not a lucky one. No, my life was far from lucky.

"When my period stopped again, I was scared. When I started showing signs, you know, signs I was going to have a baby; I cried. My mind tried to cope with the thought of having a child; the thought of a child, there in hell. My mind tried to cope with the thought of having HIS child, the man I hated. He was the man, if ever given the chance; I would put a gun to his head and blow his brains out. Could I hide a baby from him? Did I want this baby? Did I want HIS baby? I had to go to the doctor. I couldn't give birth there. I had so many emotions, all at once. I thought of nothing else. I had no other thought in my mind. I was like a junky on crack, only my addiction was what would happen to the child. I played every scenario, over and over in my mind. I thought of ways to abort the child. He could beat it out of me; but for reasons that elude me, I covered and protected the child growing inside my belly. How could I go from wanting to die, praying to die, to this?

"The man said nothing until I began to show. He asked if I was eating too much. He said I was getting fat. I didn't want to tell him. I tried not to let him know. When he started to take the food I needed to live; the food my baby needed to grow, I yelled at him, 'I'm going to have a baby!' I thought I would regret the words that flew out of my mouth, but I didn't. He brought more food, bottled water and powdered milk. As I grew, he came not for sex, but to check on me. He would touch my belly and feel the child kick. It would turn my stomach. Why would he be so nice to a child I carried, only to leave it in the hell I lived in? I never thought he would take the baby though. That thought never once crossed my mind. Why would he want a child, from a woman, he hated, as much as he hated me? The question that scared me more; why did I want a child from a man I wished dead?

"The day I longed for and dreaded finally arrived. I remember the pain. The blood; there was so much blood. I thought I would die. I thought the child would die. I labored for so long. I pushed when I thought I could push no longer. I was weak and sick the day he arrived. The pain ripped through my body. I felt as if I were being torn in two. I begged and pleaded with God, to let me go to a hospital; but my baby came kicking and screaming to life, in that hole in no·where.

"I cut his cord with a piece of metal from a can top. His afterbirth lay on the bed for days. I cleaned him with water from the sink. The water was always cold, but the baby came to life and I grew to love him. I am a part of him and he is a part of me. I can never forget that." Eliza paused and looked at Mary, with the eyes of a lost soul.

"Eliza," Mary called gently, bringing her back to her story.

"There were no diapers or bottles or baby showers. I made do with what I had, and used my old clothes to warm him. My milk flowed and the baby ate. We talked and played and he grew. The food was little though. We adjusted to this life and I had a reason to live now. The baby slept most of the time when HE came. The man brought a flashlight and looked at the baby once. He asked if he was the father. I simply said, 'Yes, he's your son.'

"What did he think?" Eliza looked up at Mary as if she had the answers to the questions she was asking. "Where would I have gone? Was he mad? Look what he was doing to me; yes, the man was mad!"

"He came and used me for sex. He told me so. Said I had no other plan in life, but to be used by him forever. I had been there for years and years and I would die there; right where I was, in that little room.

"I asked him his name once. His reply to me was, 'I am your God and that is how you will address me. I am the God of your Hell.' I knew not what he looked like. I had only a fleeting image of a man, with a scarred face, to put with my pain. He had strong arms and over the years, he didn't grow fat.

"I tried to block his visits out; to retreat to a different place and time. I couldn't block his breath on my face, his hands on my breast or his body in my body. His voice was so full of hatred toward me. He despised the thought of me.

"I told him if he hated me so, to please let me go. He replied, 'We are a family now. The most important thing in life is family and NO ONE, will break up my family!'

"I would hold and play with the baby. He would coo at me and smile and he became the center of my life. I tried to give him a name, some kind of name that would make him strong. A name has strength you know, but I just couldn't find one that fit him. I tried different ones on him, but never quite picked out the right one. I called him "Teddy" my teddy bear, but it was more of a pet name than a real name.

"I grew used to life there. This child and I, living in that place; and soon I began to dream again. I dreamt of a man, I once saw. He showed up at the house, the night of my accident. I dreamed he came out of the room and helped me. He was so handsome and nice. His eyes were pure and he was such a gentleman. He saved me from the man with the scar. I stayed the night with him. I dreamt we made love. I could actually feel his arms around me as he whispered my name. His kisses were sweet and I felt my body respond to his. He was not rushed or thrusting too deep. Our bodies melted into one another and I whispered, 'I love you,' just before we fulfilled each other. I made love to the man in my dreams; and the man of my nightmares, enjoyed my pleasure. The man of my dreams became the man with the scar. I awoke screaming. I awoke gasping for breath, as a hand on my throat choked away my life.

"The voice screamed, 'Whores don't love, bitch! You know nothing and you will love nothing. I'm taking my child.' He knocked me to the floor. I could see him picking up the baby.

"'No!' I yelled. 'Don't take Teddy!' I struggled to my feet, following the light from the flashlight he carried.

"'This baby has no name. Do you hear me, forget this child, it's not yours!' He yelled as he kicked me back. He was up the ladder in a flash. I grabbed the rungs of the ladder, as he pulled it up from outside the hole. Teddy was screaming and I was trying to reach for him. The man picked up the ladder, and then slammed it down to the ground. I fell off as I reached into the darkness for my child. The ladder was gone and the door slammed shut and the tears would not come. My child was gone and I could not cry. It felt as if a hole had been ripped through my heart. I must have been in shock for days. When the tears finally came, they stayed, and have been with me since. Is he dead? Is he alive? Is he a throw away child that no one wants? I wanted him! I want him."

Eliza stopped. Her voice was shaky and she was crying. Mary wiped a tear from her own eye.

After a while, Eliza began again. "I hope my son is alive and happy someplace far, far from here."

Mary blurted out, "You are wrong. The man with the scar could not have done this to you. He was a kind man. He would never hurt anyone. You said he tried to help you. He couldn't have done this thing to you. You have made a mistake. If you never saw him, how would you have known it was him?"

"It had to be him. How can you defend him? You just don't understand what I am saying, do you? There was no one else I remember that could have done this to me. He took my child. I never saw my first-born child again. I begged him to tell me if he was alive or dead; but nothing, never a word about the baby. After all this time, I need to know, did he kill him or is he alive someplace? I cried; I still cry for him. I don't want to talk anymore. Just leave, just leave me alone."

"I'm sorry Eliza, I spoke out of turn. Please don't stop now. Please."

Minutes passed before Eliza dare speak again, "He didn't come back after that for a long time. That was fine with me. I had no reason to go on now. I was back to the place I was before. I wished for a quick death. My food ran out and I did nothing, but lie in the bed and pray to die. I cried morning, noon and night. I drank only because I needed to. I did still have hope; hope that one day I would see my son again. Damn that man for taking him away; damn him for giving him to me in the first place. I don't know how old my son is. I don't even know when he was born. I don't know anything about him. I only have an image of this small child in my mind. At times, I think I only dreamed the child. Either way, I hold his memory close to my heart. I hope he is happy. I hope hell never touches him, as it has his brother and sister.

"I wish it had ended there, but I was soon to witness the greatest of all horrors with his return. When he finally did come back, he brought a woman with him. Together, they both raped me. She did things I didn't know a woman would do to another woman. He eagerly watched with that light of his. I begged her to stop. I looked her in her eyes, telling her this was no game. This was real. I begged her for help. She laughed at me. She flipped her hair, begging him to enter her from behind. She knelt in front of me saying, 'See, this is how a man likes it,' those were her last words. He killed her as he took her, wrapping his large hands around her neck. She reached up grabbing his hands trying to remove them and then her arms reached out to me; her bulging eyes begging me for help. I backed against the wall as she gasped for air to breathe. I finally turned away. I begged her and she had laughed at me as though it was, no, as though I were a joke. I felt nothing for the dead woman at that moment, not then and not now.

"He came for me again as her dead body lay on the ground. I tried to fight him, but it was no use. I was weak from lack of food; fighting the woman, and the exhaustion of watching her die. After a small struggle, I let him have me. His complaint now was I was too skinny. He had just strangled a woman to death and he was complaining I was too skinny? He held me in a room with no way out and no food, and I was too skinny?

"I think I was in shock. Actually seeing him kill and the twinkle in his eyes was too much for me. I don't remember him leaving or even taking the dead body out. The woman with the golden hair and young face was gone when I awoke. Her death saved my life though; I got more food for a while, enough food for months.

"Before long I realized I was pregnant again. I think it happened the night I dreamed about the other man. It was months before HE came back. When he did come, I was TOO fat. The next day I had EJ." Eliza smiled at EJ as he slept in the bed next to her.

"Do you know that EJ could hear when he was a baby? He got sick as a child and I thought he would die. I sang to him and he would smile at me. He even learned to say "Momma". From time to time the man would beat him and beat me because he was making too much noise. I'm not sure why he lost his hearing; if it was from the beatings or if it was the illness. I do think that is why he did not take him from me. EJ was not like his brother, strong and resilient; he is more like me...

"I did the best I could to teach him, but I only had some college books and a pen which had run out of ink. In college I took sign language and I taught him to talk. He does really good and can hold quite a conversation with you." Mary noticed a spark in Eliza's eyes as she spoke about her son.

"Perhaps with a doctor's help, he can hear again. Do you know a doctor I might be able to take him to?" Eliza was still looking at her son. A tear escaped her eye. "I wish I knew for sure how old he was. But the days go too fast and the months all seem to flow into one. One moment there was snow on the ground outside of the window and the next moment, green grass.

"This man continued to beat EJ and me. It was sad watching this child of mine suffer so. One night, after he finished with me, I knew he was going after EJ. I had to protect him. I couldn't sit by any longer. The man was on my back as I lay on the bed. I remembered the pen I was looking at with EJ. We would hold the clear plastic and look at the different color reflections. I had left the pen shell on the bed. I felt around for it. I finally found it. I picked up the pen, which had long ago run out of ink, and I stabbed the man in the hand. The pen went straight through his hand and into the bed that we were on. He yelled and screamed, jumped off the bed and grabbed his flashlight to look at his wound. I stood on the bed and hit him from behind, across the back of his neck. Both he and the flashlight hit the ground. The flashlight spun around the room and I went to EJ, picking him up. The ladder, get to the ladder, my mind raced. I managed to get one foot on the ladder. He grabbed my hair and yanked me back. I fell with EJ on top of me. EJ recovered from the fall and scurried under the bed. The man picked me up by my hair. I stood just below his shoulder, but now my feet dangled. I could hear my hair ripping from my scalp, and then I felt pain; I heard ringing and then I passed out. He had cut the ear off my head. I awoke to find my little EJ holding my ear. The next day he returned, but not down into my hole. He opened the top and dropped bandages and antibiotic ointment down through the door." Eliza held her hair back, so Mary could see where the missing ear had been. Mary winced and chills ran through her body.

"He came back many days later. He beat EJ and me like never before. 'You are a burden I no longer want!' He yelled to us. 'I need neither of you.' There was no rape that time, but I had broken bones and my poor EJ was in pieces. I knew I had to end the suffering. I knew I could take no more. I was never going to leave. My son was to be beaten and I was to be beaten and raped. What if he started raping EJ? What if he raped my other child? What if he threw him away? I knew what had to be done then. I had to kill EJ, and then kill myself. With no mistake this time, I had to end our suffering.

"I picked up my beautiful child the next day, and sat on the bed. I rocked his broken body in my arms and sang to this child, I knew could not hear. I held him close; so close he could feel my heart beat, feel the vibrations of my song to him. He had finally cried himself to sleep from the pain and terror he was in. I picked up a pillow; and as tears streamed down my cheeks, falling on his innocent little blood stained body; I took the pillow and slowly put it to his face. I covered his mouth, his nose and his eyes. I didn't want him to see me. I didn't want his last sight to be my face, filled with regret.

"He didn't move at first. His body was in my arms, safe and secure. He could feel my heart beat. He knew my smell. He was safe in my arms.

"'Go now. It's time to go now,' I told him. As he began to struggle, I held the pillow tighter against his mouth and nose. He struggled to breathe. His body begged to live. His arms and his legs fought against my hand pushing the life out of him. Through all his beatings and his hearing loss; through his starving and cold baths; through everything he had been through, he still wanted to live. I held a pillow against his face and took the one thing I could give him. I took the air that he breathes and he fought me to his last breath.

"Soon his body went limp. He stopped fighting and he drew no more air into his lungs. I wanted him back. I didn't want my son to die. I didn't want him to die! I was no better than his father. I was now the monster, the monster to my sweet innocent child. I grabbed him and gave him life back. I did CPR like I was taught in school and I blew air into his lungs and compressed his heart until his body could do it.

"What kind of a person does that make me?" Eliza yelled at Mary. "What kind of a mother kills her own son, and then brings him back? What was worse? I need to know. Is it beating and starving your child? Or is it taking his breath, killing him?" Eliza was crying, covering her face with her hands and hugging the pillow from the bed.

"If we have to go back there to him, live there in that hole, then I should have let him die that night. They put animals down that suffer as both he and I have." Eliza grabbed Mary's hand. "Please don't make us go back to him or we'll die. All three of us will die." Eliza got up and went into the bathroom.

Mary could hear her crying, but decided against checking on her. Mary was in shock, she did not know what to do. Should she arrest her or leave her be? Doug would know when he listened to the tapes. The confession was enough to put handcuffs on the woman, but after what she had lived through; Mary knew she would not arrest her.

As the woman emerged from the bathroom, Mary looked at her eyes. They were red, puffy and swollen. When Eliza spoke, her voice shook as if she were afraid. "I won't have my son suffer like he did, ever again. I love him, my life."

Eliza got on the bed next to EJ and curled her body around his. She stroked his hair and kissed his cheek. He turned and smiled at his mother, and then fell back to sleep. He felt safe with her, Mary knew that. Everything else, Mary was unsure of. Eliza kissed him again and slid out of the bed. She spoke again, but it was different now. Eliza seemed distant, away from her life; she seemed away from her story.

16

"The stress of my body changed after time and soon I began to flow again. We had regular food for a time, a drop at least twice a month. Sometimes he would pull me out of the hole saying the smell was too much for him and rape me under the starlit night. I just let him have my body. I had no way of stopping him and I had to keep him from EJ. He swore EJ was no child of his. He didn't want a child that could not hear; he was too perfect for that. I think that if EJ could hear he would have taken him also.

"He would climb on me and ask me if this was how my boyfriends did me. I spoke little to him, but told him over and over I had no one but him. How sick was I, trying to tell a man that raped me hundreds of times, that there was no one but him in my life? I think I lost my mind in that room; but I don't ever want to go back there to find it.

"It was a long time before I would have my last child. He would still come and beat and rape me, but his visits grew far apart, as did the food. I saved what I could. We ate only a little at a time. I was sure there would come a day when he would stop coming altogether. I prayed at times for him to come, so at least my child could eat. I wanted him to take my body; I gave it to him freely as a thank you for the food that fed EJ. Sometimes he seemed surprised we were still alive.

"'We need food to live. Please give us the food we need to live.' I would beg this man. 'I will do anything you want; just please, bring food for me and my child. We don't want to die, please.' I was a pathetic excuse for a human. I begged the man I hated; trading sex for food and fresh water. I was no longer a rape victim, but had turned into a prostitute for the basic things in life. I used to wonder why women would trade their bodies for sex. What would drive them to do such a thing? I knew. At that time, I knew. I didn't walk the streets picking up men, but I did things that only a whore knows how to do.

"I don't think he ever knew I was going to have another child. He stopped coming for sex; said the smell was too bad, I was too used up. The food would just be dropped into my hole; not much, just enough to survive. I was relieved on one point, but on another; I thought, God, the man that keeps you, no longer wants you. I felt like a wife whose husband no longer wants her. I was angry and upset. When the food would drop I would yell up, 'Why am I no longer desirable to you? Please just come down here.' I had lost all reasoning. God, my brain is so messed up. I would think at times he had someone else he was spending his time with. Why would I do that? Please tell me why I felt jealous? I need help." Eliza was talking through her tears. She knew Mary did not know what to say to her. What could she say? Could she even understand how she depended on the monster? She looked at Mary who was shaking her head, knowing she did not have the answer.

"Eliza, I'm sorry," Mary said. "Sometimes people bond with their captors, but I do not know what drives them to do so."

Eliza began again after she wiped her eyes. "She was a beautiful baby. EJ helped deliver her. The man didn't even seem to know I had another child; to this day, I don't know if he knows. She has never felt the wrath of her father. She has never felt the complete starvation that plagued her brother and me. She was breast fed, and up until a few days ago, I had milk. He dropped food only once after she was born. I was sick for days after giving birth to her. I was lost in the fog of a fever. EJ kept me alive. EJ kept Hope alive. EJ would get her and bring her to me to feed. I had her set up on a comforter. EJ watched over her and seemed to know her every need. She is a bright baby. I think she was EJ's will to go on. He was mine, she was his."

Eliza looked over to the crib that contained the baby. Hope had perked up quite a bit since she got milk earlier. She would stretch in her crib from time to time, but never fully awake. She whimpered for only a second. "I'm really tired; can we stop for now?" Eliza asked. She had talked for so long and tried to tell Mary everything she could.

"Well Eliza, we are so close to the end. Can you tell me how you managed to get out after all of those years?" Mary probed.

Eliza began, "I think there was an earthquake or something. The hell hole we were held in shook beneath our feet. A fracture formed on the floor and I watched it climb up the wall to the small window sill. The window cracked as it absorbed the energy of the earth as it moved. EJ screamed. He couldn't hear the cracking cinder blocks, but he could feel the earth shake, throwing him off balance. I was frightened at first, and then I hoped the walls would tumble down freeing us. I was wrong. We were left with a cracked window. I went to the window cursing. I looked up at the crack and there before my eyes, were legs. Blue jeans and work boots. He had come in the daytime. I heard him yell, 'What are you doing there? Get the hell away from there!' I motioned for EJ to come to me. We hid under the bed. I don't know why we hid; he could open the door and come in anytime he wanted, but we hid.

"I heard a loud thump and then there was a yell. Not a woman's yell, but a man's deep, dark yell. I figured he had hurt himself because he didn't come down. That was the last time I ever heard him or saw him.

"I waited for days; waited for him to come, but he never showed up. The window bothered me. I found myself staring up at it day and night. After a sleepless night, I pulled the bed over and pulled on one of the bars. It came out without any effort. I fell back on the bed and rejoiced. We were getting out. I knew then, we would be free. I got back up and I pulled at the next bar, then the next, and finally the last; my heart breaking with every tug as the three remained solid. I felt disappointment overwhelm me. 'Why?' I yelled. 'Why? Couldn't one thing be easy for me just once?' It was dark that night and I couldn't see well. I fell into an exhausted, tear-filled sleep.

"I woke in the morning and went to the window. It was raining and the water came in through the crack and soaked into the ledge. I thought it might weaken the concrete, I was wrong. We were so close to getting out a few days ago, I couldn't let this idea go. It consumed my every waking moment. I looked around the room and saw the metal frame the bed sat on. I tossed the blood and sex stained mattress to the floor. I found my old key chain and used it as a screwdriver in the oversized screws. The frame fell into pieces. I began to chisel the remaining bars loose. I could have done that fifteen years ago, but I just didn't think about it. How stupid am I?" Eliza looked at Mary.

Mary shook her head, not saying anything.

"They came out one by one, the bars that held us. It was hard work. Some days I was too weak to work, but I did anyway. I remember the feel of the metal against metal as it rang through my body. A few times I missed my mark and smashed my fingers. I kept going, working through the pain. There was nothing to stop me. There was no one to stop me.

"When the last bar fell to the floor, I cried. Finally, freedom was within my reach. I wanted to leave right then; I wanted to go, but night was falling and I knew that if he came, we wouldn't get very far. I put the bars back up and hoped they would not fall. I put the bed back together every night in case he came. That night was no different. In the morning we would leave. I was hungry and I knew EJ was starved. It had been more than a few weeks since the earthquake. I made plans for our escape. I didn't know where we would go. Anyplace; I mean anyplace would be better than where we were.

"I woke EJ up that morning telling him, 'We have to go.' He had a hard time waking up. I thought he was dead. I thought I had waited too long. I pulled him up from the pallet of blankets he slept on; feeling his breath, in and out. I placed him on my lap. His body was almost lifeless, but I knew he had to live. We were leaving. This would be the first day of the rest of his life. He had to live.

"I gave him my breast for some food. I couldn't let him starve. I let him feed for only a few minutes. I still needed milk for my other child.

"It was time to leave. I lifted him up and placed him on the floor in the far corner by his sister. I turned around and looked at the place I called home for so long, so very long. One fragmented room. A broken down bed stood in the middle. My books; some still full of their pages, others just a shell standing empty we had used for paper and napkins. There was our makeshift sink and toilet and on the ground were our blankets to keep our feet warm. The room had smells we cared not to notice. It was a dark dingy place, a hole in no·where, a place where all hopes and dreams died and we were leaving. After all that time, I would finally be free!

"I pulled the bars from the window and broke the glass that was already cracked. I tossed a blanket on the glass so my son would not cut himself, knowing deep inside, any loss of blood for him could mean death. I lifted my tiny son through the window and then went back for the baby. I handed the baby to EJ who was bent down looking back into the hole. I pulled myself up though the opening to freedom. I had an urge to again look back at the room, but decided against it. I knew every nook and cranny. I knew every bug that ever managed to find a way in, hoping to follow it out. I resisted the security the room held; at least there I had shelter. I was afraid. We were out though and there was no looking back. We were finally out.

"I grabbed EJ's hand and spoke into his anxious palm. 'We will make it.' His face lit up as the sun came our way. He smiled. I grabbed his hand and drug him toward the trees. We needed cover to survive, an open field would not do. EJ wanted to stop and look around. It was the first time in his life he had been out of our hole. I know it was beautiful to him, hell, it was beautiful to me; but we needed to go, to get as far away from there as we could. We needed to run, without turning around and looking back. We managed a slow walk; the baby was heavy, EJ was hungry, whinny and tired. It was a struggle.

"Everything was so new to EJ. His hands were busy with questions and I tried to keep up with answers. The flowers and trees and the grass and the cows and chickens and ... he just went on and on asking questions. We ate berries and carrots and stayed to the trees as best we could.

"We hid from cars. EJ didn't know about cars or why we should be afraid, but I told him the man might drive a car and come after us. I have never told EJ who his father is. I would not do that to him. He thinks you just need only a mom to have a child. I have never told him about his brother either. This sweet child of mine should not carry the burden of his father. No one should ever carry the burden of his or her father.

"I saw the police station from the bushes across the street. We were there for a long time. We finally saw you alone and after no one came in for a while, we decided to go in. You were a woman; I cannot trust a man. I was afraid you would send me away, but I hoped you would help. We really don't need too much help; we just need to leave here. Please, we don't want to make a fuss. You really have to understand. Just get us away from here, away from this place. I told EJ, don't you see, I told him we would be okay." Eliza pleaded with Mary.

Eliza's eyes, her mouth and her heart begged Mary for safety. Mary had heard the story of hell. A life she knew, she herself could not endure. She had to leave now. Her own heart was breaking. Eliza looked away, but Mary spoke to her with a tender, tear filled voice. "I will help you Eliza. I will help you and your children." She hugged Eliza. Her body was small and didn't feel like the body of a woman, mid-way through life. It was time for Mary to leave. She grabbed a tissue, dried her eyes and blew her nose. She picked up her recorder and made her way to the door.

"Thank you, Eliza. I know it's been hard on you. I'm sorry. I'm sorry for all you and your children have been through. I'm sorry for making you tell your story." Mary opened the door, forced a smile on her face, and turned toward Eliza. "Lock the door, close your eyes and tomorrow you can begin living. There's nothing to hurt you now." Mary closed the door, leaving Eliza and the children safe for the night, in the little motel.

17

Mary sat in her car before finally driving away. It was really late or really early, depending on how you viewed things. She knew the sun would come up soon, and there were already farmers out working. As she sat there she realized she was wide-awake. She had many questions to ask Eliza in the morning. She was not sure how to start, but she wanted to start with questions about Chris.

Mary was worried by her brother's involvement. She knew Eliza had seen him; after all, she had described him. Chris' face was not something people just made up. Eliza had spoken of Chris more than once in her story. Chris had been dead for a while now and like Eliza said, "It had been a while since he had come back to feed them, longer than ever." Mary was haunted by visions of Chris doing these things, these terrible things.

"Damn you Chris." Mary grabbed the steering wheel, threw her SUV into gear and pulled away. "Damn you."

She headed home; there was nothing she could do tonight. *No way, it just couldn't be,* she thought. She did not make it far. She came to the turn off for her brother's house and found herself turning onto the long, curved, one lane road.

What the hell are you doing? Mary thought to herself as she pulled up to the gate. *I just have to be sure.*

She opened the gate and drove slowly down the drive to Chris' house. Her heart was pounding. She was anxious. She had not been to Chris' house since he passed away. His death suit had been picked out by her husband. Mary had wanted to go get the suit, but she had broken down while telling her mother again, about Chris' death.

As she drove to the house, she remembered when Chris bought the house from Doug. Doug was getting married and his grandfather had left him the big house. This cabin fit Chris and he loved it. She threw Chris a house warming party and it seemed the whole town dropped by. He was liked by everyone, but loved by none.

He had been such a popular kid and good looking to boot. That is, until the accident actually cut his face in two. He almost died as the saw blade cut deep into his skull; taking an eye, his nose, parts of his lips and his front teeth. It was a stupid accident which never should have happened. He dropped something on the ground; even years later, Chris could not remember what he dropped that cost him his face. He bent to retrieve the item from under the table. When he reached to pull himself up, he pulled the saw down. While trying to keep it from hitting his face; he grabbed the trigger, turning the saw on. He locked the trigger in the "on" position. The force and weight of the saw was too much for Chris; he slipped down sending the saw into his face. The saw did the job it was made to do.

Mary rounded the corner just as it happened. Blood, skin and hair shot across the work room. Mary screamed as she pulled the plug from the socket. She was glad to have saved his life. He was, after all, her brother.

Now, she wondered if she had done the right thing. *Was he a kidnapper and rapist? Was he responsible for the torture of women and his own children? Could he be a murderer? Maybe he got what he deserved. Maybe he became this monster because of what happened to him. Maybe I made a mistake saving my brother. Maybe, just maybe I'm wrong; maybe he was the best person in the world and this woman is just crazy*, Mary thought.

Mary found the spare key under the ceramic frog and entered his house. He was a clean person and nothing seemed out of place. She walked through the living room, touching the back of the sofa as she passed. The same sofa Eliza described. It was new fifteen years ago. Now, still positioned in the same place, it was faded and worn.

Mary looked at the doors before her; a bedroom, a bathroom and a basement. She opened the bathroom door, turned the light on and looked toward the tub. She could see Eliza; full figured, bathing in the claw foot tub. She quickly extinguished the light.

She was afraid to walk down into the basement. She lingered at the entrance before turning the knob and opening the door. She took a deep breath and found once she hit the first step, she was at the bottom before the light could completely illuminate the space. Nothing was there except a pool table, a rack of pool sticks and a goofy picture of some dogs smoking cigars. She banged on the walls. There were no secret doors or windows. She breathed a sigh of relief and headed back up the stairs.

She opened the door to the bedroom and quickly closed the closet door which stood opened before her. Her mind went to Eliza crouching on the floor. She shook her head, trying to banish the image floating in her mind.

Mary looked around the room. Chris' life looked back. She began fingering and touching his papers, pictures, and things. She needed a good memory of her brother. Tonight had been full of horrible thoughts of Chris. Touching his things brought back a flood of warm and happy memories for her. There were always good times before the accident. After the accident there were still good times, but they were surrounded by bouts of depression.

She found pictures of his first and last girlfriend, Missy. They were still framed and lying in the bottom drawer of his dresser. Missy swore to stay by him after the accident, but that lasted only a few weeks. Mary remembered his pain and his refusal to talk about her. She remembered the handful of pain medication; she had knocked it from his hand as his tears stained her shirt. She picked up the pictures and threw them to the floor. She watched as the glass shattered. "Why couldn't you love him? Why?"

She moved to his desk and started rummaging. She found an old card stuffed in the very bottom of one of the drawers. The card had a faded ribbon on the front and an assortment of flowers. Mary read the card out loud:

As you begin a new journey in your life...

Mary held the card close to her heart and said, "This is good for you Chris, for now, you are on a new journey." She blew a kiss up in the sky and put the card in her pocket.

She left his room and looked to a picture on the bookcase by his television. It was a picture of Chris and Mary, laughing and playing. A halo appeared above Chris' head. Tears filled her eyes, but did not spill to her cheeks. "Chris, this can't be you. I'm wrong; you couldn't have done this." Even as the words left her lips, she did not believe what she said.

Mary grabbed a flashlight off the kitchen counter and headed to the barn. She pulled at the door only to discover a single lock keeping the doors closed. She looked around and found a shovel leaning against the barn wall. She broke open the door and stepped inside. There was nothing there; but dirt on the floor, spider webs hanging from the ceiling and Chris' truck. She closed the door keeping her flashlight focused in the air at a swarm of bats eating insects in the darkened sky.

She had to walk the property. She felt a push to go on walking, looking, and hoping to find nothing. The light shone across the ground, swinging from side to side as Mary walked. She walked around, looking for something that seemed out of place. "There is nothing here. I'm sorry Chris. I'm sorry for thinking it was you, I just had to be sure."

She got back into her vehicle, started the engine, and drove back out through the gate. Shutting and locking the gate would have to wait for another time. She turned once again and whispered to Chris, "I'm sorry; I just had to be sure."

She needed to go home. She had been gone from her own house for too long. She needed to be home with Bryan and Charley. She needed to hug them and kiss them and just be thankful for them.

18

Mary arrived home to find both Bryan and Charley sound asleep. She kissed Charley lightly on his forehead, although her first thought at seeing him was to grab him up and pour kisses all over him.

Sweet Bryan Mary thought as she changed out of her uniform and put on a pair of shorts and a tee shirt. Mary kissed his forehead trying not to wake him from his slumber. She went into the kitchen and put on a pot of coffee. She then wrote a note for Bryan, just in case he woke up and sleep had found her. She sat down at the table with a pen and paper, and began writing questions. She wanted to listen to the story again, but that would take a long time and her mind spilled over with questions.

The sun began creeping through the back window of the kitchen when Bryan walked in. Mary had been so engrossed in her writing and rereading her questions, she failed to hear him. When Bryan touched her head, she jumped.

"I'm sorry Mary; I didn't mean to frighten you. Good morning." Bryan bent down to kiss her cheek. "Or is it good night?"

"Well, I guess its morning since the sun is coming up." Mary pointed toward the window.

"Why then, I guess it's good morning, but for some reason I would say you have yet to see the bed. Would I be correct in that assumption?" Bryan was pouring himself a cup of coffee.

"Well Bryan, that's not exactly true. I did "see" the bed. I changed clothes didn't I?" Mary felt irritated.

"Would you like a refill; or are you finished and ready to jump into bed?" He held the pot out to her.

"Oh Bryan, I can't sleep. I have to get back to work soon and I have so many questions for this lady." She pointed to her pad.

"You know everyone needs a little sleep. And I can see from the look on your face that you are no exception." Bryan did not move to the table, but stood by the pot of coffee on the counter.

"Bring the coffee and come and sit down. Caffeine is the only edge I'm going to get today." She held her cup out and Bryan came to her.

"You know, I make a pretty good living right now. You can quit and let someone else handle this." His tone was soft and quiet.

"Please don't tell me I'm married to Saul. God, I would just die. Please, bring my husband back. Do you think I can't handle this too?" Mary's lack of sleep was catching up with her and she was on the edge of saying mean things; things you can never take back.

"Hey you, I never said you couldn't handle anything. Please Mary, I love you and it would break my heart if you married Saul. For one thing, you are married to me. And another, I know you don't like the guy. I would have to watch you suffer through a marriage that would make you crazy; and baby, I love you too much for that." He reached out and grabbed Mary's hand.

"I'm sorry Bryan. There's just so much that happened to that poor woman and those kids; and then the thing with Saul, and yes; since I've been sitting here, I might have grown a bit tired and please forgive me. I love you too." She was out of breath as she put her hand on top of his.

"I'll tell you what, you get a nap and I'll wake you before I leave to go to work. That will give you a little sleep. You need the sleep. When you wake up, you can take a shower and go save the world.

Anyway, you look so much better without those bags under your eyes." Bryan touched her face. Mary jerked back, and then stopped, letting her face again find his hand.

"Fine, you win, but you better wake me. Bryan, I mean drag me out of the bed and if I shoo you away, really drag me out, straight to the floor, deal?" She held her hand out to him so they could shake on it.

"How about we kiss on it and that will be your sleepy kiss too?" Bryan and Mary had always said that. It had never been a goodnight kiss, but always sleepy kisses because Mary worked different shifts.

"Oh you big lug, lay it on me." She leaned forward in her chair and waited for Bryan to meet her halfway. He pushed his chair out, walked around, took her by the shoulders and walked her to the bedroom.

As he laid her down in bed, he puckered up his lips, kissed her on the forehead and walked out of the room closing the door behind him.

"I love you too!" Mary yelled after him.

"Oh, you will never know how much I truly love you Mary." Mary heard Bryan say as he walked away.

Mary fell asleep within minutes of Bryan putting her to bed. Her sleep was poor as thoughts of her brother intermingled with the images of the family she had encountered that day.

Bryan kept his promise and woke her with a kiss and a cup of coffee a short time later. "Good morning, beautiful," he spoke in her ear.

"Oh yea, who said it was a beautiful morning?" Mary had never been what people would call a morning person. Her brain worked best at night. In fact, it was when she peaked. She could solve problems better then. Bryan however, was the complete opposite. He loved the morning and took in the beauty of the new day, as if meeting a new person. He loved the sunrise, she loved the sunset. She loved the closure of the day with feelings of being loved and happy. He loved the start of the day being surrounded by his loved ones.

"Hey lazy head, are you getting up or are you going to roll over and go back to sleep? Did you forget about your meeting?" Bryan nudged her gently.

"Oh shit, I guess I'm getting up. Where's the coffee? I do smell coffee, don't I?" Her eyes opened only enough to follow her nose to the cup sitting on the side table. "Please don't make me focus too hard honey, what time is it?" She propped herself up on her elbow and slowly sipped the hot, black coffee, her eyes opening with each swallow.

"Seven-thirty now, get a moving." Bryan patted the bed and left the room.

Mary got up, jumped into the shower, put on a clean uniform and then went into the kitchen. Charley was sitting in his chair eating breakfast and the sitter was doing the dishes in the sink.

Bryan asked, "Whose card?"

Mary looked at the card in his hands. "Oh, I got it from Chris' house last night."

"Was he going someplace?"

"No, that's from when he was in the hospital; see." She opened the card and dropped it on the ground as she screamed. It was addressed to Eliza.

Dear Eliza,

As you begin your new life in Houston, don't forget about us and your old life in New York. Find a good man and have lots of kids or at least lots of sex!

Love,

Amy

P.S. Don't forget to call.

"Mary, what is it?" Bryan rushed to his wife's side. Charley was screaming and Mary had fallen to the ground where the card lay open.

"Oh my God it was Chris! Look at the card! He took a trophy. I can't go back there and face that woman knowing that my own flesh and blood did this. No one must ever find out. Why did he do this? Why would he do all of those things to her? And the children, what about the children? He has always been so good to Charley. I let that monster, my own brother, around my son. What are we going to do? What will people say? How will they treat Charley? We have to protect him. Please help me. Chris is dead now. He can't hurt her anymore. Bryan, please help me." She looked like a child, her legs strewed out on the ground, her face tear-stained.

"Take Charley into his room," Bryan told the sitter. She scooped him up and went into the room without a word.

"No Mary, you are wrong. He wouldn't do this. He could not do that to her. It's not in his blood. Do you hear me? He was not an angry man. There's a mistake. Somehow, there has been a terrible mistake."

He held her as she cried, moaning repeatedly, "Why Chris?"

"You are going back to bed. I'll call Robert and let him know you aren't going to meet him." Bryan helped her to her feet.

"No. I have to be there. I have to know. I need to know why. Why would Chris do this Bryan?"

"Mary, if it was him, you may never know why." Bryan took the card from her hands.

"But if it was him, then those kids are a part of my family. Did you see what he did to his family? Why would he treat his family like that?" Her eyes were staring at his; waiting for answers, she knew, he didn't have.

"Mary, you know nothing, nothing at all. You need to find out the truth before you condemn your brother. I think I would've known if he was keeping someone. I was at his place at least three times a week. And when you were there, did YOU ever see anything? Were there any signs that she was at his house? Did you look in the basement? Did he own any other property, anyplace else? I know the answer is no. Now you need to get your shit together, and either find out the truth or let Doug do it. I personally think you owe it to Chris to make sure his name is NOT in the middle of this." Bryan held Mary's arms as he spoke.

"I have to go." She pulled away from Bryan walking toward the door. "I have an abused family; which might be my family, waiting for me."

"Mary," Bryan called after her.

Mary walked on, not turning back. She jumped in the SUV, slamming the door as she sped away. Her mind was not on Bryan or Charley. Chris and the woman filled her thoughts. *No wonder he only came at night. No wonder he wore that mask.* Mary knew who it was. Her brother had done this. He had not had a girlfriend since his accident. *All men have urges; all men need relief, don't they?* The thought of her brother doing those things to Eliza made her stomach turn. She managed to pull the SUV to the side of the road and open her door just as her morning coffee was coming up. She wiped her mouth and grabbed a tissue from her visor. She pulled the mirror down to look at her face. Her eyes were blood red and her mascara had run onto her crimson cheeks. She did not know how she was going to make it through the day.

Mary saw Robert as she pulled up a short time later. She always beat him to work, but today was different. She knew he was preparing to say something smart to her, but as she got out he could only ask, "God Mary, are you alright?"

"Robert, I don't want to talk now. I'm having a tough time of this. Please, just go get some food and we'll talk later."

"What kind of food?" Robert asked.

"Shit Robert, just ask what they want." Mary started feeling woozy again, but didn't want to throw up in front of Robert. "Can we just go in please? It's going to be a hot day and my stomach is doing flip-flops."

"I don't think you are in any shape to go in," Robert said as he grabbed her by the arm.

"Leave me alone Robert." She replied as she twisted away from his grip. "Why can't you just leave me the hell alone?"

"Hey, you need to calm down Mary. I don't know what your problem is, but you can't go in there like this. I mean it Mary." It was the first time in his life that Robert had talked to Mary in that tone.

Mary stopped walking. "I'm sorry, I didn't get much sleep and I'm tired and sick. Just go get some eggs and toast and I'll see you in a few moments." Mary touched Robert on the arm. She wanted to push him away. She wanted to go into the room and hide Eliza and her secret. She just wanted it all to go away. She forced a small smile on her face. "I'm fine." Mary did not want any questions. She did not know how to answer them. "Really Robert, I am fine."

Robert looked at her. "No Mary, I don't think you are fine, but I'll give you some space and time and when you are ready, you know where to find me."

19

The morning arrived too soon for Eliza. Her sleep had been sporadic. She kept waking to check on the children. She was reluctant to get out of the soft, clean bed. She still needed sleep, she was tired. She rolled over and looked to her still sleeping children. She felt for the first time in their small, little lives, they would be okay. She pulled the covers off her body and sat on the edge of the bed, waiting for her dizzy head to stop spinning.

When Eliza opened the door to Mary a short time later, she could not help noticing how Mary looked. She recognized a fake smile plastered on Mary's face, the red puffy eyes and the slight smell of vomit. She saw her looking at the children. She did not want to move them, to wake them from their peaceful slumber, but she did because Mary asked her to do so.

Mary looked at the children with new eyes. She looked for any sign of her brother in the children; any sign of her family, but she found no resemblance. That really did not matter now; the children barely looked like children.

The women stripped EJ and put him in the tub. Mary wiped a tear as she looked over the little boy's body. She knew Chris could not have done this. She was sure he did not do this. He had loved

Charley and spent so much time with him. She left the room. She was falling apart.

Mary could hear EJ playing in the tub. Joyful sounds of a deaf child made her weep even harder.

Robert returned with the food. Mary divided the eggs, toast and bacon onto two plates. EJ ate everything on his foam plate and drank all of his milk. He found a ball and rolled it to the door just hard enough for the ball to roll back. The baby finished her bottle and was bright eyed and ready to enjoy her new life. Both children looked happy. Robert noticed, Mary noticed and Eliza beamed.

Robert phoned the sheriff. Mary did not want to talk to him. She would not tell him about her brother or the card. She could not tell him.

Robert escorted the children to the doctor's office. It took fifteen minutes to get EJ from his mother's side, but a promise of food and more toys, finally won the child away.

"You'll bring them back to me, right?" Eliza asked.

Mary assured her the children would be fine, grabbing her hands and staring her deep in the eyes. Finally Eliza agreed.

"Is there anything you forgot to tell me last night? Are you sure you never saw his face while you were locked in the room?" Mary needed to know if it was her brother. She needed confirmation from the only person that would know. Her heart was breaking as she waited for the answer.

"I just remember the good looking man and the man with the scar. I don't know if it was either one of them or someone completely different. I think it was the man with the scar; why else would he wear that mask. Why else would he hide his face? I really don't want to talk about this again." Eliza sat on the edge of the bed, looking toward the television. "I'm ready to go, to get out of this nightmare. I really could care less if you ever get this guy. I need to protect the two children I have left. I told you all you need to know and now I'm done, finished, I'm ready to leave right now. I should not have let you take the children." Eliza got off the bed and began pacing.

When the knock on the door came Mary found herself very nervous. She reluctantly answered and found the sheriff standing before her. After the long drive and being up all night, Doug looked perfect. His face bore little signs of age, although he was at least forty. His jaw was strong and his lips were the perfect curtain for his show business teeth. His hair, a light brown, swept to one side. He stayed tan all year and his body was the perfect amount of muscle and fat. He stood six feet two inches, and his body weight was no more than two hundred pounds.

"Doug?" Mary asked, as though she was not expecting him. She stood in the doorway blocking his entrance.

"Mary," Doug responded his hands paused on his sunglasses. "Are you going to let me in or do you want me to conduct my interview outside?"

Mary paused. With the moment of truth before her, her mind grappled for the words. Mary knew she had to tell him the sordid details of what Chris had done. She started, "Doug, I need to talk to you for a moment. I think we need to be alone, outside."

Doug brushed past Mary. As he walked into the room, he pulled the sunglasses from his face revealing sky light blue eyes, fixated on the woman before him.

"Doug, I really need to talk to you," Mary's voice was begging.

"No. Not just yet. I want to be alone with her for a few minutes. I need to see firsthand what is going on. I heard she doesn't like men, but she's just going to have to get over that. From this moment forward, I'm taking over this investigation. I heard about your conversation with Saul; there'll be none of that with me." He paused for a moment as if waiting for Mary to say something smart to him. She knew he was ready, willing, and able to fire her.

"But Doug, I need to talk to you. It's about something I found out," Mary whispered.

"Tell me later. I told you, I need to talk to her alone. Now go outside and wait for me." He looked her straight in the eye, "I mean it Mary, Now!"

Mary walked over to Eliza. "Everything will be fine. The sheriff wants to talk to you alone," Mary said. She wanted to protect the good that was Chris, but she knew the truth would come out. She wanted to tell Doug, she did not want it to come from an outsider. Although Chris had raped and tortured Eliza, she needed to be the one to tell Doug. There was no need to protect Chris now, he was dead. He had been a monster, but he was dead. Maybe though, Doug could help this family that Chris had abused. Perhaps he could keep the information out of the papers to protect her family, her whole family.

Mary quickly left the room. She ran to the side of her vehicle and threw up, again.

20

Eliza stared at the man Mary had left her with. He had been one of the last people she remembered seeing. His good looks were still there, only he was a little older. Eliza wanted to say something to him, but did not know what. She had hid in a closet, while he could have saved her from years of pain. He was the man she made love to in her dream; the night EJ was conceived. She rose from the edge of the bed with her mouth open, ready to say something, but nothing came out. Eliza again opened her mouth. She was ready to speak; she was ready to say what a fool she had been. He had been the other man in the room that night. Help had been right there, so close and she had let it slip through her fingers.

Eliza finally found the words and began to speak, "I know you, you are the man ..." She did not finish her sentence. She watched the sheriff lock the door. She noticed his size, his shape, his voice. For a moment, just a moment, she was confused, but as the realization registered in her brain, he began moving toward her; his face twisted and she knew. She turned around; looking for a place to go, a place to hide. Eliza knew she had just been delivered into the hands of evil. The devil himself had come up from the bowels of the earth and was now in the room with her. His voice was full of hate as he advanced toward her.

"What did you tell these people? How did you get those bars off that window? Why the HELL did you do this to ME?" His hands were now around her neck and his mouth was close to her ear. "You tell me now what you said, so I can fix this mess you have made. I have taken care of you all these years and this is what you do? I told you never go to the cops, don't you remember?" The veins running through his face and neck were protruding; his brow wrinkled. "I told you as soon as you went to the police I would know; why didn't you believe me you stupid whore?" Doug's eyes were now glowing light purple as a fiery red mixed with the blue. Eliza swore she was staring into the eyes of the devil himself. "What did you tell Mary? Tell me what you said and I want to know now!" He shoved her on the bed, pushed her dress up, and then ripped her baggy panties from between her legs.

Eliza tried to fight him; she tried to yell for help. She kicked and squirmed. It was no use. He had his pants down and was inside of her in seconds. Burning pain shot through her as he ripped her body and mind in two. His weight on her was heavy, crushing her tiny frame. Her windpipe allowed no air in or out; as his hand was wrapped tightly around her neck. Soon, she passed out on the bed, with the devil himself positioned above her, raping her.

Eliza awoke to Doug yelling, "A hole is nothing but a hole if you die." He released her throat letting her lungs fill with air.

Eliza screamed a blood curdling scream with such force the windows in the small motel room shook. The sound crept under the door and out into the parking lot. She screamed a second time and felt the air rip into her throat leaving a raw butchered meat sensation. *Mary will come,* Eliza thought, *Mary has to come.*

The handle on the door began to shake. There was knocking, not loud yet not soft; then the banging started and the words came. Eliza relaxed her body ever so slightly. "Open this door!" Mary yelled. "Open this damn door right now!" The door shook with each bang. "Is everything okay in there? Doug, Eliza can you hear me?" *She's here,* Eliza thought. *Thank God she's here.*

Doug covered Eliza's mouth while responding, "We … are … fine." Eliza felt him let go of his hate juice and wondered if Mary's banging on the door excited him. "You just get better with time, don't you whore?" Doug whispered, sounding exhausted from his morning romp. "You are going to give me a heart attack one day." He stayed on top not moving; lingering inside of her.

Eliza could feel his heart pounding to the beat of her own heart. She tried to slow her heart rate. She wanted nothing to match his. She heard Mary still pounding on the door. She wished she would knock the door down and see what he was doing to her. She wanted Mary to believe her, to know that she was not making anything up.

"God, I wish she would stop that." Doug now sounded frustrated. "Mary, stop pounding on that damn door!"

"Why couldn't it be today? Why can't you just die right here, right now so the world knows what a monster you really are?" Eliza whispered.

Doug laughed and then got off Eliza. "Now, tell me, did you tell them it was me?"

Eliza stayed on the bed; not moving, not talking. She was happy he finally pulled out of her, but she could feel his wetness haunting her insides.

"Answer me." Doug grabbed her hair and yanked her head back.

Eliza could feel the tearing of her scalp, the strain of her neck as he pulled harder and harder. "No, I didn't know. I didn't know it was you."

He slapped her in the throat. She could feel her windpipe close. "Now, get your ass up and put your clothes on." He threw a dress that was laid out on the back of a chair in Eliza's face. "Leave that other dress in the bathroom; I'll take care of it."

Eliza refused to move. She had bitten her lower lip and blood was now on her mouth, dripping to her chin. She struggled to breathe.

"I said, get up and get into that bathroom now!" Doug's teeth were clenched as he spoke to her. His hand was raised, ready to strike her again.

"Please, don't," Eliza managed to whisper.

"Which child have you decided to kill today?" Doug asked. "It seems to me I now have another to choose from. In fact, how have you managed to stay alive? It's been months since I've put any food in that hole. I thought you and that misfit would be long dead. But a daughter, now that is a total surprise."

"What? What do you mean, which child?" Eliza struggled with the words.

"A daughter, I always wanted a daughter." Doug smiled and winked at her.

Tears gathered in Eliza's eyes, but none spilled over. "You're a sick bastard." Eliza was up and into the bathroom in no time. She was crying and shaking and scared. Scared for her children and scared for her own self.

She heard Doug open the door and say something to Mary, and then the door closed. She hoped he had gone. She prayed he had left, but then she heard Mary's voice. She opened the bathroom door slightly. She could hear the deep voice of the devil speaking to Mary, and then she heard Mary almost yell, "She said what? That can't be."

Eliza strained to hear what was being said, but the rest of the words were spoken so low, she could not make them out.

With her face still red from the tears and her dress wrinkled, she walked back into the room and sat on the bed. She wondered what was going to happen now. Doug was there, sitting on the chair by the door, and Mary was sitting next to him.

"Go on now woman; tell her what you told me, that all of this is just a mistake. How you and your old man got into a fight, and you just didn't have any money to buy food for your children." He turned to Mary and said, "It's just amazing what these people will do. I told her if she filed a false police report, we would take her to jail; and then she came clean."

He turned back to Eliza. "You thought your children were going to die, so you went to the police department and made up this whole story. Where is that husband of yours? Why would he leave you and those kids to starve to death? Perhaps we need to find him and teach him how to care for his family?" Doug smiled at Eliza and she felt her skin crawl.

21

Mary could not believe the words coming out of Doug's mouth. "Eliza, is this true? Did you make this whole thing up?" Mary was waiting for her to say, "No," that she was just scared of Doug because he was a man. Mary waited and waited, she needed to know the truth. *Was it my brother?* "There was no way Eliza made this story up. I have seen her body. The pictures Doug, have you seen the pictures I took?" Mary thought to herself. *Had Eliza told Doug about the man with the scar and Doug was trying to protect my brother? No, Doug would not do that.* Mary finally got up, walked to Eliza and pulled her face up to look at her.

"Eliza, I need the truth. You have to tell me. No matter what, you have to tell me the truth."

"Eliza? Miss Johnson? Are you listening to me?"

"What about the other boy?" Eliza asked. He was on her mind. She had to know what had happened to him. She needed to know he was safe.

"What?" Doug asked.

"She said she had another boy from the man and he took the child away." Mary replied.

"Oh, you know what I think? I think this man, husband, boyfriend, lover or whatever; if indeed took a child from you, that child is doing fine right now." Doug looked at Mary then added, "What do you think Mary?"

"Please Eliza, tell me." Mary was still holding Eliza's face.

"I made the story up." She jerked her face from Mary's hand and lay on the bed, curling up like a child in the womb of a mother.

"Eliza, what are you saying? You told me all of that stuff last night. You made it all up? I don't believe what you are saying. It's okay to tell the truth." Mary could feel her anger rise inside of her. "You need to tell the truth. Stop lying about what happened." Mary grabbed Eliza off the bed and looked her in the eyes. "Tell him what you told me last night. Tell him about the man. Tell him Eliza, you need to tell the truth. You need to tell him about my brother. You need to tell him about Chris." Mary was now crying as she released Eliza.

"It's all out now. Doug, I know it was Chris. I found a card; I found her card at his place last night. She described him, his face. I don't know why he would do something like this. I didn't believe it was him, but I've come to accept the fact there are things I didn't know about my brother. When his accident happened, I guess it changed him. It turned him into some kind of monster." Mary turned away, her head hung as she walked across the room toward the door. She needed to get out of there. She needed some air. She needed to go home. She wanted to crawl under a rock and hide. She needed to get away; away from this woman that had turned her life upside down.

22

Doug was shocked. He was at a complete loss for words. *What had this poor pathetic excuse for a woman said to Mary last night* he wondered? Damn, Doug thought, *I tipped my hand. She thought it was disfigured Chris and I walked in here and screwed up.* Doug began to chuckle quietly, and then it turned into a roar of gut splitting laughter. He looked toward Eliza and winked.

"Stop Doug, it's not funny! What's wrong with you? Stop laughing. I have the card outside, it's addressed to Eliza." Mary said, un-wiped tears trickling down her face.

"It was not Chris. I can tell you for a fact, it was not Chris that did this to her." Doug laughed once more, and then turned toward Eliza, "Tell her you made it all up and tell her now."

Mary touched Eliza on the arm. "No, it was Chris. These children are my family. I don't know how Chris could do this to her and the children. I'm so sorry Eliza. I'm so sorry for what he did to you. He's dead now. He has paid for his sins upon you."

Doug took in the scene before him. He wanted to feel bad, but he could not. He thought back through all the years he kept Eliza. The fights, the rapes, and the lies he had told. He never really thought about getting caught. Through the years he had wanted to rid himself of her, but he did feel something for her. Was it love? He shook his head. No, love did not look like the shadow of the person in the room with him. Doug knew at that moment Eliza would die very soon. Not tonight, he needed to make arrangements, but soon, very soon. "Let's wrap this thing up. I've got things to do today."

23

Tears ran down Eliza's face. She did not look at Mary or Doug, but she looked at the picture hanging above the bed. It was a cheap picture of a flower garden covered in sunshine and a little girl picking flowers with a bonnet on her head. There was a boy running in the background, flying a kite and laughing. Then out of the corner of her eye, she saw yet another boy, sitting on the limb of the tree that covered the garden.

Eliza found herself being drawn into the painting. She let her mind run with the boy flying the kite, stopping to pick flowers with the little girl. She was laughing and playing with the children on the ground. The little boy's kite got stuck in the tree and as she climbed the branches, she saw the boy sitting watching her and the other two children playing.

"What's your name?" She asked the boy.

"I can't tell you," he replied. "Who are you?" He asked.

"Why, I'm your mother and I have come to play with you and I love you. Please come out of the tree and play with your brother and sister." They climbed out of the tree and the children gathered in a circle. They all held hands, laughing, as they collapsed in the field of flowers.

Eliza left the painting and found herself again in the room with Mary and the devil.

Eliza looked at Mary. This poor woman, Eliza felt sorry for her. She could not let her suffer. "Mary, it was not your brother. I lost that card when I had a flat. It fell out of my car. I told you a man with a scar stopped to help. I guess he kept that card all these years. The person that kept me is still alive, still full of hate. He will kill me now. I know you did your best Mary. We shouldn't have stopped at the police station. I'm sorry I brought you into this. I'm sorry, please remember your brother with a light heart. He tried to help me once and I turned him away. I was afraid of his looks, never judge a book …"

Doug cut Eliza off. "I'll take you home. You need food for these children and a secure place to live. Tell Mary you made the story up. Tell her what you told me. Tell her you needed help and didn't know how to get it."

Mary looked at Eliza. "Is that true? Is it?"

Eliza looked to the floor, her head bent, staring at her feet. "It's true. I lied about the whole thing." She lifted her head and looked at Mary. "I'm sorry." She dropped her head down again.

24

Mary was now looking at Eliza with different eyes. "What's wrong with you? Why didn't you just say you needed food? Why make up this story? Why hurt my brother like this? What kind of sick person are you? Your little boy, where did all the scars come from? I don't believe you."

"I'm sorry; the man that ran off did this to us. He was never really a man." Eliza looked toward Doug.

Mary's anger grew. "I just don't understand you. Why would you allow him to do these things? You cannot protect this man, what is his name?"

"I don't have his name. I just ..."

Mary cut her off. "It's your responsibility to care for the children you bring into the world. You can't let just anyone around your kids. We can't let you take these children back." Mary looked at Eliza. "Look at me when I talk to you." Mary grabbed her handcuffs out of the holder, "In fact, you're under arrest until you tell the truth."

Mary could not believe how fast her mood had changed. She wanted to believe what Eliza told her. As much as she didn't want the monster to be her brother, it had to be her brother. Mary would frighten Eliza into telling the truth. She would take her children from her.

"Where are the kids?" Doug asked, breaking in. He watched as Mary grabbed Eliza's arms and placed the handcuffs on her.

"At Dr. Denton's getting a full checkup," Mary answered.

Mary knew that Eliza loved her children but said, "Should we take the kids? I just hate the thought of leaving them with her. What kind of mother would let some man do this to her children?" Mary felt guilty as the words left her mouth, but she could not stop them. She was angry and there were just too many emotions and too many questions left unanswered.

"Mary stop this, you are out of line. I told you what she said; now back off." Doug looked at Eliza, smiling a hateful smile.

Eliza was now crying and saying, "I'm sorry, I shouldn't have come. I love my children however, if you think they would be better off without me then you take them. I love them with all my heart, but if I can't protect them, then maybe you can Mary." Eliza looked at Mary with such pity in her eyes, Mary wanted to cry.

"Oh now, don't get all upset. Mary, take those cuffs off of her. I'm taking her home." Doug raised his hand as Mary started to protest. He rose from the chair and said, "Mary, call and see how long until the kids are finished at the doctor's office. And then, go get her some food to last for a few weeks; you know stuff that will keep. Use the emergency fund at the station. I'll wait here for the kids, and then I will take her and the children where they need to go."

"Eliza now is the time to tell the truth. If it was my brother I can help you." Mary was trying to look Eliza in the face.

Mary saw Doug walking toward her out of the corner of her eye. She spoke almost shouting, "I'm not going to let her go. She needs to tell the truth."

Doug grabbed Mary by the arm. "She is telling the truth. Now you either take the cuffs off or else. She said she doesn't know the guy that did this and quite frankly, I believe her. I'm the sheriff in this town, not you."

Mary stood stunned. She had nothing to say. There was nothing to say. She took the cuffs off of Eliza and sat down on the chair by the door.

Doug spoke softly to Mary. "Mary, go get the food."

Mary got up to leave.

"Mary, please wait," Eliza whispered.

"What? What is it that you want? I've tried to help you; I listened to your story believing the words you said. I cried for you. I wanted to help you protect your family. Unless you speak up I cannot help you. Say something, anything, just say something!" Mary waited.

"I can't help you Eliza, if you don't talk to me." Mary pleaded.

"The food." Doug said.

"Just go Mary. I'll go with the, him." Eliza put her head down.

"Don't worry Doug; I'll go get her food and then I'm taking the rest of the day off. Tomorrow you can decide what you want to do with me." Mary left the small motel room. Her emotional rollercoaster was over, at least for a while.

25

Doug spoke, "Now see what you've done? I told you I would feed you and keep you alive. You are going back in your hole and if you ever think about getting out again, I WILL kill those kids you love so much. You, I will cut into pieces so little, no one will ever find all of you."

Eliza glanced over to Doug his eyes glared back as if daring her to say anything. She said nothing. Eliza kept her head down. Her fate now sealed. Doug might kill her children, he might kill Mary, and he might kill her. She would welcome her own death.

Eliza's mind disappeared from the room as her body dropped to the bed. That was the best she could do. Neither said another word, but as time passed Doug decided it was time for round two. He rolled Eliza over on the bed, dropped his pants and forced her to take him in her mouth. He finished on her face and stared down at her as she stared off into space. "You know you used to be a pretty good-looking woman. What the hell happened to you?"

Eliza spoke very low and Doug asked, "What, what did you say?"

Eliza gathered all the strength she could and rearing up yelling, "YOU! YOU HAPPENED TO ME!" She collapsed back on the bed and not another word was spoken between the two until Doug heard a car pulling up outside. "Go get yourself cleaned up. And smile for God sake; it could be worse, I could kill you right here."

"I wish you would." Eliza said not moving from the bed. "Just kill me now."

Doug walked to her, yanked her up by the arm and shoved her into the bathroom. Eliza screamed the whole way there. "Leave me alone you bastard! Just leave me alone!"

26

Mary knocked on the door as Doug shoved Eliza to the bathroom floor. He calmly walked to the door and opened it. "She's in the restroom getting cleaned up."

Mary handed Doug two bags which he sat down on the floor next to the door. "What do you want me to do with that?" He asked.

"It's food, toys, clothes and personal items for Eliza and her children. She needs this stuff. God, I hope you know what you are doing letting her go," Mary said.

Doug responded, "Why make her suffer any more than she has to. We can't save everyone. How much longer before the children arrive? I need to get home to my own family. Little Doug has a game tonight." Doug was now looking out of the window.

"Tomorrow we will sit down with Saul and talk about what happened at the station. You know sometimes a man has a better sense about these things." Doug looked at Mary as he spoke. "Yea, some men just have an instinct about certain things."

"Mary, I need the pictures and the tape of your conversation. And while you're at it, I need all the notes and anything else you have."

"Why?"

"Mary, you are not a part of this investigation any longer. All you need to know is that I need them and I want them on my desk before you leave to go home; unless, you have them here, with you?"

"I don't know Doug. I just don't know."

"Well, why don't you walk out to your vehicle and find out."

Mary walked out of the room. She gathered the pictures, her notes and the recordings. As she flipped through the pictures they spilled to the floor. She saw Doug open the door. She quickly gathered what she could. Two pictures stayed behind.

27

Eliza sat on the bathroom floor wiping her face with a washcloth from EJ's bath. She could hear Doug call and ask about her children. She needed to speak to Mary alone, but she knew Doug would have none of that. She had her chance to talk to Mary last night, to tell her how important it was for her to leave this town. *It's too late now* Eliza thought.

Eliza heard Mary come back in. She listened at the bathroom door as Mary spoke. She knew the children would be better off anywhere but with her. She knew that at least they would get food. She loved her kids, but they needed a home and a real family. They needed a mother that could protect them and a father that would love them. She knew neither Doug nor herself could do that for the children. She could not protect them and he could not love them.

"You know I think this has been good for her. I think she has learned a lesson. I think she will be fine." He looked toward Mary and added, "Let it go Mary. She will be fine. I'm sure; no I guarantee, you will never hear from her again; not ever again." His eyes fell to Eliza as she exited the bathroom.

"No, you won't ever hear from me again. Not as long as I live. Not as long as I die." She mumbled the last of her words, but no one was listening.

"Mary, help get my car loaded. I want to leave as soon as the children arrive. You better put all this stuff in the trunk; I need all the back seat for the kids. I will take you anyplace you need to go, Eliza."

"Will you take me home? I just want to get home."

"Oh yes," Doug said "You'll be going home. Don't you worry; I'll personally make sure you get back where you need to be."

Eliza stared at him knowing what he meant. Doug smiled and Eliza felt hatred fill her. If she had had the strength, she would have rushed across the room, pulled the gun from his waist and shot him dead. She would then kick his body over and over again. Eliza looked at the little badge on his chest and the words "protect and serve" made her cry again. *He was protecting and serving himself.* She wondered, *how in hell he managed to put the badge on every day and not fall down laughing at the ass he was making of everyone.*

Outside the room a horn blew. Robert had returned with the children. Eliza was thinking about making a run for it. *At least the children would be safe,* she thought. *Doug would hunt me down and kill me, but the children would be fine.*

Mary and Eliza started for the door. Doug smiled at Eliza and said, "Mary put the children in my car. Eliza and I will be out in a moment. Eliza stopped in her tracks and looked at him.

Mary said, "No, I'll take them home. You look so tired Doug."

Doug replied, "Now look, you have things to do and I'm off today. Mary, put the children in my car and send Robert back to the office. We'll be out shortly."

As Mary walked out of the room, Doug followed her and Eliza stood in the doorway listening. "I'm sorry about all of this Mary. I didn't know you would get so involved."

"What?"

"I know how upset you are about the woman and the children. She'll be fine. She never should've come here. She should've stayed where she was."

"What, what are you saying?" Mary sounded confused.

"She told me her boyfriend was arrested for drugs in another state and she needed food. She made up everything to draw you in, to help her. I've got her now. Don't worry about her, I've got her now." Doug lightly pushed Eliza inside, shutting the door behind them.

Doug grabbed Eliza by the arm and said, "If you say anything, I promise you tomorrow when you awake, the children will be gone, dead and buried."

Eliza jerked her arm away from Doug; opened the door and went outside straight to her children. "I'm sorry kids," she whispered. She hugged them close to her body. "I'm sorry." She started crying again and made her way to the car. It was now loaded with the children's car seats, food, clothing and toys. *At least we'll eat tonight*, she thought as she made her way to the backseat.

Doug walked out and said, "No, you ride up front." He grabbed Eliza by the arm and moved her to the front seat opening the car door for her. "There is no room for you with the car seats. I need you to give me directions."

"You need me to give you directions, to HELL?" Eliza could barely move as she spoke. If it was not for Doug pulling her, she would not have gotten into the car. She did not want to go back to that place. She wanted to run as fast as she could. She wanted to be anyplace but where she was. She did not want to go back there to die. Her taste of freedom was too much. She looked back at the children and lowered her head. *Why me, why us?* She was conquered.

Doug gave Eliza a slight shove hitting her head on the door frame. No one seemed to notice. Doug smiled, and then grabbed the door. "Move your legs into the car."

Eliza did as she was told. Her head stung and she knew that Doug could, if he wanted to, slam the door on her. Doug did slam the door, missing her leg by only a fraction of an inch. He then walked to the driver's side of the car and got in.

Mary walked to the window and motioned for Eliza to roll it down. Eliza looked at Doug as though she didn't know how to work the window. She actually was afraid to touch anything. As Doug put the window down a picture on his sun visor caught her eye and she turned back to get a better look. "Those eyes," she said. "Is that ... son?" Tears welled up in her eyes.

"Oh that's Doug Jr." Mary then added, "Apple of his father's eye. Do you see how well he's taken care of? Maybe Doug can give you some pointers on how to care for children on your drive home."

"How old is he?" Eliza questioned. She had not heard a word Mary said.

Doug said, "Now don't you worry with my child. You have two of your own to worry with. You know, making sure they don't die."

"He's a beautiful boy. Where is he now?" Eliza was not listening to anything Doug was saying either.

"Oh Doug, I don't know why you won't answer her. His mom is Patty. She used to be the waitress at the diner before Doug swept her off her feet. How old is he now; ten or something like that? Patty takes really good care of him," Mary said.

"Can I see the picture please?" Eliza held her hand out to Doug for the picture.

Doug looked at her, rolled his eyes and then took the picture down. "Here, take a look."

"You know we really have to go now. What do you want Mary?" Doug was sounding a little impatient.

Mary said, "Oh I just wanted Eliza to know if she needs anything, if I can help in any way, she can call me. Here's my card." She pressed the card into Eliza's hand.

"Eliza, I just want to wish you good luck. I hope that you'll get yourself together and you find the help you need. Please Doug, take her someplace to get the help she needs. Please do it for the children."

Mary was still talking as Doug was putting the window up. Eliza was staring at the picture in her hands when Doug grabbed it from her.

"Good-bye Mary," Doug said as the window made its way to the top.

28

Doug waved one slow wave and Mary looked at his hand. She saw an old scar in the center of his hand. It was such a small scar; one she had never really noticed before. Now it stuck out like a sore thumb. A small circular disfigurement was in the center of his hand. Mary then looked to Eliza. Terror filled her eyes. Not remorse for lying, as Mary had first thought, but pure terror. Eliza mouthed the words, "It's him. He will kill us. It's him." Eliza's body shrunk toward the door; putting as much space between Doug and her as the car would allow.

EJ looked out of the back window as the car drove off. Tears slipped down his cheeks, his arms reaching toward Mary. Mary could not move. Her head was spinning, her mouth slightly open. She was frozen. The reality of what she had done crept into her mind. She understood why Eliza was acting as she was. She had handed the family back. *Oh shit.* Mary touched her forehead. *What have I done? I need to get them back.*

"Wait!" She yelled running after the car. Her arms were waving and she was yelling so loud, the manager of the motel came running out. "Please stop Doug! Wait, don't go! Come back!" She yelled. She was quickly out of breath, but ran a few more feet. Her legs burned and her heart was pounding so hard, she thought she was having a heart attack.

The clerk from the front desk came out and asked, "Is everything alright?"

"I don't think it is. Damn." Mary said as she made her way back to her SUV. She grabbed the radio and although out of breath she said, "Bring the lady and the children back to the motel. Doug, do you hear me? I need you to bring that family back!" Mary knew she could not let them go.

Doug's voice calmly replied, "Mary, I'm off duty now. Call Saul if you have a problem and I'm turning this radio off. I won't be in contact with the station for the rest of the night, over and out."

"Come back Doug." Mary yelled into the radio as she started her SUV. She took off, showering the motel manager and the clerk with small pebbles from the parking lot. Doug did not answer.

Saul answered after Mary yelled into the radio for the tenth time. "Mary, come to the station if you have a problem. You heard what Doug said; I'm in charge."

"Screw you Saul." Mary said to the radio. Saul did not get the message. Mary did not send it over the airways. She failed to push the button on the hand mic.

She drove a few miles, but could not see Doug's car. The sky grew dark and moments later the clouds released their fills, soaking the earth with its shower. For Mary, it meant seeing Doug's car was no longer going to happen. Visibility turned to zero. Doug's few minutes head start, had given him a lifetime to kill the family. This time Mary knew it was her fault.

29

"What the hell is wrong with that woman? Did you forget your panties?" Doug asked patting Eliza between the legs.

Eliza recoiled closer to the door. She knew Mary had seen her mouth the words, "It's him." She watched Mary run after the car as they drove off yelling for them to stop. She wished Mary would pull out her gun and at least try to shoot at the tires. She heard Mary's voice over the radio. Mary sounded frantic. *Come on*, Eliza thought to herself. *Chase us down. Stop him.* Seconds passed, and then minutes. She watched, looking for Mary in the side mirror wondering why she was not following them. She looked over at the speedometer and her heart sank. He was driving fast, way too fast for anyone to catch up with them. Eliza knew where he was taking them. She hated where they were going. Her heart broke. Not just for herself, but for her children. She turned her eyes to the visor. She stared at the picture of her son.

"Are you good to him?" She asked.

"Good to whom?"

"Teddy?"

"Who the hell are you talking about? I don't know any 'Teddy'," Doug shot back.

"My son, the one you took." Eliza glared back at Doug. "He is mine, isn't he?" Eliza asked.

"No you whore, he's mine."

"No you bastard, just because you gave sperm doesn't make him yours. Now I asked you a simple question and the very least you can do is tell me, are you good to him?" Eliza was angry. She was angry she lost her son, she was angry she was riding in a car with this man and she was angry she was going back. She had finally found her voice.

"Why are you so worried about him? It's not like you are ever going to meet him, talk to him or even see him in person. He doesn't know you! And look at you, who would want you for their mother?" He paused. "I didn't know about the girl. I wonder if my wife might want another child. I've been thinking about another child."

"What? I see how you treat women. She goes over my dead body!"

"Don't tempt me. And by the way, I stopped by your place this morning before I came out and let me tell you, there have been some changes. I let you keep a window all these years and what did you do? You broke it. I told you I would only replace that window once." Doug hit Eliza in the face sending her head into the passenger's side window. "And don't you ever talk to me like that again!" The children were crying in the backseat. "Shut them damn kids up or else!" He yelled at her.

The rain started falling, pounding on the windshield. "Oh shit, this is just what I need now." Doug said as he wiped the fog from the window.

Eliza, bleeding from the mouth, did her best to console the now hysterical children. "Please stop, please," she begged. She looked in the food bag on the floor and found lollipops. She opened one for EJ and let the baby suck on one as she held it. Both seemed to enjoy it. Soon, besides a couple of deep breathes and sniffles the children had calmed down.

Eliza turned back around in the seat and begged. "Please, let us go. I promise, I won't say anything. You can drop us off around the corner and we will disappear. Just let me and the kids go. I see my son, your son, is happy. You have done a wonderful job with him. I will leave this place and never return. I trust you will take care of him. Please just let me take these kids and go. We need a life too."

"Oh, but you have a life right now. What I can't figure out is why you left. I didn't tell you it was time for you to go anywhere. Stop thinking for yourself; you do a lousy job of it. I wonder what would have happened to you if I had let you go all those years ago. It makes one wonder, if indeed, you would have died out there that night. You were bleeding, knocked out in the freezing cold. I thought at first you had gotten away, but no, there you were lying flat on your face. See the favor I did for you? At least you are alive; I don't know for how much longer, but right now you can still breathe." He patted Eliza on the leg and she began to scream.

"Don't touch me you bastard. Don't ever touch me again!" Eliza was terrified of speaking, but could not seem to stop herself. She was, at that moment, more afraid than she had ever been in her whole life. Waking in the dark that first night had scared her, but now she was not in the dark. It was no longer a nightmare that only came when the sun was down; now she was living the nightmare during broad daylight. She pulled at the door handle of the car. She was going to jump. She was sure Mary knew it was Doug. She was sure Mary would save the children. She yanked and she pulled and she screamed as loud as she could, "I HATE YOU!" The door refused to open. Eliza began slapping him and punching him. "I hate you with all my might. I wish you would drive this car off the road and kill us all. You have no reason to put us back in that hole, just kill us now." She kneeled on the seat and decided he would not take her alive this time. She reached for the steering wheel and pulled as hard as she could. She found strength only a crazy person could harbor in their soul. Doug's soul was evil though; and one thing Eliza knew from all the time she had spent in the hellhole, good doesn't always win; in her case, good had never won.

The wheels of the car slid from one side of the road to the other, but Doug managed to stop the car on the side of the road. He grabbed her hands off of the steering wheel and used his head to push her back on the seat. She started biting him on the head, taking in mouths full of hair. He shoved his elbow into her stomach and as she gasped for breath he screamed, "Bitch, calm the hell down or I'll shoot you where you sit." His face was red with rage.

"Then do it! Just do it. I won't go back with you. I won't be put back in that hole. I won't do it." Hair fell from her mouth and into her lap as she spoke. She felt his hands let go of hers and she stopped fighting him. She ripped open her dress top; exposing her boney chest to him. "Go on, just do it. Put your gun here and shoot me. Right...here...in...my...heart." She spoke the words slowly, patting her chest after each word. "I, I don't want to live." She looked back at the children. EJ was crying and Hope was screaming at the top of her little lungs.

"Bitch," was the last word Eliza heard him spew out of his mouth. Eliza didn't feel or even see the punch come.

30

When Eliza awoke, she gradually opened her swollen eyes. Her head was throbbing and it was dark. Had she finally made it out? Was this death? No, she was sure death did not hurt this much. Death had eluded her again. *It's never my time to die*, she thought. She could not see where she was; but the old smell that came with the place she had called her home for so many years, was thick in the air. She was home, back in the dingy little place where she knew her punishment would not be death, but life. Why did he want her to live, when all she wanted to do was die?

She tried to look around, but her eyes hurt and her head ached. "Kids, are you here?" She heard nothing. She stayed quiet, not breathing, begging her ears to do what her eyes could not. She was scared. She was scared she was all alone. She called out again. No answer. An ache built in her heart. "Why?" She yelled over and over. There was a rustling noise to her left. She heard the steady breaths of her children sleeping. She was relieved and upset. She was back and the children were back. She failed. She felt she was a bad mother. She could not now, nor in the future, protect her children. The taste of freedom was too much for Eliza. *"Be careful what you ask for,"* ran through her mind. She had asked for freedom. She had asked for life outside of the hole. Right now, she wished she had never climbed through that window. She wished she had starved to death and died right there in her little hellhole. She knew, in the whole world, there had never been a mother that destroyed their children like she had. The throbbing going through her head was too much to take. She was beaten both physically and emotionally. She wanted not to sleep, but to die. Pain ate at her every movement and her every thought. She curled up and cried herself to sleep.

31

Mary drove around town for an hour. She looked everywhere. She drove by Doug's house; she drove by Chris' house. She drove up and down the old rural roads that did not go anywhere yet led everywhere. She even drove by the old plant. It was no use; Doug was not to be found. She reluctantly drove back to the station. Saul was there. He was sitting in Doug's office; watching her. Mary went to the door, opened it and asked, "Where's Doug?"

"Well now Mary, it's not my day to watch Doug. What are you doing here anyway? Doug said you were taking the rest of the day off, yet, here you are."

Mary turned to leave.

"Go home Mary, Doug said you were upset and after the way you acted yesterday ..."

She turned back, "Saul stop. I just want to know if you know where Doug is. I didn't ask, nor do I require any input from you, other than if you know where Doug is. If you can't answer THAT question, then don't say anything else to me."

Saul stood up.

"No, really don't." Mary put her hand up. She turned and left Doug's office. She stopped by Robert's desk and left a note: *I'm going home. I'll call you later. Mary*.

She got in her SUV and again drove around town. She saw Doug's car at the ball field. Doug was standing in the dugout. No teams were on the field. The rain was now just a little drizzle. She drove slowly past Doug's car. There was nobody inside. The car seats were removed. All traces of the family erased. She saw Doug glance her way. She thought about stopping, but she did not have proof of anything. What would she say to him? Nothing, he was the sheriff; there was nothing she could say. With the family out of the picture she would have to do things differently. She quickly drove away hoping he did not see her, but knowing that he did.

She needed to talk to someone. Maybe Robert, but Robert had not seen what she had seen. Robert had not heard everything the woman had told her. She trusted Robert, but to bring an allegation like this against Doug; she did not know whose side he would fall on. She did not know if he would believe her. She did not know if she herself believed. She had handed all the tapes over to Doug. All Mary had were the fleeting words of a dying woman. *A dying woman*, Mary shivered. She needed help and it would have to come from outside of her department. Doug had friends in high places; that is how he secured his position as sheriff. *No*, she thought, for now she was leaving Robert out of the loop. She was not trusting Saul, he and Doug were really close. Did Saul know about Eliza and the children? Was Saul also a part of the rape and kidnapping? *Oh my God*, Mary thought; *I work for a police department that terrorizes women and small children*. Her mind was working too hard. She needed to talk to someone she trusted and right now that person was her husband, Bryan. In fact, he was the only person in town she trusted.

Bryan was at work when Mary got home. She sent the sitter home and spent the afternoon playing with Charley. She had a few crying spells. She hugged Charley a little longer and a little tighter, closer to her heart, trying to protect him from the evil all around.

Her mind pictured Doug doing the things Eliza described. Chills ran through her body. Had there been signs of this before?

Had she been so blinded by an easy life, she had missed them? By the time Bryan returned from work, she was emotionally exhausted. She clutched a tissue as she held the two pictures that were left behind.

Was it Chris?" Bryan asked as he walked in. "Why didn't you call me?"

"Momma cries Daddy. It kay momma, I take care of you." Mary burst into tears again and scooped up Charley hugging him tight. "Mommy hurt me Daddy," Charley said squirming to get free.

Bryan walked to Charley and took him from Mary's arms. "Mommy has had a bad day. She just wants you to know how much she loves you. Now give mommy a big kiss and go play in your room for a few minutes."

"Loves you Mommy," Charley said as he ran over. He kissed Mary on the cheek and raced from the room.

"Now Mary, tell me what's going on here? If it's Chris, then we'll deal with it. That woman can live in his house. We can help her with the children. We cannot make up for what Chris did, but for God sake, we can try to make things better. We will get through this and she will get through this."

"Oh Bryan, I really messed up. It WAS NOT Chris. It's Doug. DAMN, it's DOUG! I gave the family back to him," Mary sobbed. "He took her back only, I don't know where back is." Mary handed the two ghastly pictures to Bryan.

Bryan winced. "Is that her?"

"Yes, Doug did this to her."

"Wait a minute Mary, what happened? We've known Doug for a long time. Are you sure? I mean, this morning you were sure it was Chris. You were so sure."

"No, I'm not one hundred percent sure, but I am about ninety-nine percent sure. I'm sure that Eliza mouthed, "It's him" to me as they were driving away. What am I going to do? I tried to stop them. I called on the radio. Doug refused to answer me. Damn,

I should have gone after them sooner. I stood there like an idiot yelling into the radio. By the time I went after them, they were gone and it was pouring down rain. What if I'm wrong? Maybe my eyes were playing tricks on me. Oh Bryan, what if I'm right and it is him? What have I done?"

At that moment Charley walked back into the room. "Mommy, I hunger," he said as he rubbed his belly.

"We have to talk about this later." Bryan touched Mary on the head. "Tell you what; Charley and I will make dinner, and you go take a hot bath. You look like you need one." Bryan knelt down to Charley and asked, "Would you like to help me make dinner for Mommy? We can make some cheese and macaroni." Mary knew that Charley would jump at the chance of helping Bryan.

"Yea Daddy, me cook too," Charley said as he jumped up and down.

Later that evening as they put Charley to bed, Mary begged off the normal book and asked Bryan to read to him. She went into the room, undressed, and got into bed.

When Bryan walked into the room, Mary knew he wanted to finish their conversation, but she pretended to be asleep. He bent down and kissed her.

"Sleep Mary, we'll talk in the morning." He patted her on the hand and started toward the door, then turned and said, "I love you," before closing the door.

Mary tried to go to sleep, but her mind was too busy. *How can I help her now?* She deliberated as she pulled the covers around her shoulders.

When Bryan came to bed later, she was still awake. He kissed her on the forehead and fell right to sleep. Mary did not move. She again faked sleep. She wanted to sleep, but somehow it eluded her for hours.

When sleep finally came, it was restless. She tossed and turned waking every few hours. She finally left the bed and crept out of the room. She went into the kitchen. "I can't get that woman out of my head. I asked her if it was the truth. I begged her to tell me. Why would she go back? Why would Doug take her back? I need to see her. I need to know she'll be okay. What happened in the motel when I left? Why did she change?" Mary was talking out loud unaware that Bryan was standing in the doorway.

"You should be sleeping." Bryan said as he entered the room.

She did not hear him. She stared out the back window, looking at the darkness that surrounded the field beyond their home.

"Mary, are you okay?" Bryan asked as he touched her shoulders.

Mary dropped the glass she was holding. It shattered as it hit the floor.

"Mary, you need to tell me what's going on here."

"We need to get this glass up. Bryan, I messed up. I really messed this up." Mary was now crying as she bent to the floor, picking up the glass.

"Hey, it's only a broken glass. We have more. Here, let me help you." Bryan took her hand, it was bleeding.

"You should have seen this lady after Doug got there. She changed from a woman that begged for help, to a woman that wanted nothing. I wanted her to tell me, I begged her to tell me. She could have told me it was him. I could've helped her!"

"He took her and I let him." Mary sat down at the table. "I just don't get it. You know how Doug is with Little Doug. I just don't get it. And the way she looked at Doug's child; Little Doug's eyes, he has the same eyes as Eliza. She looked me in the face and told me to keep her kids. Then the shocked look on EJ's face when he saw Doug. His hand, his hand had the scar from when she stabbed him, I never noticed it before. And the description she gave of the man at Chris' house that night. Oh my god, I gave her back to him. I have to go. I have to find her. I have to save her and the kids before it's too late. He has killed before; he killed a woman in front of Eliza."

Bryan wrapped his arms around Mary and said, "There is nothing you can do right now. What are you going to do; bust in his house?" He turned Mary around to face him. "And Mary, if what you say is true, do you know what could happen to you if he finds out that you know? If it is Doug and he has them, what are you going to do? Will he kill them to keep his secret? You need to come up with a plan. I don't mean a half ass plan; I mean a real plan. A plan that if what you are saying is true, then it will take him down. If you are wrong Mary, you need to be able to hold your head high and walk into the station every single day."

"God, why does this have to be so hard? I've known him all these years. He takes care of his family, and I don't know a person in town that has anything bad to say about him. He works with all of those kids in little league. Just the thought of him keeping kids locked up like animals; beating and starving them, it makes me sick Bryan." Tears welled up in her eyes, "You didn't see them and I just let them go. I gave them back. I was so sure it was Chris. I let that guide me. Do you understand that woman came to me for help? I gave her back with a lecture on how to take care of children. What kind of person am I? If they die, it will be my fault." She cried then. She cried for the woman, she cried for the children, but she also cried for herself.

Bryan held her for a long time and finally sat her down at the table. "Okay, what can I do to help? Tell me what I can do; I can sneak around his house, see if I see anything."

Mary looked at her husband, and then started to laugh. He was not the most handsome man in town, nor was he the thinnest or even the shortest. Bryan's weight was 275lbs; his height was 6'4". "Oh yea, like you can hide behind a tree."

"I could do a DNA test on them. I'm sure Dr. Denton took blood. I can have that tested. I will have to get something from Doug to compare. His hair, his spit, I might even get lucky and get his blood."

"As long as you don't shoot him to get it."

"I don't know about that," Mary smiled. It was a terrible thing to smile about, but Mary could not help herself. "Bryan, what if I'm wrong about this?"

"I think the question you should be asking yourself is; what if you're right? This is the only way you are going to know. Hell Mary, if someone had you or Charley, I would move heaven and earth trying to find you. Maybe Eliza and her kids don't have anyone to move heaven or earth. You may have to do it for them."

"You're right Bryan, they have no one. Her own mother wanted nothing to do with her. Her parents turned their backs on her. It's so sad." Mary was thinking back to the phone call Eliza made.

"You know, you are a wonderful man Bryan. Maybe one day, Eliza will find a man like you."

Mary looked at the clock as the sun rose over the back hill. "You didn't get much sleep last night and you have to get ready for work. I'm sorry for keeping you up."

"Mary, we've been married a long time and there's something I need you to know; if you are sad and upset, then I'm sad and upset. You are so much a part of me and I love you so much. I wake up every single day and thank God you are in my life. I guess that means, if I have to lose a night's sleep every once in a while, then that's just the price I have to pay. You, my dear Mary, are worth the lost night's sleep." Bryan pulled Mary toward him.

"If you need me to miss work, I can do that too. If we always help each other through these times, we will always be together. That's what marriage is, right? Being together through good and bad; and right now you're having a bad. I love you. Now get a plan together and we'll go get those kids. Mary, one thing; don't tell anyone until you know. I mean really know the truth. You know how small towns are." Bryan leaned down to kiss his wife and trotted off to the bathroom to get ready for work. Mary sat at the table and made a plan. A plan she hoped would keep everyone safe.

32

When Eliza awoke again, the sun had not entered their home. *Had I been dreaming,* she wondered? Had we gotten out, only to be brought back again? She sat up on the bed and cringed as pain in her midsection caught her by surprise. She wondered what time of day it was. She never knew what time it was, but she usually could gauge morning, noon or night. She looked toward where the window was, hoping to see a star or something, anything. She saw nothing.

The children were making noise. How long had they slept? Was it a day, days or weeks? She wished she knew. She wished she knew what time it was, what day it was.

She stumbled around the room. She followed the moaning of her son. She followed the cries of her daughter. They were alive. She felt a moment of relief, and then she felt their lifetime of pain. They were together on the pallet. She touched them; picking the crying baby up in her arms, and rocking her battered son next to her breast. She strained, trying to see them; to see what damage their father had inflicted upon their small bodies, but her eyes saw nothing but darkness.

It had not been a dream. We had gotten out, but being back this time, was worse than the first time. This time she did not scream; she did not tremble in fear. *This time the playing field had changed. This time,* she thought, *I know my tormentor.*

Matches, the thought came to her suddenly. She remembered picking up matches at the motel. She checked her pockets. She found what she needed and with shaking hands, she struck the match. The light blinded her, sending pain through her eyes. She dropped the match and it quickly extinguished itself. She decided another approach was necessary. She turned her face away and lit the second match. Better. Much better she thought.

She looked at the children while covering their eyes. EJ had a bruise on the side of his face and dried blood at the base of his nose. She touched him softly on his cheek. The baby appeared fine, not a mark on her. She remembered a candle one of her friends had given her as a going away present. She located it using up two more matches. She lit the candle and with shaking hands placed the light on the floor.

As she looked around the room, she found that Doug had brought all the food, toys and clothes into the room with them. She was surprised, "I guess we can have some breakfast soon." She then turned to the window and almost tripped over the candle. The area was now filled with wood and concrete. Eliza wondered how long she had been knocked out.

She got the children up. EJ seemed fascinated with the light coming from the candle. Eliza had to tell him three times to keep his fingers away. "Burn," she said into his hand.

She needed the light that came from the candle, but she knew soon she would have to return to the darkness of their hole. She fed EJ and fixed a bottle of powdered milk for the baby. She then blew the candle out.

EJ complained. He used the voice he hardly ever used to scream. He grabbed in the darkness until he found her hand. With anger and frustration he signed, "I'm scared, please mom, turn it back on."

She refused. "No son, not now, we need the light for later. Oh please EJ; I need you to be a big boy now."

Eliza was astonished to see a small slit of light coming into the room. She followed the rays and saw light pouring in from the cracks around their ceiling door. She was thankful she had the light. A short time later the light began to fade. She and the children were plunged back into total darkness.

She wondered about Mary. She hoped Mary had seen her mouth, "It's him". She thought she had, but then again, she was not sure. She hoped Mary would find them, but then she had many hopes over the years; nothing ever happened. Her mind was playing tricks on her. Mary had not seen her. Mary was too busy saying good-bye. She and her children would live there until they died. She cried.

She fed the children again and kissed them goodnight. *Thank God, HE had not come. Today had been a good day, no not really, today had been a safe day.* Eliza did not know which was better; before, she could not put a face to the devil that kept her, and now, she had a face to go with the pain. He did not look like a monster. This man was not a monster that crept from the pages of a book or leapt from a movie. He was worse. He was handsome and looked like a man starring in a love story. Only Eliza knew the truth behind his rugged good looks and his soft gentle manner. Only Eliza knew the evil behind his eyes which lurked deep in his soul. Only Eliza knew when he did come, the devil himself would be arriving. She may not make it out alive, but she knew she must try or die trying. Getting out once had given her strength she did not know she had. Right now however, she was simply going through the motions of living.

Eliza pulled her children to her and rocked them to sleep. She would wait. She would eat and gather her strength and she would wait. He was not finished with her yet. She knew he was not finished because she was still alive. Eliza would now make him pay. As she laid her children down to sleep, she examined her soul. She had a heart full of anger, ready to explode. Getting out had done her good after all. She fell into a semi-sleep state. One eye open, one eye closed. She waited.

33

The phone rang at the doctor's office at 9:00 a.m. sharp. "Dr. Denton's office, may I help you?" Mary knew the voice. It was Debbie Hills, also known as, "Cider Bend Times" to all who knew her. She told everyone's medical business without a care. Dr. Denton would not fire her. He and his wife had raised her after her parents died. They were in a car accident when she was seven years old. When the doctor moved to the country, she followed even though she was a grown woman. He did however, keep the real important things from her, but that did not stop her from sometimes working late and checking out everyone's medical records. Anyone in town, who could afford it, would travel into one of the bigger cities to receive their medical advice.

"Good morning Debbie, it's Mary. How are you today?" Mary asked. She hated that "Cider Bend Times" had answered the phone.

"Oh hi Mary; what's ailing you this morning?" Debbie inquired.

Mary could hear the curious tone in Debbie's voice. "Nothing, I just need to talk to Kathy for a few minutes." Mary decided not to say anything else.

"Now Mary, you know I can help you just as well as Kathy can. Why don't you just tell me what's going on. I'll do my best to help you. If worse comes to worse, I can always find an answer, just like Kathy."

Mary rolled her eyes and wondered, *why do I have to put up with her today?*

"Debbie, some things are personal and this is one of them. I know that you and the doctor are very close, but Kathy and I have known each other for years. We went to school together and I need to ask her about personal things. I really don't mean to be rude but ..."

Debbie cut her off. "Well excuse me! Why didn't you just say you don't want me to know? Just hold on, I'll try to find her." Music filled the other end of the receiver. Mary couldn't help but smile. Mary did not dislike Debbie; she just did not trust her.

Mary waited for Kathy to pick up the phone. After a few minutes, Kathy's voice was clear and bright.

"Kathy I need a favor," Mary started to say.

"Oh so you're the one that pissed Debbie off. Thanks, now I have to put up with her all day." Kathy was laughing on the other end of the phone.

"Well, I don't know how you put up with her every day," Mary said.

"It's not always bad, she makes me laugh sometimes."

Mary immediately felt sorry for what she had said. "I'm sorry Kathy. Would you please apologize to Debbie for me? Just tell her we had personal business to talk about. I've had a bad night and I need a great big favor. The kids that were brought in for Dr. Denton to look at, did you guys do blood work on them?"

"Yes we did, but right now it's not back from the lab we sent it to. It'll be about a week before all of it is back. What happened with that woman? Is she still staying out at the motel? What's going on with that case? Are you looking for something in particular? If it's a special test, let me know and I'll make sure the lab runs it."

"Well, I need you to run a DNA test on the kids. I need it compared to another blood sample. And Kathy, please, YOU make the call, and don't tell anyone; this is police business. I mean, no one in the office is to know that you are making the call and requesting a DNA test."

"Mary, I need a purchase order for police business so we can get reimbursed. DNA testing is not cheap. Have you talked to Doug about running these tests?"

"Yes Kathy, Doug and I have spoken about this. What kind of person would I be if I hadn't spoken to Doug? We need you to call the lab and have the test run. We need to make sure the kids belong to whom we think they do. I mean, we are pretty sure they belong to the woman, but we still have questions about some things." Mary was hoping Kathy would not ask for the purchase order number right then. "I'll have two other samples that need testing."

"Are you bringing those samples into the office?"

"NO. All I need you to do is call the lab and get working on the first three samples; you do have the mother's don't you? I'll drop the other samples off myself. The lab is in Lexington, isn't it? Please make sure you call so they can get started first thing. We have no time to waste on this. We have no time at all."

"Okay, I'll do it as soon as I hang up. Let me give you the address," Kathy said.

"Kathy, please remember no one is to know; I mean no one at all. And Kathy, thank you." Mary hung up the phone after getting the address.

She called work. She was unsure if she was going in. Right at that moment, she did not even know if she had a job. She picked up the phone three times before finally dialing. Her heart was pounding so loudly she could hear it as the phone rang in her ear. When Doug answered the phone, she almost hung up.

"Cider Bend Sheriff's Department; do you have an emergency?" Doug's voice was bright.

"Doug, what are you doing in so early? I thought you were taking the day off." Mary could not hide her surprise.

"John's wife had an accident at the house and cut one of the electrical wires while hanging a picture. That woman, I'm glad she's not my wife. I still don't understand how she did it. What's up Mary? Please don't tell me you're calling in today. Remember we have to have that talk with Saul."

"No. I need, I need to get off early today. I have something personal to take care of.

"Something personal?" Doug sounded suspicious.

"I have to have some blood test run." She was not really lying.

"What's wrong?" Doug's interest increased.

"If I knew the answer to that question; I wouldn't have to have the blood test run, now would I?" *Breathe*, Mary thought.

"Okay, just be at the school when the school lets out. You know those high school kids love to speed by the elementary school. Today, I plan to put a stop to that. Driving like that, they are going to kill some poor little kid. I can't have the death of some poor innocent child on my hands, now can I?"

"You're right Doug; I wouldn't want that to happen. I'll be in shortly. Goodbye."

Mary's plan was coming together. The middle school was right next to the elementary school; and if she played her cards right, she would run into Little Doug.

She went to her SUV, climbed in and headed to work. *Hold on Eliza,* she thought to herself; *if I am right, it shouldn't be too much longer. If you're still alive, and I hope you are, I will find you.*

When Mary arrived at the station, she found Doug sitting at his desk in his office and Saul sitting at his desk. Doug's blinds were up and he was talking on the phone and laughing. After he hung up the phone, he motioned for Mary to come in.

Mary reluctantly walked toward his office not even looking at Saul. She poked her head in the door and said, "Hey, what's up?"

Doug pointed toward a chair. "I know you're still thinking about that woman, but I took her to the social services office. Did you know she lives over in Madison County; over one hundred and fifty miles away? What she was doing here or how she ended up in our small town is beyond me. After I dropped her off, I stopped in the station over there and told them to look after her and those kids. It's just a shame to see how they look in the daylight." Doug stared off into the distance.

"Wow, that's quite a walk she took getting over here," Mary said.

"You know, I thought the same thing, but as we were driving back, she told me everyone around there knows her husband. She just wanted to protect him. Talk about love; he treats her like shit and she just loves him. You just can't figure some women. She's not like you is she, Mary? I bet you wouldn't take any shit from Bryan would you? I bet you wear the pants in your family. No woman I'm ever with would wear my pants." He laughed then and looked at Mary. "Oh, don't worry, I don't keep Patty locked up in the basement or anything." He looked at the picture of his wife sitting on his desk.

"Maybe I'll go over and see the family, see how she's getting along." Mary waited for Doug's response.

"She's not our problem, Mary. You need to just let it drop. Even if we found the person she loves so much, we can't do anything. It happened out of our district. I placed a call to Peter Lynne, the sheriff in Madison County, told him everything this morning. He was out yesterday. He said he would watch out for her. So let it go Mary. You have other things to worry about. Now let's talk about Saul."

"Do you mind if I call Peter?" Mary asked. She knew she was pushing.

"And say what? I dropped that family off. I don't have her damned address. I'm telling you, drop it Mary. The family is back where they belong and we can go forward with our day. It's going to be you and me for a while. Robert will cover part of the night shift." Doug paused and stared intently at Mary. "Tell Saul you are sorry. You owe him that much. And Mary, I mean this, so listen. I know you have worked here for a long time and you come from an outstanding family, but I will fire you if you get out of line like that again."

Mary shook her head thinking, *like Saul apologized for coming on to me?* "Whatever." She got up.

Mary knew Doug knew she was not happy. She could feel him watching her from the door as she walked by Saul. She whispered, not quite looking at Saul but seeing him. "I'm sorry I yelled." She felt like a little child or a dog that had been beat as her head and shoulder slumped downward. She glanced slightly upward and saw Saul's shit eating grin. She heard Doug's door close. She bit her lip as she walked back to her desk.

Saul left shortly after her apology. She sat at her desk. She wanted to pick up the phone and call Peter, but she knew better. It would do no good to call Peter; Doug had surely covered his bases. She let everything drop for now. After sitting at her desk doing nothing, Mary found the picture EJ had drawn shoved under some papers. She smiled at the trees and thought they were very nice, even if it was the first time he had seen trees. There was a bird flying in the sky. He really was a talented artist. Mary felt bad. She sent them back. She was such a fool. How could she send them back? She walked to the restroom and had a cry.

At two in the afternoon, Mary walked to Doug's office and knocked on the door. The day had been very slow. No calls at all. She was tired of sitting there and she was ready to go to the school. She was ready to put her plan in motion.

"Why are you leaving now? Classes at the high school don't let out until three." Doug inquired as Mary told him she was leaving.

"I know what time classes get out. I just want to get a good spot and I'm bored."

Mary knew the middle school let out at two-thirty. She wanted to get some DNA from Little Doug. With her plans in place, she was ready to follow through. She knew she should have acted differently yesterday, but she could not change the past. She hoped she could change the future.

Mary saw the coffee cup sitting on the corner of Doug's desk. It had been there for years. She knew Little Doug had given it to him and he took pride in showing off what his son had accomplished. Mary reached for a pen out of the holder and as she was drawing her arm back, she hit the cup, sending it falling to the floor. Mary watched the cup as it fell to the floor and did nothing to stop it. "Oh my God, I'm so sorry, I didn't mean to." Mary stopped talking as the cup hit the floor. She watched, waiting for the cup to shatter into pieces, but the cup bounced off the floor and landed straight up, not a crack in sight. "Damn," escaped Mary's mouth as she looked at her bandaged finger. She could still see the glass shattered on her kitchen floor.

"I'm glad that didn't break; Little Doug gave it to me for Father's Day." Doug laughed. "What a break that was," he laughed again. "Pardon the pun."

Mary looked at him then said, "You know Doug that was really stupid."

He glared back at her and then said, "I wasn't the one that knocked the damn thing off. What the hell is wrong with you? I was only joking." He picked up the cup and put it back on his desk close to where he was sitting.

"I'm sorry; I just didn't sleep well last night or the night before. That woman really got to me I guess." Mary was losing her mind. She had knocked the cup off and it did not break. It was not Doug's fault the cup did not break and she could not afford to let him know she knew anything. She was tired, confused and she felt really bad.

"I told you that woman's in good hands and nothing is going to happen to her that she doesn't deserve. Now get out on those streets and start protecting. And if you still feel like shit later on, just write a few tickets to those kids. You can preach to them and give them the ninth degree and you might even make a drug bust. I heard through the grapevine we have a little weed on the streets of our small town." Doug laughed.

Mary started to leave. She had her hand on the door when Doug said, "Mary, just drop the thing with the lady, trust me; it's best for everyone if you just drop it."

Mary wanted to say she could not just "drop it". Eliza had touched something in her. She wanted to say she knew it was him. She wanted to beg Doug to tell her where the children were, where Eliza was. But Mary said nothing. She left the station, got into her vehicle and drove off.

34

Mary needed a back-up plan. She needed to get DNA from both Doug and his son. As she sat thinking, she pulled out her phone bill and began writing the check. She stuffed it in the envelope and licked it, closing it tight. *Oh shit I've got it!*

Mary walked into the drugstore, bought a box of envelopes and carried them out to her SUV. She began folding papers and writing on the outside of the envelopes. She finished twenty and then drove to the school and parked. One envelope she left empty, she sealed a few and waited for class to let out. She got two evidence bags out. She saw Little Doug walking out of school. She got out and made her way toward him. His friends all made fun of him as Mary called him over.

"Is something wrong?" Little Doug asked.

"No, not at all, I was just waiting for the high school kids to let out. I'm doing a little sting, but hush, please don't say anything," she paused as she looked into his eyes. They were the same as Eliza's eyes. A chill ran up her spine and she had to look away from him.

"Hey, can you help me with something? I need to mail all of these letters today and I've been licking and licking and I'm a little out of juice. Do you think maybe you can lick a few for me?" Mary walked Little Doug over to the pile of envelopes.

"Sure Mary I can, but I have to hurry. I need to get to baseball. It starts soon."

"Okay how about one or two? It sure would make my life so much easier."

Little Doug started licking. When he came to the empty one he pulled it up to his lips and licked the envelope.

"Wait, don't seal that one. I forgot the letter."

Little Doug handed her the licked unsealed envelope and then said, "Sorry, I didn't notice."

"Hey, you better get going so you're not late." She patted Little Doug on the shoulder. "Thanks for helping me out."

"Mary, are you sure there's nothing you want to talk to me about?" He asked.

Yes, I want to tell you about your father. I want you to know about the monster he is. I want to take you to your mother, your real mother, and let her see that you are a good boy. I want to see her wrap her skinny arms around you and give you all the love she has kept for you. I want you to see what your father has done to your mother; how she has been kept. I want you to meet your brother and sister. I want you to be a friend and a big brother to the sweet little child that has been so abused. Mary kept her thoughts to herself and only said, "No sweetie, there's nothing I need to talk to you about. Have fun at baseball."

Little Doug went on his way and Mary put the licked, unsealed envelope in the bag and then said, "One down, one to go."

After sitting on the street in plain view, not a car sped by. Mary was happy she had completed her task of sitting by the high school watching the kids. She headed back to the station.

When she got to the station she noticed Doug's car was still in the parking lot. She thought long and hard about how to get something from him for testing. Blood, it had to be his and it had to be today. She stayed outside for a while looking through everything she had. She went to the back and opened the toolbox Bryan made her carry around. You never know when you may need something, he would tell her. She spotted the razor knife. It had never been used. It was, in fact, still in the package. She grabbed gloves out of the box and placed them on her hands. She pulled the razor out of the handle and placed it in her pocket. She took some tape from her evidence box and walked to Doug's car.

What am I doing? She questioned herself over and over as she made the short walk to his door. She looked from side to side making sure no one was watching her. With her heart beating almost out of her chest and her blood pounding in her ears, she placed the razor under the door handle. She pulled the gloves off her trembling hands, stuffing them into her pants pocket, as she walked toward the station. She looked around, swung her head quickly from side to side, but saw no one.

What if someone saw me? She made a quick scan of the parking lot. *Can I act like nothing is wrong? Can I follow Doug out to his car and him not think something is up?* Her brain was working overtime. She hated doing it. She hated cutting Doug, but there was no other way. She only hoped that he would not be too hurt. *No, I hope he cuts his hand off. No, I hope he has had nothing to do with this and I'm just overreacting.* She knew she was right and doing this, was the right thing to do.

At five, Doug said good-bye and started to walk to his car. Mary followed, making sure she had a few tissues and a bandage in her pocket.

"Hey Doug, do you remember you said I could get off early? I really have that thing to do today." Mary walked a little behind him, but tried to catch up so he would not stop.

"Oh, I forgot about that. Just let the guys know you are leaving and you should be fine," he said as he reached for the car door.

"I'm one step ahead, I let them know already." Mary said then added, "I just wanted to remind you."

"What the hell?" Blood poured from Doug's hand as he pulled the handle up.

Mary asked as if totally surprised, "What happened?"

"Oh my God, would you look at the blood, Jesus Christ what the hell?"

Mary was now very nervous. Doug's hand was covered with blood.

"What the hell is under there? It cut me. God, I'm bleeding." Doug looked a little woozy.

Mary ran to his side and then handed him tissues and peered under the handle.

"It's a razor! Hey, hold on a minute I have a towel in my car. She grabbed the evidence bag off the front seat, shoved it in her pocket and grabbed the white towel lying next to it. She carried the towel to his side. "Here, put those tissues in here." She pulled the evidence bag from her pocket and handed him the towel."

"You know I don't have AIDS, I better not have AIDS." Doug said as Mary pushed the plastic baggy toward him.

"I know you don't, but, well, we have our training. Let me see." She took the tissues from him and put them in the plastic bag. His three fingers were cut inside between the second and third knuckles. "You might need stitches. You better get to Doc Denton's office."

"Get that thing off of there and I want it checked for fingerprints. Oh God, now I have to have all kinds of test run." Doug sounded really upset. "What kind of sickness can I get from this? What kind of a sick shit would do something like this?" Doug winced, "Damn this hurts."

Mary went, got a pair of gloves, and went back to Doug's car. She pulled the razor along with the tape from underneath the door handle.

"I want fingerprints and whoever did this, is going to pay. What, do we have to put cameras outside of the police station now?" Doug was holding his wrapped hand in the air while trying to get in his car.

"Who the hell did you piss off Doug?" Mary asked.

"I bet it's that Robertson kid. Wait till I talk to his father." Doug had tears trickling down his face as he spoke. "This really hurts and don't you dare tell the guys I had tears in my eyes. Men don't cry; do you hear me? Real men don't cry."

"Do you want me to drive you?" Mary asked, praying he would say no.

"No, I'll go, but I swear that kid's going to pay and there is no way his father is going to buy his way out of this." Mary closed the car door as he spoke.

"Don't take that off until you get to the doctor's office!" Mary yelled after him.

Doug took off with his lights and siren going. Mary got in her vehicle and headed the other way, out of town, to the crime lab sixty miles away. She had the two samples and wanted answers. Was this one big family or did Mary owe both father and son an apology? She really hoped she would owe the apology. Not that they would ever get one; for that to happen, she would lose her job and might be up on criminal charges herself. Right now though, it was worth the risk.

35

Mary arrived at the lab and found her way to the right department. She was unsure how long it would take, but was willing to wait all night if she had to.

Mary handed the evidence bags to a young lady in a lab coat. "These are two different cases, the razor blade is one and it needs a full work up. The envelope and the tissue need a DNA test." She then asked, "Did you get the other samples in? How long will the test take? I have to make a phone call to my husband, and then I'll be right back."

"Oh, we won't have the results back tonight." The lady responded as she marked the plastic evidence bags that were handed to her.

"Please, I'll wait," Mary's voice was demanding.

"I'm sorry. We'll call with the results. I know you are in a rush, but what you fail to understand is, everyone is in a rush. Everyone wants everything yesterday. We'll get to it when we can and not a moment before." The snooty lady responded while rolling her eyes at Mary.

"Look," Mary checked out her name tag, "Laura, I know you think I'm just some dumb hick cop, but I need these results. Lives depend on this." Mary beseeched the lady.

"Everyone's life always depends on everything we do around here. Look, I'll do my best to get these plus, the other samples done as soon as I can. I'm really not trying to put you off, but we have a process and these tests take time. Please just go home and I'll call the station as soon as I have anything." Laura's demeanor had changed.

Finally understanding, but not too happy, Mary left with nothing. She hoped when they did call she would be there to take the call.

The drive home was long. She seemed to get to the lab quickly, but going home took almost two hours. It did not matter that the road was the same. It only seemed that right at this moment, Mary had nothing to rush to. The answers she needed would have to wait and there was nothing she could do to make them come quicker. She just did not know if she had time to wait.

Mary went home and fell into the arms of her husband. "I almost called looking for you. You are never this late. Hey, what's the matter?" Bryan held Mary in his arms.

"Where's Charley? I need to see him. I just need to look at him. I just need to kiss him." Mary was now crying.

"Bryan I did the most horrible thing today. Do you know I could go to jail for what I did?" Mary pulled Bryan's shirt close to her face.

Bryan pulled her away from him and looked at her, "What did you do?"

"I cut Doug and I had Little Doug lick envelopes."

Bryan stood there a moment before speaking. "Licking envelopes? Yea Mary, I hear you can do life for something like that." Bryan's laugh quickly sobered as he asked, "You cut Doug?"

She told him what she had done and after a promise that there were no fingerprints to be found; Bryan held her close and together they promised it would never be discussed again. "If he did father those kids and he is guilty, then another DNA test, the proper way, can be completed. No one would ever have to know a thing." Bryan reassured her.

Mary and Bryan went into Charley's room. He was sleeping like a beautiful baby. "I'm not willing to trade him Bryan. I just want you to know that."

"What do you mean, trade him?" Bryan asked.

"I mean, I'm not willing to trade Charley for that woman and her children. I know how much she has suffered and I'm sorry for that, but I refuse to let anything happen to Charley or you."

"I know Mary, and that's why I'm here, because I'm not going to let you. We'll keep him safe."

Mary fell into another restless sleep and woke early the next morning. She kissed Bryan and her son and then left for work. She wanted to make sure if the phone call came in, no one would answer it but her. She had to make sure no one got that call but her.

36

Mary sat at her desk all day. She requested office duty instead of splitting the shift as normal. Robert was confused but happily agreed. She jumped every time the phone rang. She passed on lunch, saying she was on a new diet. By three, she had picked up the phone and called the lab twice to see if the results were in, no luck.

A few minutes later, Doug came into the office. "How's your hand?" Mary felt a little remorseful as she asked; he was, after all, innocent until proven guilty.

"Oh, it's funny you should ask about that. Last night after I went to Dr. Denton's office, I stopped by the Robertson's house. Do you know what that shit of a father said? He and his son had been home sick all day. Hell, the damn kid didn't even go to school. I made him call the kid downstairs. The little bastard even looked sick. Yea, like I believe him. I called both the school and the lumber yard; both said they called in sick. The old man was most likely passed out on the sofa and the kid was out running the streets. You did send the blade in for testing right? I might have to get AIDS testing just to be sure. And I had to get a tetanus shot. I'll kill whoever did this to me, if I ever find out. That, you can bank on!" Doug was shouting.

"Oh, something else, Kathy said she sent the kids blood over for the test you ordered." Doug looked her straight in the face.

"You know those test cost money. I told Kathy to nix them all. Really Mary, we aren't a rich town."

"Okay. I forgot to tell her to cancel them after you took the family back." Mary waited for Doug to say something else, but he said nothing. He went into his office. She needed those test run and she needed Kathy to not tell Doug what she was doing. Mary called Kathy as soon as Doug closed his door. "Kathy, did you cancel those tests Doug told you to stop?"

"Oh my God I told him I would call this morning and stop them. I forgot. Hold on and I'll do it while I'm on the phone with you. Thanks for reminding me. I cannot believe I forgot."

"No Kathy, stop. I need those test run. There was a slight mix-up and those test need to be run. Kathy, I need them back fast. I've been waiting all morning. If you want to do something, then do nothing. And Kathy, please don't tell Doug."

"What?"

"Kathy, we've been friends for a long, long time. I really need this favor. If he asks you, tell him what you just told me, you forgot."

"Is it that important, we could both lose our jobs?"

"Yes, it's that important." Mary tried to express how important the tests were.

"What's going on?"

"I can't tell you. I'm really, really sorry, but I just can't. You have to trust me."

"Then I won't call at all. I'll forget to cancel the test. Are you sure, I mean really sure you want me to do this?"

"Yes Kathy I'm positive and I can't tell you why, and you can't say a word, to anyone."

At five-thirty that evening the phone rang, and as she had done all day, Mary jumped to answer it. It was Mrs. Wisdom. She wanted someone from the station to stop over and find out who was running through her flowers. Mary tried everything to get off the phone with her. She told her someone would try to stop by later.

Mrs. Wisdom was not ready to hang up. When the second line began to ring; Mary asked Mrs. Wisdom to please hold on, but she continued talking. She talked about who she thought it was and when she thought it had happened. On the fifth ring Mary said, "I have to answer the other line now, hold please." By the time Mary finally put her on hold and tried to answer the other line, it had stopped ringing. Mary looked into the office of the sheriff. Doug was talking. He looked at her and still he kept talking. Finally he hung up the phone and walked out of his office. Mary quickly picked up the first phone line; trying to get back to Mrs. Wisdom, but the line was dead.

Mary could feel her heart beat. She looked down at her chest to see if she could see her chest moving. The blood was rushing through her body and the only sound she could hear was the thud, thud, thud of her beating heart growing faster. She felt dizzy. The room started to spin. She looked up and saw Doug walking toward her. She forgot to breathe. Breathing is something that you do all the time without thinking about it; but at this moment, in this time, Mary forgot to breathe. Her body started gasping for air and finally she inhaled; gulping large amounts of air into her lungs. Her head hurt and her eyes tried to focus on Doug, but his face changed as he walked. She wanted to look away but she saw his eyes. They were burring holes into her. He knew. *Breathe*; she reminded herself, *don't look at him. Breathe. Calm down. If he knows he won't do anything now; there are too many people around. Breathe. If he does not know, then why give yourself away? Breathe.* His eyes were not blinking. His face looked distorted. Pain, Mary felt a sharp ping of pain in her head. *Breathe.* She looked away. She picked up a pencil and began writing on a pad; Mrs. Wisdom needs to be spoken to about calling. *Breathe.*

"Hey Mary, that was the lab. I told you to cancel the test; I told Doc's office to cancel the test. Seems they wanted to know which results we wanted first, the one on the blade or the test you ordered. What test did you order Mary? Which brings me to my next question, why are you sending test to the state lab that I have not approved? What do you think you are doing?" He sat on the edge of her desk. "You know, I think you overstepped your bounds here. Only I am allowed to approve any testing of evidence." He studied her as he spoke.

Mary's face was getting red. She could feel her blood pressure rising. She knew he was toying with her. *Breathe. Damn, just breathe,* she said to herself. She gathered her nerve then spoke, "I wanted to make sure that lady really is the mother of those children. Please don't be upset. They had blood work at Dr. Denton's office and I just couldn't sleep until I knew for sure she had not kidnapped those kids." Mary put her pencil down and looked up. "Well, what are they going to do?" She lost her nerve and again looked down at the note she had written.

"Well they said they had five other samples to test. I said, 'Five other samples' and they said, 'Yes, five samples.' I then inquired as to what type of testing they were to do, and do you know what she told me? DNA testing. Now who in the world would you need DNA testing on from five samples? Let's see, there's the woman and the two children. That's three by my count. Who were the other two samples from Mary?"

Mary felt her mouth fall open. Her brain was working overtime. "I, um, I." She needed time to think. She looked at Doug; he was staring at her. She quickly looked away. She watched him slowly rub his bandaged hand.

"Who did you have tested?" He spoke slowly as he leaned down. "Mary, look at me; I'm waiting for an answer."

"The woman and her kids," she mumbled not looking up at him.

"No, I don't think so, there were FIVE samples. Who else did you test?" Doug placed his bandaged hand on the desk in front of Mary's face.

The phone rang startling Mary. She jumped. As she grabbed the receiver, she knocked Doug's hand off the desk causing him to lose his balance. She lifted the receiver to her ear and started speaking before Doug could stop her.

"Cider Bend Sheriff's department, how may I help you on this fine day?" Sarcasm filled Mary's voice.

"Mary, are you okay?" It was Bryan.

"I'm sorry Mrs. Wisdom. Did I hang up on you? The other line was ringing."

"Mary, answer me. Are you doing okay?" Bryan anxiously asked.

"I'm not sure about that right now." Mary looked up, smiling at Doug as she spoke.

Doug grabbed for the phone as Mary swiveled out of his reach.

"I'm coming down there," Bryan insisted.

"No, you really shouldn't do that Mrs. Wisdom. Can you hold on for just a moment please?" Mary covered the phone with her hand.

"Doug, I really need to take this call. Can I meet you in your office in a few minutes? We can talk as soon as I finish with Mrs. Wisdom; something about her flowers. She wants to shoot the kids that are running through her yard. I'll be with you as soon as I hang up." She forced another smile on her face.

Doug looked at her. His face now filled with anger. "We need to finish this conversation and the sooner the better."

Mary went back to the call. "No, Mrs. Wisdom; that's not a good idea. Are you sure those boys on Elm Street are smashing the flowers? Why do you think they would come all the way from Elm to smash your flowers?" Mary was speaking into the receiver.

Doug tapped on the desk impatiently. Finally, after listening to Mary say, "Yes Mrs. Wisdom," for the tenth time, he said, "Hang up the phone Mary. I want to see you in my office, NOW!" Doug walked away without waiting for a response from Mary. He went into his office, let the door close, and stood staring at Mary through the glass. Mary could feel him glaring at her. She looked up briefly and gave a brief wave of acknowledgement. Doug did not wave back. He stood staring at her. She turned back to the front of the station.

"Mary, what the hell is going on?" Bryan asked for the tenth time.

"Call back in five minutes and tell me it's an emergency with the baby. Please Bryan, I think he knows." She was covering her mouth as she spoke quietly into the phone.

"What the hell are you still doing there? Get out of there now!" Bryan yelled.

"No, I can't. I don't know for sure that he does know, but Bryan, I think he knows. Just call back in five minutes please." She hung up the phone before Bryan could say another word. The phone rang back as soon as she hung up, this time she let the phone ring.

Robert walked into the station as the phone was ringing. He picked it up on the fifth ring, looking at Mary with a large question mark on his face. "Well hello to you Mrs. Wisdom."

Mary walked to Doug's office, poked her head in the door, and said, "I have to use the restroom. I've been sitting at that desk all day long. I won't be but a minute."

He glared at her not saying a word. She crossed her legs, made a face and pointed in the direction of the restrooms.

Mary turned and went to the bathroom. She could feel his eyes burning a hole in her back, but she refused to turn around. She walked straight into the bathroom holding her head high. As the door closed behind her, the blood which was pounding through her body seemed to disappear, as did all the strength in her legs. She slid to the floor securing the lock on her way down.

Shit, what the hell am I going to do? She felt her bladder suddenly full. *Why do I have to pee now?* She crawled to the toilet, used the handicap rail and lifted her weight off the floor. *What if he comes in here?* Mary thought as she quickly finished and pulled her pants up.

She washed her hands and looked at her reflection in the mirror. She wished she felt as confident as she looked. "What are you going to do now? Look at the mess you created. Damn, I'm so stupid." She saw a tear forming in her eye. "Come on, keep it together. Don't lose it now." She spoke to the reflection staring back at her. She felt scared.

She left her reflection and moved to the door. "On the count of three, open the door. One, shit. Two, damn. Three, no, it's too soon." She waited a moment and then willed herself to grab the door handle, open the door and walk out. She immediately turned back around, grabbed the door handle, opened the door and turned the light out. She wanted to step back in, to stay in the refuge of the bathroom. She pulled the door closed behind her. As she removed her hand from the handle, the phone rang. She listened to the ringing, waiting for Doug to pick it up. Robert was standing near the front door ready to walk out. Mary did not move toward the phone.

Robert threw his hands up, "What the hell Mary?" He headed back to the phone. He looked at her with both confusion and impatience written on his face.

"No don't," she said. She was waiting for Doug to answer it. She knew it was Bryan.

"Mary?" Robert asked.

"Not now Robert." She shook her head and headed for Doug's office. There was a fake smile plastered on her face, again.

"Well Doug?" She inquired.

He had the phone to his ear and waved her to a seat. After a few moments he said. "I'm sure Mary didn't mean to hang up on you Mrs. Wisdom. I have to let you go. There's a bank robbery taking place right now and I have to go."

Mary wanted to laugh. It was common to make an excuse to get off the phone with Mrs. Wisdom, but usually, it was something she could never find out, but a bank robbery? Mary wanted to cry. She thought Bryan would be on the phone, not Mrs. Wisdom.

"Mary, we need to talk about this—test." Doug moved toward the open office door.

"Robert!" Doug yelled as Robert was exiting the building. "Answer the damn phones, we're in a meeting!" He slammed his office door not waiting for a response.

Mary was shocked. After all the years she had known Doug, his normal mild manner had all but disappeared. He knew. He knew and there was nothing Mary could do about it. Where the hell was Bryan? Why didn't he call? She had to pee again.

"Mary, I told you to drop this thing with that woman. Maybe you don't understand what I am saying and I don't know how to make it any clearer. We've known each other a lot of years. It's okay to tell me what you know. Why did you send in...no... whose blood did you send in? What is it you want to know?" Doug was now standing almost on top of her. "Mary, I need to know what you are thinking." He sounded cool, in control, and arrogant. "Mary, you are really putting me in a bad position here. You need to tell me what you know and stop the bullshit, after all, you have a family to worry about now and sometimes you need to make choices that effect your family, just like I have."

Mary wanted to respond. She tried to put her fake smile on, to think of something clever to say to Doug. She opened her mouth to speak, but nothing came out. She closed her mouth again. She looked into his eyes. He meant business. He was not going to back down and Mary knew it. She got scared. Maybe she could plead stupidity. No, that would not work. She felt her shoulders slump slightly. She lowered her eyes and a chill ran through her body. Any bit of nerve she had managed to muster, was now gone.

Mary wanted out of his office. She felt trapped. She felt trapped with not only a rapist and murderer, but with a sick human being. Doug was making her very nervous. She wished he would back up and move out of her way. She wanted to leave and stared at the door.

She moved her chair back slightly trying to put a little distance between her and the insane man in the room with her.

Doug moved in even closer to her, towering above the chair she sat on. He whispered in her ear, "I had the test canceled and all the evidence destroyed and the woman, the woman is gone."

Mary felt a cold chill run through her body as Doug's hot breath crossed her ear. A tear filled her eye.

A door slammed and the office window swayed. There was yelling in the outer office. Doug turned his head and Mary looked behind her. There, standing in the middle of the office, was Bryan.

Mary, at first feeling relieved, jumped up from the chair, knocking it over as she pushed past Doug. When she opened the door, it flew back almost hitting Doug as he followed her out. Mary's relief quickly turned to concern as drops of blood hit the station floor. Bryan's left hand was bleeding profusely.

"Bryan, what happened?" Mary asked as she raced through the small station.

Bryan yelled, "I've cut my hand Mary. Take me to the hospital now!" His voice scared Mary worse than Doug's did.

Doug grabbed her arm back saying, "Wait, we'll call the Doctor. Mary, we need to finish our conversation, now."

"I'm taking care of my family now you bastard." She jerked her arm away from Doug, grabbed Bryan's arm and headed out the door.

Doug called after her; his voice commanding Mary to do as he said.

Neither Mary nor Bryan turned around; Doug's imposing voice fell on deaf ears.

37

"What the hell happened to you?" Mary yelled. She was trying to help Bryan get up and into the truck.

Bryan scooted past the passenger's seat to the driver's seat. "You shouldn't be driving. Are you okay? Did you lose any fingers? Oh my God Bryan, answer me!" Bryan started the truck with his right hand. Mary stood outside of the truck shouting at him.

"Are you getting in or what?" Bryan yelled back.

Mary looked behind her. Doug and Robert were getting closer. "Fine," Mary said.

She jumped into the truck. The door closed by itself as Bryan shoved his foot onto the gas pedal.

"Are you trying to kill us both?" Mary momentarily forgot about Bryan's hand as she was thrown back and forth in the truck, almost landing on the floor. "Bryan, slow the hell down!"

Bryan eased off the gas, but not much. He took the crimson rag from his hand and threw his unused blood capsules on the seat.

Mary, now confused said, "What the...?" Her eyes were not seeing this. She needed a moment to take it all in. "I don't understand."

"It's fake blood. I'm fine. Remember last Halloween, we had the haunted house at the station? Well, we had this blood left and I thought, well, I did good, didn't I?" Bryan smiled at Mary, and then got serious. "I didn't like what I was hearing on the phone and then when I got there Doug was standing over you. Tell me what happened."

"Oh Bryan, it is Doug. I'm sure he knows that I know he knows. It's a big mess and he threatened you and Charley. You have to take the baby and go someplace safe. There's no way I'm risking your life or the baby's life. This is my job Bryan, I have to do this." She leaned toward Bryan.

"That poor woman, what he did to her. I turned my back on her and gave her back to Doug. God Bryan, what if he killed them? He said she was gone. What have I done? What did I do? What if he really did kill them? My job is to protect and serve. I served all right; I served that woman and her children up on a silver platter. Bryan what have I done?" Mary shook her head and tried to hold back the tears that were forming in her eyes.

"Let me think. First, we have to call the state police and get their help. Call the sitter and have her meet us at Chris' house. I don't think Doug would go there, do you?" She did not wait for an answer. "Bryan, you and Charley need to get out of town. Go to your sister's house." She grabbed Bryan's shoulder. "Please take care of our son. Please."

"Mary, the baby is taken care of. When I got off of the phone with you, I called the sitter to take Charley to my sister's house in Maysville. I told her not to tell a soul. She knew you were upset about a case and I told her that you would be working long hours and my sister would care for him. She will keep him safe. My sister loves him like her own child." Bryan pulled diaper wipes out of the glove compartment and began wiping the sticky goop from his hand.

"Mary, I know this is your job and I have no right, but honey, you are my wife and I love you more than the world itself. I'm not letting you go up against this man without me. Call the state police and have them meet us at Doug's house." Bryan drove on as Mary aired her protest. It did no good. "Just call the state police Mary. The only place I'm going is with you."

"I'll call them before we get to Doug's house. If he's at the station that means Patty is home alone." Mary sat back in the seat and worked on what she was going to say to Patty.

Mary was scared. She felt sick to her stomach and her heart would race every few minutes. This was not the sheriff's department she had joined. Traffic tickets, a few drugs and some underage drinking were what she had expertise in. She was in over her head and she felt like she was drowning. What if she found the family when she arrived there? What if Patty knew they were there and she knew how he kept them? Mary remembered when Patty and Doug got married. She remembered when they found out Patty was barren. Then later, Doug told everyone a one-night stand, while he and Patty were separated, produced a child. The woman, whose name was never mentioned, left the boy there for him. Of course, he had test completed on the child, and of course, the test proved the boy was his. What else could they prove? Little Doug was his own flesh and blood, but so were EJ and the baby girl that lived in a hole in the ground.

They approached the house quickly. Mary had made a decision. She looked at Bryan, "Please pull the truck over to the side of the road."

Bryan did as he was asked. He turned to Mary and saw the sick look on her face. "Mary, everything is going to be fine. It's all going to work out."

"Bryan, why are you doing this? You need to go home. This is not your job, it's mine. I can't let you go with me." She held his hand tight and looked into his eyes, "You need to be here for our child."

"Yes Mary, our child is an important part of my life, but you my dear, are the person I plan on growing old with. But WE need to be there. The only way you are going over to Doug's house, is if I go with you."

"The hell you are!" Mary jerked her hand from his.

"Well then to hell we go. I'll tell you one thing; you're not going to that house alone. You told me he has already killed one person you know about. How many others are there? You can go inside and I will stay outside and watch for him. But you my dear are NOT going alone. If the state police were here, I would be the first person to let you do your job. Hell Mary, if Robert were with you I would understand more, but that isn't the case. Either you do it my way, and I go with you, or I am putting my foot down and you aren't going at all. Mary, I love you too much and you have no back up. I know this is your job, but the bottom line is, you are MY wife and the mother of MY child! I have never asked you to choose between me and your job, but I am doing it now!" Bryan's face was red. He was shouting.

"Yes you have Bryan. When I was pregnant with Charley you asked me and I chose you and my son, but this is different. I'm not expecting a child. Please, just let me do the job I need to do. Bryan, don't interfere."

"Just forget it, Mary. You are so caught up in your woman's crap, you can't see the forest before your face, and damn Mary, that forest is pretty black. You CANNOT do this alone."

Mary knew there was no chance of changing Bryan's mind. "Fine, go with me, but you WILL sit in this truck! Let's go, I want to get there before Doug gets home." Mary was very agitated. "Do you hear me? You will sit in this damn truck!"

Bryan pulled the truck back on the road toward Doug's house and stepped on the gas. He said nothing as they approached the house.

"I love you, you stubborn old fool." Mary whispered just above the sound of the engine.

A smile crossed Bryan's lips. "Okay, I'm glad you finally see it my way. So what's the plan?"

"We call the state police and tell them to meet us there. I hope they hurry." Mary got on her cell phone and placed the call to the state police. As she was talking to Detective Milroy, a call beeped into her phone. She let the call go to voice mail. Mary gave the state police a very short version of what was happening; saying simply there is an issue with the sheriff and an involvement with murder and kidnapping and she was not on a secure line. They would be there soon. Soon however, would be at least an hour.

Mary retrieved her voice message. "Shit," was the message. It was from Doug. He was calling from the station. Mary had fifteen minutes to look at Doug's house.

38

Doug's house had always been beautiful. It sat in the middle of three hills. Beyond the hills lay a five-hundred acre pasture. The house and the land had been in Doug's family for many generations. It always passed to the eldest son, in Doug's case, as with his father, he was the only child. His father passed away when he was young. His grandfather passed, right before he married Patty.

A large porch covered the front of the house. There were three steps leading up to the porch bordered by bushes on each side. The house was grand for an area filled with farmhouses. The door and the front windows were made of cut glass that gathered the sunlight, turning it into a beautiful rainbow of colors on the wooden floors inside. The large house was painted white, but trimmed in a charcoal gray. It was a two-story house that was built in the late 1800's. The walkway from the street was quite long. Beautiful oak trees bordered the property around the house. The driveway, made of stone, ran up the left side of the property and pulled either straight to the back of the house where an old carriage house had been converted to a modern day garage or around to the front of the house.

Once inside the house there is a breathtaking set of oak stairs. Following the glorious set of stairs up, a crystal chandelier hangs evenly to the top of the stairs over a beautiful inlayed wooden floor in the foyer. To the left of the staircase is an old fashioned parlor; where two grand pillars, also oak, serve as an entrance way. Inside the parlor, eighteenth century European furniture fills the area. To the right of the stairs there is a large study with an enormous fireplace; the hearth six feet tall. Leather sofas and chairs along with a cherry desk give enough seating to read any of the thousands of books which decorate the walls. Beyond the stairs is a family room with modern furniture and an old stone fireplace. The huge kitchen is on the left side of the family room. It is filled with all modern day appliances in which Doug spent thousands of dollars to update a few years before. The kitchen leads to the dining room where an oversized table displays fine china imported the year the house was constructed. The dining room exits into the parlor which was used for after dinner drinks, and entertainment with a beautiful harpsichord as the center piece of the room. The family room, in the back of the house exits to a screened in porch with a bathroom and pantry which also exits into the kitchen. On the other side of the family room a door leads to the study which again would put you back in the foyer.

Upstairs are four large bedrooms, each with its own bathroom and a playroom unused for the last two years. The house and the land are prime real estate; it is the best estate for two counties.

All of the walls in the house were covered with wallpaper. Some of which Patty hated. She wanted to change it when they first decided to move to the house, but discovered the job was too much to undertake on her own and Doug did not want to help her do it. In fact, he flatly refused, telling her that if she did not like the way the house looked, to move out. Patty still lived there.

The house remained empty for years before Doug married. His grandfather had been locked in a nursing home; Alzheimer kept him there, while congestive heart failure killed him. His grandfather left him the house and a large inheritance when he died.

39

Mary and Bryan arrived at Doug's house. Bryan drove his truck up the driveway slowly. As he stopped the truck, Mary took off her gun belt and handed it to Bryan, "You may need this if Doug comes home."

"No Mary, I'm not taking your gun."

"Please Bryan; I'm sure Patty is the only one in the house. I don't think I need protection from her." She grabbed the door handle, "Bryan, stay in the truck. And stay down; I don't want Patty to see you."

Bryan protested but it did no good. Mary left the gun belt on the dash board out of Bryan's immediate reach. She got out of the truck, closed the door and walked up to the house.

It had been a while since Mary had seen Patty. Patty used to go to the station all the time when she was first married, but after about a year, she stopped going. Her visits into town also became less frequent. Mary thought it was strange, but never questioned Patty or Doug about it. She just figured Little Doug had kept Patty busy all of these years and quite frankly, they did not run in the same circles.

Mary rang the doorbell and waited. She rang the doorbell again. She stepped back off of the porch and looked. Mary was sure Patty's car was parked by the garage. She wondered where she was. She wondered if Doug had called her. No, Doug would not do that. She wondered if she knew anything about what was happening. Mary was pretty sure Patty did not know a thing, but then again, you never know; some women do strange things for the men they love.

"Hello!" Mary yelled out. Just then the front door opened.

"Yes, who is it? Can I help you?" The voice belonged to Patty.

"Hi Patty, it's me Mary." Mary walked back toward the front of the house.

"Oh Mary, you scared me. I was lying down. I've had such a bad headache. I guess I fell asleep. I'm glad you came by. I have to pick up Little Doug from practice in half an hour."

Mary climbed the stairs to the house and looked at Patty. She had on dark sunglasses and pulled at her hair to cover the left side of her face. "What's wrong Patty?"

"Oh you know me. When Doug got home the other night, I was helping him with his suitcase. I pulled as he pushed and the damn thing just jumped up and hit me in the eye," Patty explained.

"Wow that must have hurt. Can I see?" Mary was now standing right next to Patty. She could see how swollen the left side of her face was. Purple and yellow colors mixed with at least three shades of red.

"No, I'm fine." Patty turned toward the door. She could feel Mary's eyes on her face.

"You must have the house pretty cold for a sweater. I bet Doug is going to have a fit when he gets the electric bill. You guys did put that AC in a few years ago didn't you?" Mary wondered what surprises the sweater held, but she decided not to push her luck. Patty was a grown woman and she could walk out the door if she wanted to. Eliza could not. She had to stay the course she was on. Mary knew Doug hit Patty. She had not always known, but right now looking at the meek woman before her, she knew. Patty was once the life of the town. She planned and organized parties. Mary was surprised she had not put it all together before, when Patty stopped showing up for events. Doug always made her apologies. *I must be a really bad cop,* Mary thought as she stood looking at Patty.

"You know the last time I saw you, you had a broken arm. And come to think about it the time before that, you had fallen off the ladder and broken your leg. Patty, have you ever thought about going to work again? Life out on this farm may kill you one day." Mary could not help throwing that in. Why, in this day and age, would a woman let a man beat her was beyond her. Surely there had been signs before they got married, right? But then Mary remembered the man she worked with. He was never out of line at work. Doug never yelled or threw things or hit anyone.

"Two lives," Mary said out loud.

"What?" Patty asked.

"Oh nothing, I was talking to myself." Both women stood there. Mary was waiting on Patty to ask her in.

"Mary, you know Doug's at work right?" Patty asked.

"Patty, I was having a little trouble with Bryan's truck. I had to drive it today. Anyway, I was wondering if I could call Bryan." Mary found lying to Patty easy.

"Well, I, are you going to have to wait for Bryan? I have to pick up Little Doug." Patty asked sounding uneasy.

"I'm sorry to inconvenience you Patty, but you don't really mind, do you?"

"Sure Mary, come in. The phone is in the back. I'm going upstairs to change. I have to get going soon. I can't keep Little Doug waiting. Really, I can't keep him waiting." From the sound of Patty's voice, Mary understood.

Patty headed upstairs and Mary headed to the sun porch. She reached the phone and called her house. The machine picked up and Mary talked into the receiver. When she hung up the phone, she opened the back door and looked at the doors leading down into the cellar.

Mary went back through the house to the stairs. She yelled up, "Patty, I'm going now." She wanted to be sure Patty was still upstairs.

Patty said from the top of the stairs, "Okay, thanks for coming by, but please don't tell Doug you were here. He thinks when women get together all we do is talk about men." She was wearing a robe and Mary thought she would have plenty of time to check out the cellar.

Mary went out the front door, gave a quick wave to the truck, and then ran down the side of the house. She knelt down by a small window frame of the cellar, the glass long gone, and pulled her flashlight out. She stuck her head in to look around. It was dark and there seemed to be a wall in the way of her looking any further. The smell of mold mixed with dirt, stung her nostrils. A mouse ran across her hand. It scared her making her jump, bump her head and drop her flashlight sending it crashing to the ground in the cellar. She withdrew her head from out of the small wooden frame. Mary wiped her dirty, mouse touched hands on her pants.

She went around to the back of the house and found the doors to the cellar. She did not think she would find anything, or anyone inside just her flashlight, but she had to look, she had to be sure.

The doors were white washed and each had a small weathered metal handle. She struggled, pulling at the first door to no avail. She pulled on the second door, finally jerking it open. She peered in looking for her fallen light. There were spider webs hanging across the top of the entrance and Mary ducked as her foot found the first creaky step. She descended slowly; following a cleared path on the other wise dusty stairs. As she neared the bottom, she almost fell as one of the rotten steps gave way under her weight. After retrieving her light, she maneuvered around a cinder wall finding yet another set of steps, these carved from the earth itself. She bent down to look further in, shining her light through the space. Half of the lower cellar was collapsed in upon itself and was filled with dirt. In the other half contained a large cardboard box sitting next to the wall by the dirt steps. Mary peered into the box. She knew it was Eliza's box. The cheap toilet paper, powdered milk, and the few cans of cheap food gave it away.

Mary felt her lungs plead for oxygen and she took a deep breath filling her lungs with dust from the dirt that covered the ground. She was unaware that she had been holding her breath until that moment. She coughed deeply and spat out what she was sure was stale rotten dirt. She started walking back and noticed another set of footprints that seemed fresh. She put her foot next to one of them and saw the size compared closely to her own. "Oh Patty how could you?" Disappointment overtook Mary and she stood in the cellar trying to understand.

The sight of the mouse brought her back and she began making her way to the door, this time only breathing shallow breaths. As she reached fresh air, she refreshed her lungs, coughed again and took another large breath. She then turned to close the door. She could not take a chance of the door slamming and alerting Patty she was still there. She held the heavy door, slowly letting it descend back into place. She turned to leave and found herself standing face to face with Doug. She jumped and let out a long scream.

"What are you doing there Mary?" He asked as a smile crept to his lips.

"I, I'm just looking at your cellar Doug. What are you doing here? I thought you were at work." Mary asked as she took a step back.

"Oh no, I'm right here at my house. Why are you at MY house Mary? It's kind of funny because I was at YOUR house before I came here. Are you looking for something or should I say, looking for someone?" Doug grabbed for her arm, but Mary jerked back.

"What were you doing at my house?" Mary started to panic.

"I was looking for you, but I found your babysitter and Charley."

"What did you do to Charley?" Mary started to panic.

"They were leaving as I was driving up. Thank goodness my lights and siren worked. She pulled the car right over and we had a nice little chat. Now, what are you doing at my house?"

"Where is Charley? What did you do to my son?"

"Nothing yet, but that can change Mary. I'm just letting you know. Back off or I'll go to Maysville and pay a little visit to his aunt."

"I want to leave now Doug."

"Leave? No not yet; the fun is just starting Mary. I'm really kind of glad Charley is at his aunt's house. This way, when I'm done with you and Bryan, well, he won't have far to go to be with family."

"Please Doug, Patty is right inside. She knows I'm here." Mary looked up and saw Patty standing by a bedroom window watching below.

Doug followed Mary's eyes and saw Patty looking at the two of them. He waved to his wife and motioned for her to come out. She slowly emerged from the house moments later. Doug's eyes stared at Patty. Patty looked scared. Mary wanted to go to her, to tell her it was okay to leave, but Mary was cornered between Doug, the cellar and the house.

"Mary tells me you know she's here? I thought we talked about having people over, remember?" Doug's face was turning red and his voice was changing from a controlled person to a person on the verge of losing it.

Mary felt she needed to come to Patty's defense. She could now see his handy work completely. Patty had a deep cut on her cheek and a few small scratches next to her eye. Her eyelid was swollen shut and Patty looked only from her right eye. Her arms, which were now exposed, showed distinct finger mark bruises on her skin. Her neck bared similar marks.

"No Doug. Leave her alone. It was me. I came and she knew nothing about it."

No one said a word or moved for a few minutes. It seemed the whole world was in a quiet hush. Patty looked at Doug. Doug looked at Patty. Mary looked first at both Patty and Doug then looked for a way out.

"Doug, I need to go and Patty didn't you say something about picking up Little Doug? Perhaps now would be a good time to leave. You mustn't be late."

Patty headed back into the house. When she got to the door Doug said, "No Patty, I need you for a moment." Patty stopped and turned back around. He turned toward Mary and said, "Last time I looked, this was MY house. Remember, we went over that a few minutes ago? I give the orders at MY house. You know, if anyone should leave, it should be you." He turned toward Patty and said, "Patty get dressed in something else and go get Little Doug while I talk to Mary. I really don't know why she's here."

Patty looked forlornly at Mary. She said nothing doing as ordered, leaving Doug and Mary alone outside.

Doug grabbed Mary's arm. He pulled her to the side of the house.

"You're hurting me," she said as she struggled to break free.

"Oh, you think I'm hurting you now? You haven't seen anything yet. Where is that husband of yours? You left with him and that fake blood. What do you think, I'm stupid? And you bitch; you cut me with that damn razor. I looked like a real asshole going over to that boy's house. Oh you are so dead for what you did. No wait, I think I'll just send you to prison. You know that might just work out so much better. I don't even have to do anything to you. You are under arrest for assault with a deadly weapon on a police office. You screwed up and do you think anyone will believe you once I get done?" He laughed a sneering laugh.

Mary felt goose bumps growing on her arms. She also felt his fingers digging deeper, only stopping because of her bones. He shoved her face into the side of the house.

"And that lady and her kids will be long gone. Never to be seen again. You just couldn't let it drop could you?" He sneered in her ear.

"Does that include Little Doug? He's one of her kids isn't he?" He jerked her arms up behind her back and she screamed out in pain.

"I've called the state police and they're on their way." Mary managed to say. Her arm bones felt as if they would snap in a moment. Doug continued to shove them further behind her back.

"Oh that's fine, they will find nothing here. Why would you think I would keep them here? Oh stupid woman. Why are all the women in the world so very stupid?"

He pinned her body against the house using his body and she felt his penis harden. "You are under arrest Mary. Do you want me to read you your rights or do you know them already?" He still had her against the house. He held her arms with one hand and pulled his cuffs out with the other. She pushed back against him, but it did nothing but add pain to her already sore arms.

"Hold still, will you? You know you are just making this harder." He finally managed to get the cuffs on her, but kept her pinned against the house with his body. "Oh yes Mary, you are making this so much harder." He rubbed against her again. "I guess I have to check you. Where's your gun Mary?" Doug felt down the front of her body. "I'm glad you decided against the vest today," he whispered as he fondled her breast.

Mary jerked her shoulders from side to side. "Stop it Doug! Get your damn hands off of me! I don't have my gun, I, I left my gun in the truck. Stop touching me you sicko!"

"Oh not so fast my dear; let me see what you have down these pants." He ran his hand over her butt; reached her thighs and made his way, inch by inch, toward her private parts.

Mary squeezed her legs together, but Doug kicked them open; exposing her most intimate parts to his wandering hands. He grabbed her and she winced in pain. "Got a tight little package there Mary? You know I can tell. I know Bryan can't be that big. I saw him in the shower at the pool one summer. I bet he doesn't make you scream, does he?"

Mary threw her head back, striking Doug in the face. He responded by striking her head on the house.

Mary was hurt. As stars danced around her head, she tried to focus on getting away. She tried again to talk to Doug. "Please Doug, stop. You don't want to do this here, not with Patty in the house." His hands were still wandering over her body. He ripped her shirt open and tore at her lacy bra exposing her breast. He reached for her nipples and squeezed until his fingers met. Pain radiated through her breast making her scream in agony. With tears in her eyes she begged again. "Please Doug. Please don't do this." Her voice was no louder than a whisper.

"You know I always wanted you." He rubbed himself against Mary again. As Doug reached for his zipper he heard a CLICK in his ear.

"What the ...?" He turned around to the barrel of a gun.

"Get your hands off of my wife." Bryan did not yell. His voice was steady and firm.

"Bryan," Mary breathed as relief swept over her.

"Doug, if you try anything, I swear, I will shoot you." Bryan took Doug's gun from his holster and tossed it at the house. The gun bounced once and went into the window frame Mary had been looking in earlier. "Now back away from Mary."

Doug took a few steps away from Mary turned to Bryan and said, "Look you caught us. We're having an affair. Now be a good boy and go home. I don't want to hurt you Bryan."

"No Doug, I don't think so, now undo those cuffs."

Doug reached into his pocket and pulled the keys out as Patty yelled, "Doug, where are you?"

"Honey, we're over here!" Doug yelled back.

"Shut up and get those cuffs off," Bryan said.

Doug did not move.

"I told you to get those cuffs off. Now move." Bryan's lips barely moved as he spoke through clenched teeth.

Patty made her way around to the side of the house. "What's going on here? Doug, I thought Mary was leaving." She pulled her sunglasses up exposing her face.

Bryan looked at her and then exchanged glances with Mary. "Patty, what happened to your face?" Bryan took a step forward exposing the gun in his hand.

"You all should just go now, I'll deal with Doug. I'm sure they meant no harm Doug. They don't know anything. I swear, I didn't say a thing Doug." Patty's voice pleaded with her husband.

"Deal with me? Who do you think you are? And they know you stupid bitch. So just shut up." Doug took a step forward. Patty shielded her face.

Mary asked, "Patty, do you know where she is?"

"Shut up Patty!" Doug yelled.

"The lady and her children, where are they? It's okay Patty, just tell me where they are. I can help you." Mary took a few steps forward leaving Doug at her back.

"No, you don't understand. I can't say anything. You don't know what it's like Mary. You don't know what he will do. I don't know anything. Do you hear me? I don't know anything. Doug, please let them go. Don't do this, I ..."

"Just shut up Patty." Doug looked over at Bryan, dropped his keys and lunged toward him. Bryan, Doug and the gun went to the ground.

As the gun hit the ground two hands wrapped around the gun's grip and trigger. A shot pierced through the sounds of the men's struggle. Everyone stopped moving and looked around.

Patty looked down at her sweater. The red of her sweater began to leak down the front; landing on the ground directly in front of her. Patty grabbed her stomach. She pulled her hands up and turned them over. Blood covered her dainty white hands. "Doug, I didn't tell them anything about that woman and the boy. I fed them when I could so they wouldn't die. Who is going to feed them now?"

"Oh my God Patty, please tell me where they are!" Mary yelled.

Bryan scrambled to his feet and rushed toward Patty as she fell to her knees. "Hold on Patty." He whispered as he helped her to the ground.

Bryan glanced over his shoulder, "Get help, Doug!"

"No, I don't think so," Doug said.

Mary looked over at Doug. Doug was now holding the gun. It was pointed straight at Bryan.

"She's your wife for God sake." Bryan said. "It was an accident, no one meant to shoot her. She needs help."

Patty lifted her arm and pointed, "Over there," was all she managed to say before Doug shot her square in the head.

"I told her to shut up." Doug's voice was cold without emotion. "I think this is the best thing that could happen to her. Just think Mary, now we can add murder to your little list of felonies." He pointed the gun at Mary. "I have to clean up a little mess first though. Bryan, do you want a nice clean shot to the head or somewhere else?"

"Doug, have you gone mad? Let him go, you have me, you don't need Bryan. Please Doug, just let him go." Mary was begging for her husband's life.

"No, see that won't work for me." Doug said calmly. "Come on Bryan, now get a move on and get over here."

Bryan did as he was told.

"Any last words?" Doug asked.

"I" was the only word that left Bryan's mouth.

"See how easy that is?" Doug asked as the shot rang out.

"No!" Mary screamed as Bryan fell forward landing on Doug. "Bryan!" Mary yelled.

"Go, just go." Bryan said as his blood poured out of the hole in his chest, soaking Doug.

"Don't worry about me. Just go."

Mary looked at her husband, "Bryan, I'm sorry." She took off running, her hands still cuffed behind her back. She headed up the hill behind the house.

"Bitch don't you run from me! Get off of me Bryan." Doug struggled as he rolled Bryan off of him.

Mary heard another gun shot, but did not feel any pain. She then turned and saw the gun pointed in her direction. *Oh my God, he missed me. I cannot believe he missed me.* She ducked behind a tree.

Doug started yelling, "I'll just tell everyone we were having an affair; and you killed my wife and then killed Bryan! You bitch, come back here! I'm not going to kill you Mary!"

Mary was in shock. Bryan's blood had spattered on her. "I'm sorry Bryan. Why didn't you just stay in the truck?" She moved farther into the woods that surrounded the house and hid behind an old oak tree. She peered down at the house. The evening sunlight threw a spotlight on Doug, his wife and her husband. She reached for her phone then remembered it was still in the truck in the front of the house.

"Damn those state police; where are they?" Mary quietly asked.

Doug was looking down at his wife. He bent down next to her and then looked to the hills behind his house and yelled, "You will pay for this bitch! I loved her and you will pay for this." He wiped what Mary thought were tears from his eyes. He moved past his wife and walked to where Bryan lay on the ground. Mary saw him kick Bryan in the back. Doug again pointed the gun at Bryan; then bent down and appeared to be talking to him.

She did not know if Bryan was alive or dead, but he was a big guy and he was shot only once. Maybe he was still alive. She watched Doug with the gun then heard Bryan yell, "Go Mary, get out of here!" Doug pointed the gun at Bryan's head.

Mary cried out, "No!" She covered her mouth.

Doug yelled, "Come out, come out, wherever you are or I'll huff and I'll puff and I'll blow this fucker away!" The gun was still pointed at Bryan's head.

Jesus Christ, he's gone crazy; he's completely crazy, Mary realized. *I don't know what to do. God, what do I do? Please tell me what to do.*

"You have until the count of three. Let's count by piggies shall we?" He yelled into the woods.

Oh my God, he's going to kill him. Mary was shaking. *Stay put or he's going to kill you too*, she thought to herself.

"One little piggy, two little piggies!" He yelled.

"Three ..."

"NO, STOP, please Doug! Don't kill him, I'm coming out." She moved slowly and he raised his gun toward her.

A bullet passed by her ear at the same moment she heard the shot. She slid down next to the tree she had been hiding behind, landing on her already sore left shoulder.

"Are you dead bitch?" He yelled as she fell. He shot again and the bullet landed between her legs with a poof, as it made its way into the ground. "I know I'm getting closer, just yell out when I hit you!" A few more shots rang out hitting the ground around Mary.

"Oh my God, STOP!" The bullets kept missing her.

Doug fired a few more shots into the woods as Mary rolled from side to side.

Mary watched Doug turn back toward Bryan. She needed to get her handcuffs off or at least get her arms in front of her body. Pain ripped through her arms and neck as she managed, after much struggling; to bring the cuffs under her butt, around her legs and to the front of her body.

Mary needed to get to Bryan before Doug killed him. He was pacing back and forth in front of Bryan. Mary stayed low to the ground trying her best not to disturb the leaves and branches. She slowly made her way down the hill.

"Are you watching this Mary? I hope you are still alive; I wouldn't want you to miss this." She heard the click of the gun as it neglected to fire. Doug had the gun at Bryan's head.

"Now I have to go get MY gun." Doug gave Bryan a swift kick in the face and headed into the house, his back to Mary.

Mary ran to Bryan.

"Bryan, are you still alive?" She shook him.

"What?" Bryan replied.

"Can you get up?" Mary was not waiting for an answer as she began pulling Bryan up by his shoulders.

"I don't know," Bryan replied.

"Help me Bryan, please get up. You have to help me or we are going to die here." She pulled on Bryan, finding strength she never knew existed.

"Where are the keys Bryan? Do you have the keys?" She patted his pockets as she helped him stand.

"Keys?" Bryan asked. "What do we need keys for?"

She managed to get Bryan moving, but he was losing blood. "Just get to the truck; everything is going to be fine. We just have to get to the truck." Mary watched the blood drip from her husband as they stumbled toward the truck. Bryan fell three times and each time Mary would coax him back up and closer to the truck.

Mary leaned him against the passenger side of the truck and patted his pockets again. This time she found what she was looking for and reached her hand into his pocket.

"Not now honey, wait until we get home. What will the neighbors think?" Bryan slurred the words coming out of his mouth.

"Bryan, come on; we have to go, get in the truck." She opened the door and pushed him in. His legs got caught on the handcuffs that were still attached to her wrists. Mary winced in pain. "Please Bryan, help me, move your leg." He did as he was told, but fell backward onto the driver's seat.

Mary did not care. She slammed the door and ran around the truck. She could barely see as tears blocked her view. She thought about Patty and going back for her; she knew she could not. They needed to get out of there and fast. Bryan was her first concern now. "Why didn't you just stay in the truck?" she mumbled.

Doug came out of his house and said, "What's this, the walking dead? Are you going somewhere?"

Mary did not stop moving. She jumped in the driver's side as Doug ran down the front steps. He had his gun in hand and began firing at her and the truck.

"I hope you left that husband of yours. I wasn't finished with him yet!" He looked to the side of the house as Mary started the truck. She threw the truck in reverse and mashed on the gas. Doug followed the speeding truck; shooting. Each time a bullet made contact with the truck, Mary screamed. She was preparing for the pain of a bullet ripping through her body.

"Forget you Doug; we ARE going someplace, someplace away from you!" Mary slammed the truck into drive, barely missing Doug as he jumped out of the way. She turned the wheel, running through the pretty flowers she assumed Patty had planted. As she sped off; the truck kicked up small rocks, dirt and flower petals straight into Doug's face.

The truck was hard to control and Mary realized Doug must have flattened some of the tires. She was driving on the rims of the truck. The big half-ton barely seemed to move and seemed to have a mind of its own. Mary pushed the gas pedal to the floor, but it did no good. She was only inching down the highway.

She managed to get the handcuff key off the gun holster she had left in the truck. She had a hard time putting the key in the hole, but finally managed the feat. The truck wanted to drive itself off the road and her hands were shaking. She repeated over and over, "Hold on Bryan. Just hold on."

Mary wanted to call and talk to Charley. She needed to call and make sure he was okay, but right now she could not. Bryan was bleeding to death in his own truck.

The sun began to disappear from the sky. Mary reached for the head-lights, almost sending the truck into a ditch.

She took her shirt off holding it on Bryan's bleeding chest, keeping pressure on his wound. A flicker of light caught her attention in the rearview mirror. She saw a vehicle fast approaching. It had barely taken Doug any time at all to catch up with the pair. He was now shooting his gun out of his car window. He hit the back window of the truck and the crashing sound of the glass scared Mary, "Stop, why don't you just stop?" She yelled.

She drove down the long road and knew there was no way she would ever get to the hospital. Doug was getting too close and Bryan was bleeding too badly. She took a sharp turn left and slammed on the brakes causing Doug to smash into the driver's back quarter panel. "Screw you," she said as the car bounced a few feet back. Mary took off again, momentarily losing control of the truck. She heard metal grinding from the rims as they gripped their teeth into the road. She had finally taken back command of the large truck. She looked in the side mirror and saw smoke pouring out of the front of Doug's smashed car. A moment later he was standing outside of his car; gun in hand, shooting the air between where he stood, and the truck that was now barreling down the two lane country highway.

When Mary looked back a few minutes later, there was nothing but road in the mirror. She felt elated. She and Bryan had made it. They had gotten away. They had won. She turned on the inside light and looked down at Bryan; he was no longer on the seat. She could hear him breathing, not an easy quiet breathing, but a rattle. A shiver ran through Mary's spine; it sounded like a death rattle. The joy she had felt moments earlier fell from her heart. She had won the battle, but was losing the war.

40

The control Mary had on Bryan's truck was quickly fading. It now seemed almost impossible for Mary to control it as it grunted and grinded around each turn. Going up the hills of the road were even worse, and seemed at times unattainable, as the truck choked and hissed. Steering down the hills only worked if Mary kept her foot firmly planted on the brake. Mary moved on. She needed help for Bryan. With the hospital so far away, Mary steered the truck toward Doctor Denton's house. She was quickly becoming exhausted. "Hold on Bryan," she whispered. The pain in her shoulders, arms and legs screamed, but she did not have time to listen to her muscles. Bryan's breathing was becoming shallow.

Mary hit the edge of town. There was nobody out. She was a little surprised people were not looking to see where all the noise was coming from; but then again, she had more important things to worry about, then how much noise the slow moving truck was making as she pulled onto Main Street. "We're here Bryan, just hold on." She placed his hands on her shirt covering the bullet wound. She did not have to worry about turning the truck off as she jumped from the vehicle, setting the parking brake. The engine lost all power and merely coasted the last hundred feet.

Mary raced to the front door of Doctor Denton's house. As she banged on the door she yelled, "Help! We need help! Please Doc, we need help!"

Mrs. Denton finally answered the door. She wore a bathrobe, slippers and curlers in her gray hair. "What is it? Who's there?" She asked as she fumbled with her glasses.

"Bryan's been shot and I need Dr. Denton. Where is he?" Mary walked past Mrs. Denton into the house. She looked around the living room as if she expected him to be sitting there watching TV.

"He ran to Kenny's house to get me eggs for breakfast. I forgot to buy them at the store. Mary, what's going on?" Mrs. Denton looked at Mary. Mary was covered in blood and wearing nothing but her uniform pants and her torn bra.

"Please, help me get Bryan out of the truck. Doug has shot him. Bryan's lost a lot of blood. Patty's dead I think. I left her at Doug's house. He's gone crazy. He tried to kill me." Mary grabbed Mrs. Denton's hands and begged. "Please help us. Call Doc and tell him to come home now and don't tell him Bryan and I are here. We don't have much time." Mary let go of Mrs. Denton's hands and went to the door. She opened the door and said, "Please hurry Mrs. Denton. Doug's not done with us yet."

Mrs. Denton placed the call to Kenny's house and simply said she needed Doc home. She told him there had been a call and he might have to go out tonight. She sounded old and confused on the phone and Mary hoped the poor lady did not raise any unwanted suspicion. Mrs. Denton hung up the phone. She went to her closet and pulled out a wheelchair.

"Here, I've got this. I don't know how you and I are going to carry Bryan. He's such a big man." Mrs. Denton pushed the chair toward the truck. "I should have put on better shoes," she said as she arrived at the truck. The ground was wet from night dew and her slippers slid as she pushed the wheelchair through the grass to the truck.

It was hard getting Bryan out of the truck. He was dead weight. Mary thought he was indeed dead. It had been a while since he responded to her. She felt his neck for any sign of life and finally found a weak pulse. She pulled him by his legs bringing him to the edge of the floor board. She then pulled his arms up, bringing him to a sitting position. Sweat rolled from her brow. She had Mrs. Denton hold the chair as she pulled and twisted Bryan. He fell to the chair rocking it back and forth. Blood squirted from his mouth and as Mary reached to wipe it, she felt him breathe. "Stay with me Bryan," she whispered in his ear. The two women managed to get him in the house.

Mrs. Denton felt for his pulse again. "It's weak Mary, but still there. "I don't know. He looks really bad." Mrs. Denton shook her head. "I should call Kenny's again and find Doc."

The front door slammed a moment later, "What the hell happened?" Doc asked as he walked into the house. "I followed a trail of blood across the yard."

His eyes first went to Mary who was covered in blood. He raced to her, his limp seemed to disappear. Mrs. Denton turned exposing her blood filled robe. Doctor Denton stopped, put his hands out and asked, "Who's hurt?"

"Not me, Bryan." Both women said in unison, dropping their hands to Bryan, who was slumped over in the wheelchair.

"Doug shot Bryan. I can't explain now. I have to go. Please take care of Bryan." Tears were streaming down her face.

Doctor Denton went to Bryan. "He's in real bad shape and he has lost a lot of blood. Mary, I don't think he's going to make it." He shook his head as he examined him. "I just don't know." He wheeled Bryan to his office at the back of the house, Mary following behind. He reached in his bag and put a tight bandage packed with gauze around Bryan. He then started an IV. "We need to get that bullet out and he needs blood fast. I just don't have what he needs here. Help me get him to the van and I'll take him to the hospital.

If we wait too much longer he will surely die!" Doc's voice was full of the urgency Mary had felt from the moment Bryan was shot.

Doc Denton wheeled Bryan out to his van. "Help me get him in. We only have a little time now."

"Bryan must not die Doc. If Doug finds out he is with you, he may kill you too. I'm sorry; I just didn't know what to do." Mary was out of breath. Bryan was heavy and she held most of his weight.

"Bryan, hold on honey. I love you. Do you hear me Bryan? I said I love you." Mary moved away from the van.

"Mary, I'll do my best. And don't worry about Doug; I don't think anyone is going to see Bryan for a while." He grabbed Mary's hand, "I'll do my best to save him." Doctor Denton then started the van and drove off.

"Mary," Mrs. Denton said. She waited for her to respond. "Mary!" She said again.

"What?" Mary turned around.

"A shirt, I thought you might need a shirt." Mrs. Denton held out a tee shirt and a wet washcloth.

"I'm sorry Mrs. Denton. I'm really sorry to bring this to you and your family. It's real important though; if anyone asks, we have not been here. Please get your hose and clean this blood up before someone sees it."

"Go now Mary, don't worry about us. We'll be fine." Mrs. Denton said as she pushed Mary toward the truck. "I'll clean the blood and follow Doc to the hospital. You go now."

Mary ran back to Mrs. Denton and hugged her. She looked her straight in the eyes and said, "No matter what happens, no matter what you hear; I didn't do this. I love Bryan, and I liked Patty. I thought Doug was a different man. I'm sorry for bringing you into this. I'm sorry for bringing Doc into this. God, I'm so sorry."

Tears fell from Mary's eyes as she ran to the truck. She got in the driver's side, pulling on the shirt Mrs. Denton had given her. She tried to start the truck, but it did no good. She took the brake off and started rolling. She needed another vehicle. The truck bounced and the steel rims grinded in the road as she slowly went down the hill away from Doctor Denton's house.

Her hands stuck to the steering wheel. Mary pulled them off one at a time and wiped Bryan's blood on the wash cloth. "I'm sorry Bryan, there is so much blood, I'm so sorry." There were no tears in her eyes. She had nothing left to cry.

Mary tried to focus. With shaky hands she picked up the phone and dialed Bryan's sister's house. Sara answered on the third ring. Charley was safe, secure and sleeping. He had missed his afternoon nap. Mary's phone battery went dead. Her heart picked up though. Charley was safe.

Mary's whole plan had gone to hell and she needed to think. She needed a vehicle and she still needed to find Eliza. *One thing at a time,* she told herself.

"The station," She yelled.

She knew where she was going. It would be difficult, but she had to go back to the police station to pick up her vehicle. She pointed the truck east. Going less than one thousand times the speed of light; she went back, to what had been her second home. How things can change in the course of an afternoon.

41

Mary parked down the road from the station. She had no choice; the truck found level ground and stopped rolling. She pulled it to the side of the road as best she could and made her way to the station on foot. She was watchful of the few passing cars. She did not know what Doug was telling people. She felt as if she was being hunted like a wild animal.

As she neared the station, she realized taking her SUV out of the parking lot would be a challenge. She looked at the keys in her hand and saw she had Bryan's keys; hers were still in the station. She would have to go inside.

She crept around the back of the station and saw a motorcycle was the only company her vehicle shared. Robert was the only one there. He was her friend. *Well, it could be worse*; Mary thought to herself, *it could be Saul. Hell, it could be Doug.* She edged her way toward the back door and tried the handle. The door was locked. "Damn," Mary said a little too loud. She covered her mouth. The roads were too quiet for comfort; the street-lights a little too bright, and Mary a little too shaken. She pushed on despite all these facts.

She made her way to the front of the building and looked in the glass doors. Robert sat at his desk with his back in the direction of the door. She turned the doorknob, not a sound. She pushed the door open slowly, the bell rang. Mary stopped in her tracks; however, Robert did not turn around.

"Hold on a minute," Robert said with a wave.

Robert continued talking on the phone. "Yea, everyone is out looking for her. He said she shot his wife and Bryan. No, I can't believe it either. Do you know he told me they were having an affair? I thought she really loved Bryan. Now I could see Doug sleeping around on Patty, but Mary sleeping around on Bryan? I have to go Saul; I have to get Doc Denton on the phone and call the coroner. Saul, let me know if you find her." There was a pause. "You know we were friends. I just want to know what happened to her." His conversation ended.

Robert was a great guy and a great police officer, but Mary had noticed the "were friends," and her heart broke just a little.

"Now what can I do for you?" Robert asked as he turned.

"Mary?" Robert's mouth fell open. "What the hell are you doing here? Everyone's out looking for you. What happened? Why did you come here? I heard you left Doug standing in front of his car after you killed Patty and shot Bryan. Saul had to pick up Doug and now the state police are all over his house."

He looked her up and down. She had a clean shirt on, but blood covered her hair, face, arms, pants and even her shoes. "Oh my God; it's true. What were you thinking? Have you lost your mind?"

Robert looked at her hands held behind her back. "Please don't tell me you have a gun Mary. You're not going to shoot me too are you? We are friends, right?" Robert started to sweat although the temperature in the room was a cool sixty-eight degrees.

Within a split second he grabbed for his gun. "Just hold it right there, Mary." He said his voice and hands shaking.

"Robert wait, you have to listen to me." Mary said taking a step in his direction.

"What do you have behind your back Mary?" He pointed the gun toward her arm and waited for an answer.

Mary slowly brought her hands up so he could see the only thing in her hands was a bloody rag. "Robert please, it's not true. It's all just a lie. Doug killed his own wife and Bryan is alive. I took him to Doc Denton's house and he took him to the hospital. This is his blood Robert." She looked down at the blood that covered her. "Oh my God, he's lost so much blood."

"What are you doing here? I have to call this in Mary. I love you like you were my sister, but I have to let them know you're here." Robert reached for the microphone.

"No wait. Please, if you don't believe me, call Doc Denton's house. Just ask where he is. Please Robert, just do it. I won't move, I swear."

"Shit Mary, he said you two were having an affair and he wanted to break it off. Said you went crazy and killed his wife and Bryan." He still had her at gunpoint.

"Is that what you think? Do you think I would throw away my life on that man? He's the one who held that woman. He raped and tortured her and he knows I know. Poor Patty was so scared of Doug. She walked into this mess and got shot."

"Oh please Robert, you need to believe me. It was Doug that shot Bryan. He just pulled the trigger and shot him right there in front of me." Mary was having a hard time speaking.

"Shit Mary, I don't know what to believe." Robert found his chair and sat down. "What are you doing here?"

"I need a car Robert. I left my keys here and I need my SUV. Doug shot up the truck."

"Okay Mary, your keys are over there." He pointed to her desk where she had left the keys.

"Go get them. But walk slowly and I want to see your hands." Robert watched her as she moved to her desk.

"I need to clean up, for a moment, just wash my face. Robert, are you listening to me?" Mary waited for a response.

"Go on, but you need to hurry. Saul will be here shortly." Robert then added, "I don't know why I am doing this Mary. You know I could lose my job and go to jail for helping you?"

"I know Robert, thank you." She grabbed her keys and went into the restroom.

She opened the soap dispenser pouring the antibacterial soap up and down her arms and filled the blood soaked washcloth with the same soap. She put her head close to the sink trying to extract the blood from her hair. She washed quickly scrubbing her husband's blood from her body. She did not stop to look in the mirror, but managed to pull her hair back.

She walked back out still mostly covered in blood. She grabbed a rubber band and looked to Robert, "Can you give me five minutes to get out of here before you call?" Mary noticed his gun was back in its holster. "How about that gun?"

"I'll give you five minutes Mary. The gun, no way, but I'll give you five minutes. Now go before I change my mind." Robert yelled out as she left, "Good luck Mary!"

Mary made her way out and took off. She turned the radio on to listen for Robert's big broadcast.

True to his word, Robert waited five-minutes. "Is anyone out there?" Robert yelled into the handset.

Mary blew a kiss at the radio and knew she could count on Robert. She hoped Doug would think differently; he was killing people and she did not want Robert to be a victim.

Saul replied, "What's going on there?"

"Mary came here. She hit me on the head; I guess she knocked me out. I don't know how long she's been gone."

"Do you know where she's going?" John asked.

"No, I'm sorry; she didn't give me her agenda." Robert replied.

Sounding as sarcastic as ever Saul said, "Shit Robert, what the hell were you doing in there, sleeping? It's not like we're THAT busy."

"No Saul, I was talking to you."

The airways were quiet for a moment then John said, "Someone better inform Doug, and Robert, he's going to be pissed."

"God Robert, how could you let her get away? She murdered Patty, shot and probably killed Bryan and God only knows what she's going to do now. She may want to finish what she started." Saul sounded perturbed.

"Oh I'm sorry Saul, in case you forgot, I was getting hit on the head." Robert snippily replied.

"I suggest you start doing your job before you don't have one to do," Saul snapped.

John said, "Robert I'll come to the station. I know how close you and Mary are. I know this isn't easy for you."

"No, John. Let Robert stay there since it's HIS job tonight. You have to go pick up Little Doug and do NOT take him home. Doug wants him away from the house in case Mary comes back. The state police are there, but he wants to make sure the little guy is safe. We just don't know what she will do next and if anything happens to Little Doug, it's your ass."

"You know Saul, if I was you, I would surely watch my back. You've been such an asshole toward Mary lately; she might be coming for you, over and out."

Mary could not believe how Robert had ended the radio conversation. Maybe he was indeed still her friend and someone she could trust.

42

A moonless night overflowing with darkness filled the sky. A cloud acting as a ⬥ covered the stars. Mary knew it would soon turn into fog ⬥ ...ds fell closer covering the earth. She pulled into ... ...own and looked at the area maps of the c... ... roads, farms and the waterways. Mary k... ...to Doug's house in order to find Eliza and h... ...e area she lived in, but driving on other p... ...ing she did not do. She knew the roads wou... ...th police, both local and state. She stared at the ma... ...d her path. As the fog rolled in, she was unsure if it woul... or hinder her efforts. She prayed it gave her the cover she needed to arrive at Doug's house without being detected.

Mary slowly put the vehicle in gear and pulled away. She hated turning the lights on, but knew she needed the illumination to light her path. She had a plan to get to Doug's house, but lacked a plan once she was there. She was going to play it by ear. She drove on, quietly and slowly, she drove on.

The drive to Doug's house was risky. She dodged cows on one farm and goats on another. She feared she had hit a small dog on one, but when she backed up to see if the animal could be saved, she found it was a coyote. Although she loved all animals, Eliza and her children were more important.

She traveled slowly, opening gates and closing them. She heard on the radio the state police were at Doug's house. They discovered Bryan in the hospital. He was alive, but in critical condition having surgery. He was not awake. She wanted to be with him. To hold his hand and tell him to hold on, but she knew if she went near the hospital she would be arrested on sight. "Hold on my sweet Bryan." She whispered to the darkness that fell around her. "Hold on."

She finally arrived at what she thought was the back end of Doug's farm. She never realized just how much land he owned. It was going to be like looking for a needle in a haystack with the fog thick in the night air.

She put the SUV in low gear, turned off the lights and slowly made her way through the fields and over the hills. The drive was slow. She looked around not knowing what to look for, but she looked anyway. She was looking for something, looking for anything. She saw nothing.

A glow of light lit up the sky as Mary got closer to the house. She headed for the trees she so carefully tried to avoid on her drive in the darkness to Doug's. She needed some kind of cover. She turned off the motor and decided to sit and wait. Wait for what, she did not know, but something was telling her to be still and not move.

Mary pulled her binoculars out and watched the house. There was a frenzy of activity taking place. The police were marking off the area where blood stained the ground. In the midst was Doug, wiping his face. Mary wondered if he was trying to wipe away his sin. "That tiny tissue won't do. Hell, the whole box won't do." Mary whispered.

Mary sat in her SUV in the woods near Doug's house. The state police had come and gone and Patty had been removed. Mary was afraid they would stay all night, but Doug must have insisted they leave. Mary watched the last car pull off the property and all the lights in the house go dim. Nothing moved. The earth seemed to take the night off also. There were no sounds of crickets or sounds from bullfrogs that loomed in the ponds of the area. Silence and total darkness enveloped Mary. "I wonder if this is how Eliza felt her first night. I wonder if this is how she feels tonight. I hope she can still feel. GOD, what if I'm too late?" Mary had to be strong. She had to be right. Doug had to lead her to them before it was too late.

As Mary waited, she reflected on the life she had grown to love. Had she let it slip through her fingers? If Bryan died she would only have herself to blame. She sat and weighed the cost of life. Was Bryan's life worth the unknown woman and her children? Was Patty's life worth the cost? How many more people would die? What would the price be?

Mary thought for a long time. She cried, she felt alone; she felt helpless, and she felt brave. Mary needed to hold on to the brave right now; it was the only thing which was keeping her from running away, gathering HER family and leaving this small town all together. She knew once the sun began to rise, she would have no choice, but to leave. Right now she just sat and watched the house. She strained her eyes surveying the house; watching and waiting for any movement. She listened for any type of noise. She hoped she had not been seen, but expected at any moment the sanctuary of her vehicle would be breached. She feared her new home would be a jail cell even as her husband lay dying in the hospital.

Mary was tired. She felt her eyes getting heavy and would change the way she was sitting. Her leg would fall asleep and then her arm. She moved frequently, not wanting to give into the depression which seemed to overtake her. She did not want to fall asleep. The radio would crack on occasion, as the guys from the station would speak back and forth. At four in the morning, they called off the search for the night, ready to resume it at first light. Mary sat unyielding; she knew the next move was Doug's.

"You have to go to them Doug. Come on Doug" Mary tried to will Doug. She tried to speak to him as though she had found a way to reach inside his brain and insert a suggestion. It worked. A glimmer of light caught her eye. She looked at her watch; it was five-thirty in the morning. She watched the light and soon it reflected on a window by the house. Doug was on the move. Mary sat very still. She watched her breathing and slowly opened the door. It clicked. Mary looked up, hoping the sound did not echo throughout the land. She waited a few minutes longer and then slowly opened the door wider. The light inside clicked on. She quickly pulled the door back to its frame. She looked to where Doug was. The light was moving away from the house. He had not seen her. Her hands were shaking. She found the knob to turn off the inside light. She opened the door again. Nothing happened. She looked down to see what she was stepping on. She wanted to make no sound. No sound at all. She pushed the door almost closed.

She looked for Doug; she found the light bobbing up and down. It went to a shed behind the house. She could not lose Doug now. She walked as close as she could to him. She tried to be quiet, but that seemed next to impossible. Dried leaves and broken twigs would crack every few steps she would take. On occasion, Mary would find the light crossing the sky in her direction. She would dive for cover. The trees were good when they were large, but at times the ground met Mary. She knew she could not be caught. She knew she could definitely NOT be caught by Doug.

Doug started a four-wheeler and pulled out of the shed. Mary did not know how fast those things could go, but she had to do her best to keep up. She ran behind him. The fog was so thick in places she could no longer see him. The echo of the motor pointed her in the right direction and she followed.

Her breath was fast as she ran behind the motorized vehicle. She had to stop to catch her breath from time to time. Once she thought she had lost him as the sound was replaced by nothingness. She was running fast through the thick fog searching from side to side trying to find where he had stopped, trying her best to listen.

Then just a few feet from her she spotted him. He had stopped and seemed to be lost in thought. She scurried away before he could see her making her way behind a tree. The noise caught his attention and as he turned, her ponytail slapped the tree she dashed behind. "Damn deer," Doug said as he started the motor and continued his journey.

Still she followed. She searched the ground for tire tracks, not wanting to run upon him again. This time when the engine stopped, Doug left the four-wheeler. He stopped on the side of a hill and disappeared.

Mary checked the time. Her son had given her the watch. The hands glowed in the dark. Charley really liked it when he gave it to her as a Christmas present. "Look in dark mommy," he told her. She knew Bryan picked it out for her, but Charley gave it to her and she kept it close to her heart. It was almost six, the sun making its way into the sky.

Mary walked up the small hill. She came across a door hidden in the tall grass. It had an old door knob on it and a place where a padlock could secure the door to the frame. *An old cellar, this is her cage*, Mary thought. The wood on the door was peeling off exposing tin beneath. Mary walked around and noticed a place where a small window had once been. It was now covered with concrete.

Mary heard screaming. She did not move. She wanted to open the door and expose what was going on. She wanted to rush to the rescue of the screaming person she thought was Eliza. She wanted to save her, but she had not yet formulated a plan of attack. She did not have her gun, or a weapon of any kind. And worse, she did not have a light of any kind.

She stood there and was hesitant about what to do. Should she run back for help? She was uncertain where she was. There had been no fences, but they had crossed a creek. Mary had run full out for at least half an hour.

At that moment she heard the door pop up and she dove into the high grass. Doug emerged. He would kill her if he saw her. Mary heard some whimpering coming from inside the cellar.

Doug looked back down and yelled, "Shut up. God, after everything, can't you just shut up? I have to decide where the hell you are going to be buried now. I have to get my car." He pulled a ladder out and tossed it in Mary's direction. She rolled out of the way as it fell to the ground occupying her spot.

She waited for the sound of the motor to start up. *No chance of moving the car now*, she supposed as the sun began to rise, exposing her position. Doug limped away and was gone. She heard the faint sounds of the four-wheeler as it made its way back in the same direction they had just come from. The sound slowly dissipated completely.

Mary got up and ran to the door. He had locked it with a padlock. As she fumbled with the lock she looked in all directions. She did not like surprises and did not want one now. "Shit," she said, "How the hell am I going to get this off?" She dropped the lock causing it to bounce off the metal top.

She thought she heard a faint cry from inside the building. "Please don't worry. I've come to help you," she yelled into the cellar. She hoped they could hear her. She prayed no one else could.

She scrambled toward the woods to look for a stick. As she reached the edge she noticed Doug was sitting at the very bottom of a hill. She froze. Had he seen her? A cold chill ran through her spine making her whole body shiver. The fog had all but lifted. Doug soon got up; he was bloody and with a limp, began walking back to his house wiping tears from his eyes. The four-wheeler lay on its side.

Mary located a good sized stick. She raced back to the cellar and tried unsuccessfully to pry the lock apart. Her stick snapped in two sending her to the ground. She picked up a rock and beat at the lock. "Please," she said over and over, sweat rolling down her face. She searched around for anything. She made her way to the concrete window and noticed one of the bars Eliza had described pulling out. She took the bar to the lock and gathered her strength. She used the rock as leverage, the flat end of the bar as a crowbar, and pried the hasp from the tin. The screws screamed as one by one they detached from the door.

Guilt overcame Mary. It was her fault Eliza was there. She pulled the heavy door open, roaring as she released her frustration. The smell in the hole made her take a step back. It was a mixture of vomit, natural body waste, blood and just plain BO. She looked down into the underground room, but saw nothing. The pitch blackness echoed a bottomless pit. Her body blocked the sun that should have poured into the space. "It's me Eliza. I've come to help you. I have to get the ladder. Hold on, I'll be back." Mary yelled down into the hole.

She struggled with the ladder. It was quite long and very heavy. After trying to pick it up, she finally decided to drag it. As she placed it in the opening she called, "Don't be scared, it's me, Mary."

Mary wanted to hurry. She was scared of getting caught by Doug. When she descended three quarters of the way, she called out, "Eliza, come with me." Mary's eyes adjusted to the small amount of light filtering in. She was shocked to see how Eliza looked.

Eliza was lying on the small bed with her children around her. She picked up her head and looked in the direction of the voice. Her eyes were swollen almost shut and her hair, once mostly gray was now matted with blood. Her face wore black and blue, purple and yellow bruises as if a child had colored her. Dry blood covered her. Her lips were swollen and her left arm appeared to be facing the wrong direction.

Eliza spoke, her voice a whisper. Mary strained to hear what she said. "I'm sorry, I didn't hear you." Eliza spoke again and this time Mary understood her words although they were slurred, garbled and spoken just above a whisper.

"Are you an angel? Should I go to the light?"

Mary choked back tears as she replied. "Yes, bring your children and come to the light. Your time in hell is over." She climbed down the rest of the ladder. It was hard for Mary to breathe as the smell turned her stomach, burnt her eyes and stung her lungs. Mary felt dizzy. She continued into the cellar to help Eliza gather the children quickly. "We need to hurry. Doug will be back soon." The dizzy feeling continued and Mary found it hard to talk. She took shallow breaths through her nose and tried not to open her mouth not knowing if she would vomit or not.

Eliza's legs were bloody and her arm was indeed broken. The baby lay dead on the bed. Her little nose and ears were crusted with blood. Mary could not keep the tears in and they streamed down her face. The boy refused to leave and Mary struggled to get him free of the bed. He too was bloody and broken. Mary was surprised at the strength of the child. He kept his eyes away from hers and even though she told him it was all right, she was there to help, the boy's silent world kept her words out. Mary, tired of the struggle let go of the child. As he relaxed, she took him by surprise and carried him kicking and screaming up the ladder and out of the cellar.

Eliza, carrying her dead child, followed behind. She had trouble climbing the ladder. Mary reached down and took the child from her. With one arm broken and a leg that was like spaghetti, Eliza could not make it up the ladder. Mary handed the baby to EJ and went back down. EJ stood outside screaming. Mary wanted him to shut up. "Please EJ," she yelled over and over as she put Eliza on her back and struggled up the ladder.

After making it up the ladder, Eliza reached for her children. EJ attached himself to her leg as he handed her daughter to her. Eliza looked into the face of the baby, screamed, and fainted. The baby and EJ followed her to the ground. EJ still holding his mother's leg, repeatedly called to his mom using his broken language. He shook her leg, causing her to rock back and forth.

The scene was too much for Mary and she broke down. She stood over Eliza, put her face in her hands and wept. "We have to go! I'm sorry I didn't come earlier. Please Eliza wake up, he's coming back. What have I done? What have I done?"

43

The sound of a car traveled through the air like wind, but before Mary could react, she saw the police car headed straight at them. It stopped right before hitting the boy and his mother as neither one moved. Mary instinctively jumped, placing herself between the broken family and the police car.

Doug opened the passenger door. Saul emerged slowly from the driver's side of the car. Both had guns pointed toward Mary. "Mary, what's going on here?" Saul asked.

"God Saul, don't tell me you're involved in this too?" Mary questioned.

"Doug, is this that lady, the lady that came into the station? What's she doing here?" A look of confusion swept across Saul's face as he turned toward Doug.

"You just couldn't leave well enough alone could you? First, your brother; do you know I caught him nosing around my place? He should have just done the job the county was paying him to do. He got off that tractor and almost found them. He was walking over here, told me he was following a pipe that had trash coming out of it. I let him walk a little closer. He got in front of me and I beat him. I beat his head in until I heard his skull crack. After his skull collapsed I drug him out to the tractor and pushed him and it over the hill top. Look there Mary, see the tree branch? Do you see the one Mary; do you see the one right by your leg? I think that's part of his brain there." Doug pointed as he spoke.

Mary tried not to look down, but her head soon lowered to look closely at the branch that touched her leg. "Stop it Doug. Why are you doing this?"

"Doug what are you saying?" Saul looked and sounded dumbfounded.

Doug responded with a laugh, "He didn't have any business on my land. I liked Chris, but it's survival of the fittest. If you really look at it, he should have been put out of his misery years ago."

"You killed Chris?" Mary could not believe what she was hearing. "You killed my brother?"

Saul turned toward Doug. "Somebody needs to tell me what the hell is going on around here?" Saul repositioned his gun from Mary and pointed it at Doug. "Doug I think you had better just put your gun down before someone gets hurt."

Doug looked to Saul and said, "Saul I'm really sorry. I thought we had the same thoughts about a lot of stuff, but I'm afraid on this, you will not agree." Doug turned his body and in one swift move shot Saul in the head.

Saul's body fell to the ground; his eyes still open, his mouth paused as though he had a last thought not yet expressed.

Mary screamed. "Oh my GOD, are you mad? Eliza, get up. Please Eliza, get up."

"Look at what you made me do Mary. Why can't you just stay out of my business? You have caused me to kill my wife, shoot your husband and kill Saul. Why is this woman so important to you?" He motioned the gun in the direction of Eliza. "No wait, I take that back, all of this is her fault; I mean really, if you stop and think about it. If she would have just stayed put none of this would have happened. But NO, not her; she had to get out in the world and see what was out there. He knelt next to her and brushed her hair from her face. The boy jumped back from him and crawled on the ground back into the hole. "I guess she can't see too much now, can she?" He rubbed his hand across her swollen blackened eyes. "Look what she did to me." Doug pointed to his bloody nose and his leg.

"You're insane! What are you doing?" Mary took a step closer to him. She was in shock about her brother, but she had to do something about now. She needed to find a way to stay alive long enough to keep Eliza alive.

"Please leave her alone; you've done enough. Look at your daughter. You've killed her." She pointed at the doll like creature still held by Eliza.

"Why Doug, why did you do this?"

Mary took another step forward. "Why did you have to kill Saul? God please answer me before I die, I just need to know the truth. I think I deserve the truth, don't you?"

Doug pulled his gun up aiming at Mary's thigh, "A flesh wound Mary, nothing that will kill you. You're going to take the fall for all of this. As soon as I take you in; I'll go see Bryan. And Mary, don't worry, this time, I'll do it right."

Mary's mind was spinning. "But I need to know why, why did you do this? Why would you do this?"

"Saul saw your SUV as he was driving to my house. When he saw me, he stopped. I wondered how long you'd been watching me, if you had followed me here; and lo and behold, here you were. Don't worry about Saul. He's not with us anymore; well, I guess he is in a way. He never would have understood. Do you think he'll go to heaven? Do you think they'll open up the pearly gates and let him in after the sexual advances he made to you? What about her? Do you think there's room for a whore? What about you Mary? Will you be standing there waiting to get in? I thought I would make it in, but I guess not now. No gates of heaven for me." Doug laughed and Mary knew at that moment, he was indeed mad.

Mary moved closer; inch by inch, step by step. She could see the gun wobble in his hand as his eyes stared off into the distance.

"Why her?" Mary asked.

"Why her you ask? Why not her? Why should it have been someone else? Why not her is the question that begs an answer. She's no better than anyone else. Hell, she just fell into my hands. That night I was at your brother's house, I knew someone was there. I saw her stuff in the bathroom and I knew your brother didn't know anything about her. I drove away with your brother and I saw a reflection on the side of the road. A smashed up car with a note. I drove back. I thought about helping her, but when she saw my truck she was so scared. To be honest I really don't know what took over. So you want to know why, well, because I could. Is that a good enough answer for you? Now stop moving!"

"No, that is not a good enough answer for me. We can all do stuff, we just choose not to. Look at what you've done. There is no going back on this and you won't get away with it." Again Mary took another step.

"Don't you move Mary; I swear I'll kill you where you stand!" The smile that crossed his face sent a wave of shivers through Mary's body.

"Like I said; someone needs to take the fall for this. You don't think I'm going to do it, do you? And the best part is you are going to confess. You are going to tell the world how you killed my wife, killed your husband and killed Saul. It's really simple. After we leave here we are going to the hospital. Being the nice guy that I am, I will let you see Bryan. Of course he will die while you are there. If you are thinking about not saying what I tell you, then there is always Charley. Do they make caskets that size? Oh you already know the answer to that question don't you?"

"What?" Mary asked as her voice quivered. "You can't do this."

"I can do whatever I want."

"What about the boy?" Mary needed to buy time, her mind was racing.

"What boy? Do you mean my Little Doug? Yes Mary, Patty couldn't have children. The whore had my child, so I took him. There isn't a law against me taking my own child you know."

"What about EJ?"

"That stupid deaf boy, he's such a momma's boy. He never knew I was there until I snuck up on him. He would try to protect her. It made me laugh. I wanted to toughen him up. I knew one day I would put him out in the world; only, it would be far from here. I was never going to kill him. I just wanted him to have a chance to make it. Oh, I had plans." He kicked Eliza then said, "This stupid bitch went and screwed up everything."

"Stop it, stop hurting her. What are you going to do with this family now?" Mary already knew the answer to that question.

"They will die Mary. I do not have a use for them and I want a new start, a new family, a new police department and maybe one day, after all this mess dies down, a new whore."

The sound of a motorcycle startled him and he swung his head around keeping the gun pointed at Mary.

A few yards away the motorcycle stopped and Robert pulled his helmet off.

"What's going on here Doug?" Robert asked. He then turned toward Mary, nodded and said, "Mary."

"Go to my house and call for back-up. I have everything taken care of here. See, I found Mary."

Robert looked around at the scene. Mary had a gun pointed at her. The lady from the other day lay on the ground. Next to the woman lay a still baby. Peeking from a hole in the ground was a bloody boy, the same boy from the other day. By the driver's side of the patrol car lay Saul, a gunshot wound to the head.

Robert said, "No Doug, I think I'll take control of this scene. Why don't you go on back to your house? I know you are upset with all that happened to your wife; and I can't let you take this responsibility right now."

Doug swung the gun around and pointed it at Robert. "You know Robert, you are such a wimp, always have been, hell I've just kept you around for laughs."

"Doug, will you please put the gun down?" Robert slowly pulled his gun out of his holster keeping it down to his side. Beads of sweat began forming on his forehead.

Doug swung the gun back to Mary, "She's on a killing spree. Do you hear what I'm saying to you?" He turned back to Robert, the gun following. "Do you hear me? I'm asking you a question."

Robert lifted his gun. "Put the gun down Doug, I'm not going to tell you again." Robert's voice was calm and his hand was held steady.

"And like I said, Mary is on a killing spree; and I'm sorry to tell you this Robert, YOU are her last victim." He squeezed the trigger and Robert fell to the ground, his bike falling on top of him. Doug turned and faced Mary who started screaming. Doug grabbed his neck. "He shot me Mary. Robert, shot me." He toppled over bleeding profusely from the neck. The gun fell from his hand as his arm hit the ground.

Mary kicked the gun away from Doug and raced to Robert. She lifted the bike off of him. "Robert, are you...? Oh Robert, say something."

"You always said I was going to lay this bike down and it was going to kill me. I guess today is not my day to die." He ripped his shirt open and revealed his vest. Mary was glad Robert's wife always made him wear his vest, even in the station. She kissed him on his cheek and helped him to his feet.

"How did you get here?" Mary asked.

"Saul called and said to meet him at Doug's house. He said he found your SUV parked over by Doug's. I've been looking for you everywhere. I saw your SUV and then saw the tire tracks. I came as fast as I could. Mary, what's going on? Why is Saul dead? And is that 'the family'?" Robert asked.

As Mary and Robert talked, a gunshot rang out. They dropped to the ground. After taking cover, they looked around to find Eliza with the gun pointed down. Blood, bone and brain matter was dripping from her face, her clothes and running down her hand, splattering in the place where Doug's face had once been.

As the gun fell from Eliza's hand, it landed on Doug's shoulder then slipped to the ground. Eliza uttered one word, "Bastard."

"Eliza," Mary managed to say as she and Robert got up.

Eliza did not speak. She looked at the body on the ground and smiled. A smile that made Mary's blood run cold.

"Mary, I couldn't let Doug kill you." Robert kicked the gun away from the faceless body of Doug.

"I don't think you need to do that," Mary said.

"Better safe than sorry," Robert replied.

"How is Bryan? Have you heard anything?" Mary needed to know.

"He's going to be sore as hell, but he's going to be just fine. I went to the hospital last night after you "hit me on the head". Jeff came to the station and relieved me. Bryan needed blood and I was more than happy to share. I guess that makes us blood brothers. Hey I'm your new blood brother-in-law." Robert playfully punched Mary in the arm.

"Shut up Robert." Mary leaned into Robert. "Thank you."

"I knew, as I was sitting there getting drained, there was no way in hell you would ever kill anyone." Robert said.

"You are right, I didn't kill anyone. I should have, but I didn't. And I didn't hit you." Mary replied looking at the family.

"I know you didn't hit me, but they think you did. I smashed my head with the paperweight from your desk. Sorry I got my blood on it, but I had to cover my ass. By the way, there's a warrant out for your arrest, but we'll take care of that." Robert said.

"Wait Robert, what are we going to do with Eliza and EJ? The baby is dead. Doug was a monster. We worked together all these years and I never knew. How can I enforce the law and help people when I don't even know who the bad guy is?" Mary shook her head as she looked at Robert.

"You know, I didn't know either. I had no idea." Robert responded.

"He beat his wife and caused her death. He killed my brother Chris. He tried to kill my Bryan. Then today, he killed Saul. He even threatened Charley." Mary fell apart; she tried to be strong, but all of her strength was gone.

"Mary, you did well. You saved Eliza and EJ."

"Robert, how do you judge a life? Who's more important? Were Eliza and EJ more important than Chris? He killed Chris because he stumbled upon them. Jesus Christ, at one point, I thought it WAS Chris." Mary turned toward Eliza. "Chris was my brother. The one with the scared face, the man you were so afraid of. He was a great man. If only you would have let him help you."

Eliza stood staring at the ground where Doug lay, not reacting to a word Mary was saying.

"Mary, everyone that breathes air in this world is important. Everyone that wants to make life better for someone else is important. Chris was a wonderful man when he was alive. He touched so many people's lives in a positive way. Saul was well, you know, Saul and Patty, I guess Little Doug needed her in his life to show him the true meaning of love. Patty loved him, you know she really did. EJ will go on and be a wonderful person and that's thanks to you. You saved a little boy. You did a good thing." Robert hugged Mary.

"Let's get this family out of here. What do you say?" Robert asked.

"Eliza," Mary said.

Eliza did not move, but EJ ran from the opening of the hole and grabbed on to his mother's leg.

"Eliza!" Mary yelled this time. "Are you ready to go?"

"I was ready years ago," Eliza whispered.

Robert carried Eliza and her dead baby to Saul's car, stepping over the lifeless body of his former boss. Mary carried EJ; he put his head on her shoulder. She placed him in the car whispering, "You're safe now. You're safe now." EJ placed a gentle kiss on Mary's cheek. She grabbed him back up and held him for a few moments longer. She wanted him to feel safe. She thought he felt safe now. She tenderly kissed him.

Robert started toward his bike as Mary put EJ in the patrol car. He looked at the bodies that were close to the car. He debated on whether to move them or not. "What do you think I should do with them?"

"Leave them where they are," Mary said. "Just leave them there."

Mary climbed into the driver's seat and started the car. She carefully pulled away from the scene of the crime. Not the crime of Saul or Doug, but the crime of Eliza and her family. As they drove away Mary said, "Eliza, Hope is dead, your baby is dead, I'm so sorry."

"I know. I know she has left me. I couldn't protect her. I tried, but I could not. After he put us back in that hole, he beat EJ and me for leaving. When he left we were all alive, but he came back. This time I fought back and hurt him. I hurt him this time. He was trying to take Hope and EJ. She kept crying and crying and crying. I tried to get to her, but he pushed me away. EJ hid under the bed; out of his reach, using his voice to yell, 'NO' over and over. When EJ wouldn't come out HE said, 'I guess you keep the deaf boy. I'm taking the girl.' He tried going up the steps and I pulled him back down. Hope hit the floor first and then he fell down landing on top of her. She whimpered for a moment and then she was quiet. The pain she must have felt. I knew she was gone. See, she didn't move. She didn't scream. Hope lay on the floor broken. I killed her. It was my fault she died, but I blamed him. I yelled, 'Just kill me too!

Why did you do this? Just kill me now!' He managed to get up and hit me. I blacked out then. I don't know how long I was out. He came back and another beating took place. He told me the baby was stinking. He told me to throw her down the shithole. He said if that baby was not out of there when he came back, he would most definitely kill me and that bastard son of mine. I couldn't throw her out. I didn't want to throw her out. She was my child and even if he hated her, I loved her and I love EJ. I wanted him to kill me. I wanted EJ to die too. I wanted the pain to end. I'm sorry I didn't get help from your brother. I'm sorry I made all these people die." Eliza was crying. Her words were broken by sobs. "You came in after he left. I just couldn't leave Hope there. She spent too much time there already. I couldn't leave her there. For once in her tiny life, I want her to go someplace nice. I want her to know heaven. Do you think she will go to heaven?"

"Yes Eliza, I think she IS in heaven, looking down at you knowing you did the best you could for her. I know you gave her love. I'm sorry I didn't make it in time to save her. She was a wonderful little girl Eliza. I'm sorry I failed to keep you and your children safe. I'm so very sorry for what I said about Chris. It's not your fault. Eliza, I'm sorry I gave you back to Doug. I'm so very sorry you came to me for help and I didn't believe you. I'm sorry." Mary could not hold her tears in and both she and Eliza cried as they made their way to Doug's house.

Eliza looked at Mary as Doug's house came into view. "What now?" She whispered.

"What?" Mary asked.

"I said what now? What am I going to do? I have no home, I have no money, but most importantly, I haven't seen my son. What's going to happen to him? What's going to happen to EJ? What's going to happen to me?"

"We'll get through this Eliza. We'll figure out something. Now is not the time to worry about the little things," Mary replied.

"My son is not a little thing," Eliza answered back angrily.

"No Eliza, I didn't mean your son. I meant the money and the place to live. We'll figure those things out. I'm sure you and EJ will be in the hospital for a few days and from there we will play it by ear. Doug had money, so you can provide for your family. Little Doug is a big thing. I don't know where he is and you have to remember a few things; his father is dead and his mother is dead." She looked at Eliza and saw the hurt look that crossed her face.

"Again I'm sorry Eliza, but Patty is the only mother Little Doug has ever known. You are a new person to him and it will take time. I'm not sure how much time, but you need to prepare yourself. He may reject you and EJ. He's not the infant you remember; he is after all, almost a teenager." Mary stopped the car by the house and got out leaving Eliza and EJ behind.

After a while, Mary came back to the car followed by a state trooper. Mary opened Eliza's door. "They are bringing Little Doug here, but you need to get to the hospital. Eliza, you and EJ are in really bad shape."

"I can't go yet. I have to see him. I have to see my Teddy." Eliza said.

"Miss, I really think the best thing for you to do is to go with this child to the hospital. We will bring your other child to you." The trooper opened the back door.

"Please," Eliza begged. "Just a few minutes, I've waited so long. Just a few more minutes please."

"Mary, you go on ahead. I'll stay with her while she waits." The trooper handed her his keys. "Your SUV can't be moved. I'll ride to the hospital in the ambulance with Miss Johnson and pick up my car. I hope Bryan is okay."

"Thanks." Mary started to walk away then stopped. Turning back she said, "Eliza, don't be too disappointed."

"But he's my son Mary."

"I know Eliza." Mary then nodded to the trooper. "Tell the coroner to take the baby and get the EMT to look after EJ."

Mary walked up to Robert. "Robert, stay here and take charge. I'm going to the hospital to be with Bryan. Eliza is waiting for Little Doug; call me when he gets here." She got in the vehicle and sped away.

44

Eliza sat in the car dreaming of her reunion with her son "Teddy". She knew everyone else called him "Little Doug" but she hated that name as much as she hated the man that fathered him. *No* she thought, *I'll get out of the car and yell Teddy when he gets here. He'll come running into my arms and he'll know I'm his mother. I'll kiss him and hold him and he'll know how much I missed him. He'll know he was ripped from my arms. Together with EJ we'll leave this place and start a new life. The three of us will play in the sun in a field of wild flowers and sitting in a tree will be my sweet Hope; looking down on us. All that I know and love will surround me.*

Eliza saw the car pull up. She was anxious. She struggled to get her broken body out of the car. It was difficult and she winced at the pain that each movement caused. She leaned against the door and managed to yell, "Teddy" with a slight wave of her hand as the flash of a boy went running by her.

Eliza stood by the car holding on to the door. The boy passed her and did not even look her way. "Now what?" Eliza said to no one. She slowly sat down in the car and motioned for the state trooper. She and EJ were taken to the hospital.

45

Robert observed Little Doug as he ran past Eliza. The boy did not even appear to hear or even see Eliza. Little Doug looked focused as he took the steps to the house in a single bound coming face to face with Robert.

Little Doug said, "Hello," as he reached for the doorknob.

Robert sat for a moment watching the boy struggle with the locked door. He grabbed Little Doug's arm as the boy yelled for his father and mother.

"Let me go!" The boy yelled, wiggling away from Robert. "I need to see my dad. Where is my dad? What's going on around here? Where is my mom?" He then began to shoot off question after question, not waiting for an answer.

Robert finally managed to get a few words in and said, "Wait Little Doug, you have to wait." Robert picked up his cell phone and called Mary. He did not know what to say to the boy. All he said to Mary was, "He's here."

"Wait? Wait for what?" Little Doug asked.

"Mary, we have to wait for Mary." Robert sat outside on the porch waiting for Mary to come back; he did not want to be in charge.

46

Eliza was overcome with grief, but there were no tears to cry. She looked at the trooper and he quickly looked away. Eliza could feel how uncomfortable he was. The ambulance hit a bump as Eliza's reality crept in. She felt she could not care for herself much less EJ. *He needs a better life, he deserved a better life. All I have is love, and love just is not enough. It has never been enough. EJ has to be safe. Teddy has to be safe.* She knew heartbreak was in her children's future. She knew she could never make it better for them. She knew she was not the mother they deserved. *A mother is a person that is given a challenge and succeeds. I failed. I always fail.* She thought of her dead daughter and the pain she could not protect her from. She looked at the son lying in her lap bruised and broken. She thought of the boy that ran past her. Eliza could feel the tight grip around her heart. *I'm dying of heartbreak,* she thought as she moved her arm to her chest.

The ambulance pulled into the hospital bay. As the doors opened, Eliza's face was filled with pain. She looked out and saw Mary standing just outside the door. Eliza reached out her hand toward Mary. Mary rushed to her side. Eliza spoke almost in a whisper, "I know I don't know you very well, but I trust you. I trust you will be a good mother to my boys. I trust you will help them through this time. I trust you will love them." Her hand slipped from Mary and she grabbed her chest again, "I'm dy ..."

Someone yelled, "I think she's having a heart attack." A flurry of people ran in as Eliza and EJ were rushed away.

Eliza felt death. As the pain rushed through her body, she shut her eyes and her mind closed in upon itself. The freedom that she had hoped for, strived for, and prayed for, disappeared.

EPILOGUE

EJ, Little Doug and Mary stood in the doorway of Eliza's hospital room. Eliza's eyes were open, but a vacant stare looked out at the room. She sat in a wheelchair with her hair unkempt. She had a tube peeking out of her gown showing her only source of food. Her body was still only skin and bones and her many scars still visible. The nurse walked out of the room patting Mary on the shoulder as she left saying, "I'm sorry, there's still no change."

Little Doug walked to Eliza. "I do not believe this woman is my mother. I don't believe what I heard about my father. There is no way my dad could have done all the things they said he did. What do I say to her?" He asked Mary again as he had every visit for months. "I don't know what to say to her. Are you sure she's my mother? This is all a lie. Look at her, we look nothing alike. It's just not true." He ran from the room as tears formed in his eyes.

"Eliza," Mary spoke gently. "His recovery will take a long time. The happy go lucky boy Doug and Patty raised is gone. Left in his place is an angry, depressed and withdrawn child. He hardly speaks and goes through the motions of the day hating everyone and everything around him. Many days he lashes out at EJ as though it were his fault. But we are making progress with him. Some days are challenging, but I will keep the family together for you Eliza.

You will get better and Little Doug will get better too, just you wait and see. Today he got really close to you. Time will heal this."

EJ stood on her left hearing every word that was spoken. His body was changing as food, sunshine and freedom left positive effects. His hearing was about seventy-five percent with a hearing aid. He practiced his speech every day with a therapist, growing more confident with each word. "Mom, it's me, EJ. Mom, please wake up and talk to me. I have so much to tell you." EJ looked to Mary. "When can she come home?"

Mary did not answer. It had been months and still there was no improvement in Eliza's condition. Eliza's mind was lost. Maybe it was in a field playing with her children or maybe it was just lost in a hole in no·where.

"EJ, we've got to go, I have to find Little Doug." Mary touched Eliza's face. "I'm taking care of your boys until you can."

"I'll be right there," EJ said as Mary walked out of the room.

EJ took his mother's hand in his and signed "I love you." He turned his palm up and waited for a response. He reached around to hug her with his free arm and kissed her gently on the cheek. He turned her hand back over and said, "Mom, this is how we talk in the dark, when we are alone. I love you Mom." As he turned his hand back over, his palm begged for a response. He felt a movement in his palm. He looked toward her face. A slight smile caught her lips as a tear rolled down her cheek. "I love you too," she wrote.

"Mary, Mary, come quick Mary!" EJ yelled as he ran into the hall.

"What? EJ this is a hospital. You have to be quiet."

"But my mom, oh my God, my mom!" EJ dragged Mary back to Eliza. "Look at her, she's awake. She spoke to me. Here, in my hand."

Mary looked at Eliza. "I'm sorry EJ; you must have just thought it, wished it so hard your mind played a trick on you." Mary pulled EJ to her. "I'm sorry."

EJ knew. He knew what he saw, he knew what he felt. Even though his mother still had a vacant stare, her arms still drawn as her muscles contracted, he knew she was still there with him. He went day after day to see her, to talk to her. He was waiting, waiting for her to awake again even if for a moment, for that was all EJ needed, just a moment with his mother. A moment to tell her he was better. A moment to tell her they were no longer in the hole. A moment to tell her he loved her more than anything in the whole wide world. A moment to tell her thank you, thank you for saving my life.

The End

Made in the USA
Lexington, KY
07 November 2013